Rum Pι

by

Su García

Copyright

Table Of Contents

'The man who would be fully employed should procure a ship or a woman, for no two things produce more trouble'
Titus Maccus Plautus
(254 - 184 BC)'

Chapter One

Terri

It is said that life is stranger than fiction, so when Terri Gillingham won an all-expenses-paid, two-week holiday cruising in the Caribbean, she couldn't believe her luck but definitely believed in fate.

Two months later, as she sat, all alone, bobbing up and down in a rubber dinghy, in the middle of the night, with what could only be described as a miner's lamp on her forehead, Terri decided that fate wasn't all it was cracked up to be.

It had all started on a drab May morning at work. Terri was attending the regular weekly publication meeting on the eighth floor of the British Electricity Board headquarters in Paternoster Square, London and wishing she could be anywhere other than listening to her boss droning on about publication budgets and departmental deadlines. When her right thigh trembled from her vibrating mobile phone, she welcomed the distraction and eased her right buttock off the chair. Checking that Head of Marketing was now locked in conversation with a colleague, she eased the phone out onto her lap and read the incoming text.

'Congratulations, Terri Gillingham, you are the lucky winner of this month's True Life Movie competition. We are going to whisk you and your family off to the Caribbean for a two-week cruise. All you have to do is contact Adrian Falks at Global Adventure Holidays on 0798532664

and quote this reference number – A56395. Don't delay, he's waiting for your call!

'Terri, how many BEI brochures have we actually printed?' Terri's head shot up as six pairs of male eyes bored into her.

'Uh. . . ten thousand,' she replied, ramming her mobile back into her pocket.

'And, did we know that the Chairman was unhappy with the new logo before we went to press?' Harold's expression resembled that of a recently spayed bull mastiff.

'Logo?' Terri replied, her teeth now leaving their imprint on the inside of her lower lip. 'Er . . . you mean the elliptical world map with the letters BIE across the middle?' Obviously, Terri was playing for time.

Her boss's eyelids disappeared into his eyebrows as his finger stabbed at the front cover of a forty-six-page, full-colour brochure promoting the professional services of the British International Engineering Division. 'The very same, Terri.'

'Well . . . no . . . actually.' A collective intake of breath instantly depleted the oxygen level in the room. She scanned the furrowed brows around the table and felt a Damoclean sword hover over her head at the thought of ten thousand brochures being fed into the shredding machine in the headquarters' basement. 'As eh, . . . far as I know,' she stammered, 'the logo was approved at board level last month.' A raft of implausible excuses and possible buck passing rotated around in her head as she tried to side-step the potential cock-up. She knew that if the Chairman had not been copied into her memo requesting approval of the damned logo she would be for the chop. Sweat broke out on her forehead, all thoughts of a cruise in the Caribbean forgotten.

Back in her office, she grabbed the BIE file and extracted the memo, her shaking hands hindering progress. Terri scanned the list of names at the top of the page and felt her stomach flip. Cyril Trowbridge's name was nowhere to be seen. She had failed to include him in her haste to get the logo listed in the previous month's Directors' Meeting and no amount of wishing otherwise was going to change that. She picked up the phone and dialled the CEO's PA.

'Chief Executive's Office,' announced Anne Blakemore in her crisp, efficient manner.

'Mrs Blakemore, it's Terri Gillingham here in Marketing. I wonder if you could confirm that the Chairman attended the Directors' Board Meeting last month?' She had her legs crossed, incontinence threatening.

'Just one moment, Terri, I'll check.' The line went dead and Terri's lungs stopped functioning. 'Hello, are you there?'

'I'm here,' she choked, her face resembling a beetroot.

'Yes, Lord Trowbridge attended,' the rush of air from Terri's lungs sounded like a Boeing 737 in reverse thrust, 'but he had to leave early for a BBC interview on the *Daily Politics Show*.'

Terri collapsed into a chair and crossed her fingers. 'I believe the board approved the new BIE logo but I seem to have mislaid my copy. Could you let me have another one for my file?'

The pregnant pause went on forever. 'I'm looking through the minutes, Terri, but there doesn't seem to be any reference to the logo. Maybe they ran out of time. It often happens with "Any other business".'

Terri could feel the sharp whack of cold steel on her neck and pictured her head rolling onto the desk. Bloody hell, she thought, rubbing the skin above her spinal column, how do I explain this to Harold?

The Head of Marketing had already left the building by the time Terri plucked up enough courage to admit to her mistake, which went some way to lowering her blood pressure, but now put the whole matter on hold until after the weekend. She walked towards St Paul's tube station like a rugby player on his way to the sin bin and wondered how she was going to get through the next two days without having a nervous breakdown.

Ealing Broadway was a seething mass of humanity as she made her way through the turnstiles, her mind reliving the conversation with Anne Blakemore for the hundredth time and willing the outcome to be different. Fat chance, she decided as she left the tube station, the thought of her house being repossessed by bailiffs sending her blood pressure soaring once more. Opposite the Job Centre she stepped out into the road without looking and caused a local cab driver to slam on his brakes, nose-diving his rear-seat passengers into the glass partition as he hit his horn and gave her a finger sign.

Number 45, Deloitte Villas looked forlorn in the evening drizzle as Terri walked up the path to her front door. She had bought the Victorian semi back in the eighties with a small inheritance from her grandmother and a hefty mortgage with the Woolwich. At the time, she had optimistic plans of meeting some upwardly mobile Prince Charming with shed loads of money and a pad overlooking the Thames and would keep Deloitte Villas as an investment, but, twenty years on, she was still single and still there. A number of frogs had passed under her Victorian portal over the years but none had turned into anything resembling a prince.

Dropping her bag on the hall table she wandered into the kitchen and checked her answer-phone messages.

'Hi, Terri. Sam here. Are you going to the reunion tomorrow? If so, do you want a lift? Ring me soonest. Bye.'

Terri stared out of the kitchen window onto borders choked with weeds and a lawn full of impact dents from dirty footballs kicked over the fence by the two young hooligans next door. She felt depression slide over her like a moth-eaten fox fur.

'What does Cyril Trowbridge know about logos anyway,' she groaned, her words fogging up the window. She grabbed the half empty bottle of cheap red wine sitting on the kitchen work surface, lifted a wine glass from the draining board and headed into the lounge.

Her ancient, blue Dralon chesterfield groaned under her weight as she settled in for the evening to consider her options. Sam's message referred to the Beagle Air Reunion for over-the-hill air crew, held annually at a pub near Gatwick. In her youth, Terri had pushed a trolley up and down the aisle of a BAC 1-11 aircraft, dispensing duty-free booze and ham salads to happy package holiday makers. Twenty-five years later, she had struggled to recognise many of her fellow crew members beneath their surfeit of excess flesh and dental implants. The old jokes, which had the trolley dollies in their twenties rolling around the galley in fits of laughter now seemed immature and gauche at forty-five and the saga of the Chief Stewardess's varicose veins operation was mind numbing.

'I'm getting old,' she mumbled as she felt the cushion below her posterior fold around her hips and disappear between two webbing straps as red wine splattered across her white blouse. 'Bugger!' She drained the glass and lay back.

An hour later she was still lying there, wallowing in her own self-pity.

'Oh, do stop winging, Teresa. What else will you be doing on Saturday night? At least it will take your mind off work.'

That was her dead Grannie talking. She had been a surrogate Mum to Terri from the age of eight when her parents were killed in a car crash on the M1 in fog and, since departing this world at the grand old age of ninety-three, had taken on the annoying habit of invading her granddaughter's sub-conscious mind to proffer pearls of unwarranted wisdom.

Terri stared at her empty social diary, shrugged her shoulders and made a mental note to ring Sam within the hour then promptly forgot as her Indian take-away arrived from the local curry house and more cheap red wine filled her glass. She awoke with a rick in her neck as the ten o'clock news was finishing and decided to call it a day. Tossing her blouse into the laundry basket she turned and caught her reflection in the full-length bedroom mirror. It was not a pretty sight. Wrinkles weaved their way across her neck and upper arms like a map of the Amazonian Delta and her bats-wings flopped about her armpits making it possible for her to sky dive without a parachute. Her boobs were heading downhill, her pelvic bones had disappeared, her stomach remained stubbornly inflated even when she tensed her stomach muscles and the stretch marks on her thighs looked like tramlines. She turned to check out her backside and felt suicidal realising that her cheeky dimples now resembled a Waitrose crumpet.

'I really must get into shape,' she muttered, running her hand through the bird's nest travesty, which was her hair, knowing that no amount of exercise, dieting or spa treatments could stem the onset of middle age.

'Just be grateful for wrinkle cream, dear, and remember to stay in subdued lighting whenever you're out.'

'Thanks for nothing, Gran.' She picked up her dressing gown and carried it into the bathroom. 'Why should I be so worried?' she argued, reaching for her toothbrush. 'Middle-aged men don't have six packs. In fact, most can't even see their private parts.' Harold Crompton sprang to mind which triggered the morning's meeting and her future lack of employment.

She flopped into bed and flicked out the light. 'Damn,' she muttered into the duvet. 'I forgot to ring Sam.'

Chapter Two

Sam

Brompton Road was awash with traffic as Sam stood opposite Harrods in a gale, waiting to cross to her apartment in Pont Street. She was running late and knew that CJ would have arrived before her. He hated being kept waiting, but then he had a chauffeur-driven Bentley to transport him between Knightsbridge and the City while Sam had to struggle with local transport.

Her security card flashed green at the entrance to Beauchamp Villas and she entered the lift alongside a portly lady of the hooked nose and blue rinse variety who was shackled to a brush-on-a-lead, known to its owner as Twinkle, her Yorkshire terrier.

'Excuse me,' groaned Sam as the brush-on-a-lead tried to copulate with her right calf. 'Could you keep your dog under control?' She was not in the best of moods.

The blue rinse sniffed the air and rearranged her ample chest inside her overcoat, refusing to comment. As the lift door opened at the fourth floor the women went their separate ways, a cold stare boring into Sam's back.

Beethoven's Fifth blasted Sam's eardrums as she opened the apartment door, and her heart sank. CJ always played Beethoven's Fifth after a good day at the office and it followed that she was now in for an athletic night.

'Hi,' she called above the strains of the LSO as she dropped her bag on the hall table and walked through to the bedroom, kicking off her shoes by the bed and moving into her dressing room. Minutes later she reappeared in the lounge.

'You're late,' commented CJ, seated on the cream leather settee reading the *Evening Standard*, a glass of whisky in one hand.

'Umm,' replied Sam, not bothering to elaborate. She poured herself a Campari and Soda from the drinks cabinet and flopped into a chair, wrapping her feet under her left hip. She knew she looked good. A personal trainer, some help with Botox and a diet of salad leaves had delayed her ageing process. Samantha Hutchins was six foot in her stockinged feet and looked ten years younger than forty-eight. Clad nonchalantly in a black silk jumpsuit with matching ballerina pumps on her feet, her long blonde hair piled on top of her head and anchored in place with an amber clasp, she could have given Angelina Jolie a run for her money.

'Do you want to eat in or out tonight?' asked CJ.

'In, I think. It's been a bitch of a day and I really don't feel like going out again.'

'Right, I'll ring down to L'Escargot and order something to be brought up. Any preferences?'

'No,' said Sam, sipping her drink, 'just keep it light.' She never could perform on a full stomach.

CJ picked up the phone by his elbow and began to dial.

'I assume your day went well.' Sam flicked through *Elle* magazine.

'What makes you say that?' He looked up, his amber eyes below bushy ginger eyebrows undressing her from head to toe.

'Beethoven's Fifth,' she replied, meeting his gaze and trying to raise the energy and inclination for sex. It wasn't easy after twenty-five years. CJ had become as familiar to her as an old shoe over the decades, their long-standing affair feeling more like *George and Mildred* than *Dirty Dancing*.

They ate in silence, the scallops cooked to perfection. Sam toyed with her rocket and balsamic salad, a general malaise dulling her appetite. 'Where are we holidaying this year?' Her question hung in the air for ten seconds. She waited, fork hovering between plate and mouth.

CJ seemed to be closely examining the condiment set. 'I'm taking the family to Alaska, whale watching.' He refused to meet her stare.

'Nice,' said Sam, returning her fork to the plate. 'Where will I be . . . in the bilge?' Normally CJ rented a villa for his mistress twenty minutes from the family's exotic holiday resort so that she could placate his libido whenever the need arose. His fingers drummed the table and female intuition told her something was not right.

'I, umm . . . that's something we need to talk about.' Sam's forehead creased as she watched him shift position, his chair legs scraping across the oak floor. 'I'm going to be cruising for most of the time, so . . .' He wafted his palms in the air.

Sam sensed her annual holiday was about to go down the plughole. 'And what about me? Have I become surplus to requirements?'

'No, of course not.' He stuck his fork in a scallop, pinning it to the plate.

Sam's eyes followed his every move, anger bristling just below the surface. The silence was palpable. She knew she was being irrational in picking a fight like this, but there was nothing rational about their relationship.

CJ was a happily married man with two children and five grandchildren and, when not in London, lived in rural splendour somewhere in leafy Berkshire with a Country Casuals wife who showed little interest in his business activities, or where he was during the week. It had never been his wish to leave her and Sam had accepted that fact years ago.

Equally, he had been very good to Sam. As his mistress, she had a generous monthly allowance paid for from his company's coffers, the apartment on Pont Street was in her name and she had a corporate credit card with no limit. Whenever he went abroad on business she went with him, flying first class, staying in five-star hotels and socialising with the world's finest. In return, she was at CJ's beck and call at any time of day or night, 24/7, and had long since forfeited other male company, her lover's possessive nature having seen to that.

However, Sam didn't like change, and losing out on her all-expenses-paid annual holiday in some exclusive location did not go down well. CJ's holiday plans were now messing with her head and her jealous streak was surfacing with a vengeance. Staring through a yellow mist, she felt CJ's hand caress hers as he eased her out of her chair and led her towards the bedroom. It was time to pay her dues.

Lying on her back in the super-king-sized bed, Sam heard the phone ring and the answer phone kick-in, just as CJ climaxed, his groans masking what her caller was saying. He slid off her naked body and rolled onto his back, all sexual prowess spent. Within seconds his snores were bouncing off the bedroom walls, nasal contortions producing a sound like a cracked trombone. Sam watched his nostrils flare and wondered what she would do if he ever croaked while visiting Pont Street. He was in his late sixties and at least two stone overweight having spent a lifetime over-indulging on expensive wines and exotic foods, and taking little exercise other than sex. A sudden coronary at the height of ejaculation was not out of the question and Sam had no idea what she would tell the paramedics if they asked who she was. She eased her leg from under his thigh and decided that the last thing she needed was a media scrum outside Beauchamp Villas and a distraught wife vying for her blood, while her deceased Captain of Industry was wheeled into an ambulance in a body bag. The horrifying image doused any hope of sleep so Sam turned on her side and began to count sheep. Half an hour later she was still counting.

Over breakfast she was still fizzing about missing out on her holiday. 'I thought you hated water?'

CJ continued to butter his toast, head deep in *The Times*. 'Sorry?'

Sam knew that tone of voice, Apprentices heard it when they were about to be fired by Alan Sugar. 'Nothing.' She poured more coffee. 'What dates are you away?'

'Last two weeks of July, first week of August.' He folded his newspaper, any further conversation on the subject at an end.

'Right,' said Sam, watching CJ glance at his watch, leave his seat and pick up his briefcase.

'I'll see you Monday.' He kissed her on the neck and stroked her left breast. 'Great sex last night, by the way.' The front door clicked shut and Sam was left alone.

She was still analysing their one-sided conversation as she rewound the answer-phone tape from the night before.

'*Hi, Sam, Terri here. Sorry, have I called at an inappropriate moment. Whoops, I didn't mean to say that, I meant . . . Oh, hell.*' Pause. '*Just give me a ring when you have a mo' regarding the Reun . . . er, thingy. 'Bye.*'

Sam walked into the bathroom and poured Jo Malone foaming oil into the bath. Fortunately, CJ would not have heard Terri's garbled message, being otherwise engaged at the time, she thought, as warm water frothed and the aroma of gardenias soothed her senses. The Beagle Air Reunion was a secret Sam had always kept close to her chest, as Terri well knew. Fraternising with ex-airline pilots would not have gone down well with CJ and Sam certainly didn't want to rock the boat at this juncture. The reference to boats challenged her equilibrium so she eased herself into the bubbles and concentrated on the positives. While CJ was off whale-watching with his wife, she mused, she would have three weeks in which to do what the hell she liked. The water caressed her nipples as she leant back against the porcelain. 'Mmmm,' she murmured as she sank below the bubbles. 'Mmmm, indeed.'

Chapter Three

Terri

John Humphrys was questioning some female Labour MP as Terri's radio alarm clock sprang into life. She opened one eye to stare at the clock. Mistake. Lights flashed across her eyeball and her eyelid clamped shut as her head buried itself below the duvet like a rock crab in sand. The cheap red wine with the Madras curry seemed to be gripping her body in a vice. Is it me who's groaning? she thought. Guessing it was, she promised herself for the umpteenth time that she would never do that again.

The power shower didn't help either, the needle-sharp jets of hot water shot-blasting Terri's head producing a headache. She staggered into the kitchen wrapped in her faded pink track suit, desperately in need of some strong black coffee when the phone rang.

'Terri, Sam. Have I woken you?'

'Yes . . .No . . . Well, let's put it this way, my body is downstairs but the rest of me is still prostrate.'

'Too much cheap red wine?' said Sam, annoyingly.

'I will treat that remark with the contempt it deserves.'

'Fine, have it your own way, but I have known you for thirty years, Teresa Gillingham.'

Terri stuck a china mug under the Dolce Gusto coffee machine and pressed the espresso button. 'OK, OK! Yes, I'm a bit hungover. Why?'

'Because you rang me at eleven-thirty last night. Not a good time as you well know.'

Terri imagined CJ leaping off the wardrobe in Beauchamp Villas and groaned once more. 'Oh, hell, Sam. I'm sorry.'

'So you said, last night. Anyway are you going to the reunion or not?'

Terri watched black liquid splutter into the cup, trying to remember what decision she'd settled on. Needless to say she couldn't. 'Yes I . . . think so . . . how about you?'

'Terri, I'm the one who'll be driving us down to Crawley, remember?'

'Oh, yes.' Total recall was becoming a problem. 'Um . . . sorry, Sam, I'm having trouble with the old grey matter this morning. Just tell me where and when and I'll be there.'

'Right. Six-thirty at Pont Street, and don't be late.' With that, Sam cut the line and Terri felt hot coffee slide down her throat. It was bliss! She was on her second cup when her mobile rang.

'Hello, is that Teresa Gillingham?' asked a male voice with a strong Yorkshire accent.

'Who's this?'

'Adrian Falks.'

Terri was none the wiser. 'Ugh?'

'Adrian Falks from Global Adventure Holidays in Leeds. Am I speaking to Teresa Gillingham?'

'Yes, but . . .'

'Congratulations, Mrs Gillingham. All you have to do is answer the following question and . . .'

'Look, I'm sorry to butt in, but are you trying to sell me something because I've had one hell of a week, it's my day off and I want to be left in peace?'

'Far from it.' His Yorkshire accent was grating on Terri's nerves. 'I'm ringing about the *True Life Movies* competition. The one you entered by giving the correct answer to the question, "Where is the island of St Lucia?"'

'Did I?'

'Yeeesss.' Adrian was sounding unsure.

'I don't wish to be rude, Andy . . . '

'Adrian.'

'Adrian, but I think you have the wrong Teresa Gillingham.'

'This is 0798 521 3476, isn't it?'

'Yes, but . . .'

'And you did use this number to text the *True Life Movies* competition line last Sunday night, didn't you?'

'Did I?' She was beginning to sound like a cracked record. All Terri could remember was waking up on Monday morning with a mouth as dry as a burnt crisp, bags under her eyes which she could have used as barrage balloons and a resolve never to drink on an empty stomach again.

'Yes, you did, and you're the lucky winner. What do you say to that?'

Her mouth opened but nothing came out.

'Hello, are you there?'

Terri hit the espresso button once more and tried to concentrate. 'Yes, sorry. What were you saying?'

'All you have to do is answer the following question correctly and the prize is yours.' He sounded like Chris Tarrant in *Who Wants to Be a Millionaire?* 'Now, you will have received a text with a reference number. Can you tell me what it is?'

An image of the dreaded publication meeting flashed across Terri's retina, her mobile vibrating in her pocket. 'Right . . . um . . . hold on.' She scrolled through her messages. Flicking a few buttons, she tapped on the relevant text. 'Hi, Alan . . .'

'Adrian.'

'Adrian.' She'd never been good with names. 'The reference number's A56395.'

'Well done, dear.' He now sounded like Michael Winner. 'All you have to do is decide on a departure date and we can get things moving.'

The espresso was finally reaching the parts other beverages couldn't reach and Terri was on the case, mentally packing her bikini and lying in a cruise liner's steamer chair, browning nicely as the Caribbean Sea drifted past.

'How old are your children?'

'I'm sorry?' She felt as if a brick wall had smacked into her forehead.

'Your children. How old are they?' He waited in vain for a response. 'Your prize is for a family of four, Miss Gillingham.'

Oh, hell, thought Terri, and parried, thinking on her feet. 'When do we have to take this holiday, Ala . . . Adrian?'

'Any-time between June and September this year.'

'Isn't that the hurricane season?'

'Noooo.' He was now imitating a Highland cow giving birth. 'Well, not that you'd notice in the Grenadines anyway.'

'But St Lucia isn't in the Grenadines,' she countered.

'True, but Grenada is.' This was all as clear as mud and twice as thick to Terri.

'You start in St Lucia and end in Grenada. You'll spend the majority of your holiday below the hurricane belt.'

'Sounds painful,' she quipped.

Adrian's guffaw rattled Terri's molars and exacerbated her headache. 'I'll get back to you after the weekend,' she said, moving the conversation along. 'Must speak to those indoors. You know, check on the cricket fixtures and the kids swimming events.'

'Oh.' The silence was riddle with question marks. 'Right.'

Obviously, Adrian didn't do kiddies' activities, thought Terri. He's probably still at the binge drinking stage, she decided, and cut him off with a brisk: 'I'll ring you on Monday. Bye.'

She wandered into the lounge determined to find a way around the problem. This was the first time in her life that she had won anything, if one didn't count the goldfish in a plastic bag that she'd won at the Kursaal in Southend when she was six, and she was not going to let the little matter of a missing husband and kids foul it up.

'Is there such a thing as "rent a family"?' she muttered, as she stretched across the coffee table to pick up her iPad. She didn't have a clue and, sadly, Google didn't either.

Chapter Four

The Beagle Air Reunion

Sam pulled into a parking space at the Dog and Duck public house and cut the BMW's engine. Terri opened the passenger door and stepped straight into a puddle.

'Oh, damn!'

'Problem?' Sam enquired over the car roof as she slammed her door.

'You could have parked in a dry spot,' Terri whinged, flicking water off her left shoe.

'And you could watch where you put your feet. You seem to be miles away. I haven't had a sensible word out of you since we left London.'

She has a point, thought Terri, still busy mulling over her problem with *True Life Movies* and her surrogate family to notice what was going on around her.

The saloon was packed as they approached the bar. 'Evening, Stan,' said Terri, wiping her tights with a handkerchief. 'I see your plans to refurbish are still pending.'

Stan rubbed his chubby hands on a greasy tea-towel and wandered over. 'Yep. Can't see the point in spending good brass on new décor with you lot around.'

'*You lot*' was Stan's generic term for the various air crew who had used the Dog and Duck as their local for years due to its close proximity to Gatwick Airport and the fact that it was open all hours.

'I take it you're here for the reunion?'

They both nodded. 'Is it in the den as usual?'

'Yep.' Stan's monosyllabic responses were legendary unless money was involved. 'What's your tipple?'

'Campari and Soda,' said Sam, removing her coat.

'And a G&T for me, with ice and a slice.'

'Ice on the house, a slice is extra.'

'That's our Stan,' whispered Terri to Sam, 'the last of the big spenders.'

They watched Gordon's gin dribble into a glass from the optic at the back of the bar. 'Did you recognise any of our crowd?' Sam enquired.

'Nope.' Stan placed both drinks on the bar. A solitary piece of ice splashed into Terri's gin. 'That'll be eight pounds thirty-five.'

'Daylight robbery,' she muttered, opening her purse and slapping a £10 note on the counter. 'I'll remember to bring my own slice next time.'

'Oh, very droll,' was Stan's only comment as he wandered over to the cash machine, thick-skinned as ever.

Terri pocketed the change and followed in Sam's wake as she headed across the room, towering above the throng, her four-inch heels adding to her six-foot frame. No one had ever understood how Samantha Hutchins had managed to get a job with Beagle Air when the regulation height for an air-stewardess had been between five-foot-five and five-foot-eight, but the airline's Chief Pilot was known to be partial to wrap-around legs and Sam had never let regulations get in her way.

A cacophony of loud voices and clinking bottles assailed Sam's and Terri's eardrums as they opened the door to the den. More than twenty people were squashed together in a space the size of a small motorhome, tables and stools pushed back against the walls to give more drinking room.

Sam scanned the heads looking for other members of the A-team, their year's stewardess intake at Beagle Air, and moved ahead purposefully. 'Come on,' she called above the racket, 'I can see Evie.'

Evangelina Shapiro was sitting astride a bar stool, her rear elevation covered from neck to ankle in dark brown leather, her riot of thick black curls refusing to conform to any hairstyle as usual. Terri smiled, recalling the first time she had seen her; a pint-pot Italian beauty with 'come to bed' violet eyes, a wasp waist, and a bust which caused her a major centre of gravity problem. With an Italian father and a Cornish mother, she was a force of nature, who could flutter her long eyelashes and have every man within five square miles flocking to her side offering protection. Terri envied her ability to look helpless. When I try it, she thought, I just look pathetic.

'Hi, girls, how's London?'

Each kissed Evie on both cheeks and made wriggle room alongside her.

'You're not wearing specs, Terri?' Evie never missed a trick.

'I've had laser treatment,' Terri spluttered as someone dug her in the spine and G&T dribbled down her chin.

'Did it work?' she asked.

'Well, I had no difficulty recognising you from across the room so something must be right.' Terri placed her glass on the bar top and removed her raincoat. 'Where's George?'

'Here,' said a voice to Terri's rear. 'Our Queen Bee has been boring the pants off me about her varicose veins operation.'

George was the final member of the A-team. Georgina Stanhope, to be precise, a powerhouse travel executive who ate men for breakfast. She was a ball-buster who thought the opposite sex were only useful in bed. Many a pilot had tried to tame her at Beagle Air and had come off worse from the experience. Georgina didn't suffer fools easily and you wouldn't want to cross her. As a friend she was totally loyal; as an enemy she put Genghis Khan in the shade.

'London is great, Evie,' answered Sam belatedly as she made room for one more.

'Well, it would be, Sam,' remarked George, winking in Terri's direction. 'You spend most of it servicing CJ or in a health spa.'

Terri cringed.

'I can see you haven't lost your acerbic wit,' said Sam.

'Only jealous, Samantha. Some of us have to work for a living.'

'And you think I don't?'

Evie cut short the bickering by raising her glass. 'Cheers, girls. Here's to the A-team and long may we last out.'

Over the years the friendship between the four females had stood the test of time, acerbic wit or not, and if any of them needed help it was the A-team who they would turn to first.

They all felt that there was something special about spending their formative years together as trolley dollies, having gone into Beagle Air as innocent girls and come out as fully-fledged members of the female race.

'So, George, how's life in the travel industry?' asked Terri. 'Been on any jollies lately?'

'The Great Wall of China,' George replied, trying to attract the barman's attention.

'Were you trying to get in or out?' enquired Evie.

'Prepare to repel borders,' cut in Sam, nudging Terri in the ribs.

Before her words could register, Terri's left buttock was gripped in a vice-like clutch. 'Hello, Jim,' she said, not bothering to turn round. 'Long time no feel.' Captain Jim Taylor's mighty paw had a very familiar resonance on Terri's derrière and, she had to admit, felt rather pleasant after so many years abstinence.

'Terri, darling, I'd recognise that backside anywhere.'

A smile cracked Terri's stern expression as she tried to work out how old he was. 'This is a surprise, Jim. I thought you'd be in a home . . . another hemisphere by now.' She coughed, picturing the odd commode.

'How could I possibly miss out on seeing my A-team once more?' he replied, fingers playing a Rachmaninov piano concerto on her spine. 'Sam, George, Evie,' he acknowledged, kissing each of them on the cheek. 'How are my girls? Let me buy you a drink.'

'I don't believe it,' Terri exclaimed to George through the toilet door. 'He looks as good today as he did three decades ago; in fact, he looks better. More mature, softer round the edges. How the hell does he do it?'

'You know the old adage, Terri. You're only as old as the woman you feel,' shouted George over the hum of the hand dryer, 'and, let's be honest, Jim felt more than most.'

'Man alive,' Terri gasped, pulling up her briefs, 'I've just been goosed by a seventy-five-year-old. Do you think it's too late to claim sexual harassment?'

'You've got to be joking. If we'd claimed sexual harassment in the seventies, Beagle Air would have ground to a halt. Every pilot in the company would have been suspended. Come to think of it, so would most of us!'

Terri had to admit, George had a point.

'Are you staying over?'

'No, Sam has to get back to Pont Street.'

'On standby duty again, is she?' George always managed to cut to the chase.

Terri shrugged, acknowledging the truth. 'Duty' for Sam was always CJ – the other members of the A-team had never been given his full name, only that he was something big in the City and kept her in opulent surroundings in Knightsbridge for weekday use. They'd assumed the affair would eventually grind to a halt but Sam knew so much about CJ's business life, that any leak to the gutter press by this former mistress risked ruining him overnight. Of course, thought Terri, Sam wasn't like that, she didn't have the killer instinct. At least, Terri didn't think she had.

'How about you, Terri? What's happening in your life?' She followed George out of the ladies.

'Do you want the good news or the bad news?'

'Bad news.'

'I'm about to be given my marching orders at work.'

George stopped in her tracks. 'You're joking! How d'you get fired from the British Electricity Board? Employees don't leave, they get carried out in a box.'

'Not these days, they don't. Since privatisation, management is as keen as mustard.' Terri told George about her faux pas with the BIE logo as they made their way back to the bar.

'And the good news?'

Evie handed Terri her G&T. 'I've just won a two-week cruise around the Caribbean.'

Three pairs of eyes locked on to her face. 'Explain that statement,' ordered Sam.

'Well, you're never going to believe this . . .'

'Try us,' said George over her shoulder.

'Have you ever watched *True Life Movies*?' Terri asked. That got no response. 'It's a TV movie channel. Anyway, they have these competitions where you can win an exotic, all-expenses-paid holiday by correctly answering inane questions. You know the sort of thing. What is Tom Jones famous for?'

'Women's knickers,' answered all three in unison.

'Very funny, but no. The answer's either, A - Blue Suede Shoes, B – Delilah, or C – Waterloo.'

George stabbed her temple. 'Ugh, my brain 'urts, Brian.'

'As I said, inane. Anyway, being bored rigid last Sunday night and having had a couple of glasses of wine, I apparently texted the TV station and answered the question, "Where is St Lucia?" '

'Are you sure it wasn't the whole bottle?' asked George.

'You're becoming really sad,' added Sam.

'Either way, it doesn't do my street cred any good,' concluded Evie.

'Do you want to hear about this or not?' Three pairs of hands were raised, palms out in surrender.

'OK. On Friday morning, some guy texted me at work and told me I'd won a two-week cruise in the Caribbean. I can tell you, I hadn't got a clue what he was talking about.'

'Definitely a whole bottle,' announced George and was kicked in the shin.

'Oooh!' gushed Evie. 'When do we leave? I'd love a Caribbean holiday at someone else's expense.'

'Not so fast, Evie. It's for a family of four.'

Evie pouted.

'Does anyone have any idea where I can rent a family?'

'Well,' said Sam, 'how about George being your husband? It wouldn't be the first time she's been mistaken for a dyke.'

'Touché,' retorted George, eyes rolled heavenwards.

'And Sam and I could be your kids,' announced Evie.

'Oh, thanks a bunch. Do I look that old?'

Only in broad daylight,' quipped George.

'No offence, Georgina, but much as I love you, I don't fancy sharing a bed with you.'

'Sounds erotic,' chipped in Jim, back from working the room and busy wrapping his arm around Terri's shoulders, his hand fingering her bra strap. 'I didn't know you girls batted for the other side.'

'We don't,' said George through gritted teeth. 'As it happens, we're talking about Terri winning a Caribbean holiday for herself and her family.'

'Really. Where?' Jim was all ears.

'St Lucia,' said Evie.

'Actually, it's a cruise from St Lucia to Grenada,' corrected Terri.

'And we're all going, aren't we girls?'

'Oh, come on,' Terri said as Jim's hand slid between her armpit and left breast, 'you can't be serious. *True Life Movies* would never buy it. Apart from anything else, we all have different surnames.' She thought the whole idea was ridiculous.

'Why not?' demanded George, looking determined. 'Lesbian couples could have been previously married and both have grown-up children.' Terri's heart sank. 'What company in this day and age would dare to argue?'

'But they'd want proof, surely?'

'Not if they had a character witness,' suggested Jim. 'Take me with you as your ex-husband, and I will gladly perjure myself.' Terri's arm was now rammed against her side defensively. 'We could do turn and turnabout, George, in that double bed.'

'In your dreams,' George huffed, looking at her watch. 'Good Lord, it's past midnight. Does this pub ever close?'

Terri looked across at Sam. 'What do you think?'

Sam picked up her coat and drained the last of her Campari. 'I think we should take the back roads home, Terri. If the police stop me, I'll be going to the Caribbean via Holloway Prison.'

With Jim Taylor's handprint still moulded to her backside Terri pulled back the duvet and climbed into bed. Could we get away with it? she wondered turning out the light. The idea certainly appealed to her. Two weeks of sun, sea and bad behaviour with the A-team sounded great, and at two-thirty in the morning, with a head full of alcohol fumes, anything seemed possible.

Terri drifted off to sleep dreaming of being at 36,000 feet above Paris on a Vickers Viscount, as it flew seventy-eight passengers north on a night flight from Palma to Gatwick. Captain Jim Taylor was demonstrating the benefits of his joystick to her in the cockpit while the First Officer was at the rear of the aircraft taking a leak. She smiled in her sleep. What happened at 36,000 feet, stayed at 36,000 feet!

Chapter Five

Georgina

Prestige Travel was bedlam when Georgina walked through the door at nine o'clock on Monday morning. Ralph, her number two, was shouting down the phone to some local holiday rep in Greece, three other phones were demanding attention, and a customer from hell was sitting at the middle desk grating her dentures.

'Where's Fran?' mouthed Georgina to Ralph as she threw her wet coat onto the rack by the door and grabbed the nearest phone. Ralph nodded towards the staff room, his eyebrows touching his hairline.

Oh, great, thought George, smiling at the customer, inwardly throttling Fran for being heavily pregnant and constantly caught short.

'Prestige Travel. Can I help you?'

'Good morning. Ms Stanhope, please?'

'Who should I say is calling?'

'Adrian Falks, Global Adventure Holidays.'

Another agent wanting a split commission, decided George, and immediately put him on hold while she answered the next call. The customer stared at her watch, looked at the staff-room door and grunted. What the hell is Fran doing? thought George, making a mental note to fire her if she didn't appear promptly.

'Prestige Travel. Sorry to have kept you waiting.'

'No problem, George,' whispered a familiar voice from what sounded like a cavernous tunnel.

'Terri. Is that you?'

'Yes.'

'Why are you whispering?'

'I'm hiding in the loo at work.'

'You're where? Oh, just a minute . . . Sorry to keep you waiting Mr Falks, Ms Stanhope will be with you in a minute . . . Can't this wait, Terri? It's World War Three in here.'

'No! No, it can't. Oh, bugger!' George heard a loud clatter, some whispered expletives and a lot of shuffling.

'Terri . . . Are you there?'

'Sorry, George. I just dropped my mobile.'

'For goodness' sake, make this quick! And speak up, I can hardly hear you?'

'It's Global Adventure Holidays. They're about to ring you.'

George saw the holding light flashing on the other phone. 'They already have. I've got them on hold.' She heard a toilet flush.

'Just a minute,' mumbled Terri above the racket, 'someone's in one of the cubicles.' A door squeaked and footsteps could be heard walking away. 'Right, all clear. Now, where was I? Oh, yes. Global Adventure Holidays. You have to confirm to them that we are lesbians living together with two grown-up daughters.'

'What?'

'You heard me.'

Georgina hadn't a clue what Terri was talking about. 'Why do they need to know that we're lesbians living together with two grown-up daughters?' she asked, her strident voice causing Ralph to choke on his coffee and the customer from hell to leap from her chair and shoot through the door onto the High Street, leaving the glass vibrating on its hinges. 'That's it,' announced George, 'Fran has to go.'

'What?'

'Nothing, Terri. Well, everything actually. I've just lost a customer because one of my staff spends more time in the loo than at her desk.'

'You're being a lesbian has nothing to do with it then?' muttered Ralph, wiping cappuccino froth from his nose.

'Don't you call me a lesbian,' huffed Fran at the staff room door, hitching up her knickers over her rotund belly under her voluminous tent dress. 'I'll have you know I'm happily married, Ralph Parker, so don't you go spreading malicious rumours about me.'

Georgina looked up and frowned.

'Better dash, George, or I'll be for the chop.' A toilet flushed for a second time.

'I thought you were fired already,' George replied, beckoning Fran to her seat like a demented headmistress.

'Look, just confirm everything I've said to Adrian Falks this morning. Have you got that? And, Georgina, make it sound convincing or our Caribbean cruise will be a non-starter. Speak later. Bye.'

Georgina swapped handsets as in her mind the conversation at the Dog and Duck rose like a phoenix above the chaos of the morning. She coughed, swallowed hard and lowered her voice by two octaves.

'Mr Falks, Georgina Stanhope, here. Sooo sorry to have kept you waiting. Now, how can I help you?'

Harold was standing by Terri's desk when she appeared from the general direction of the ladies. Her stomach did a quick Lambarda and ended up somewhere between her knees and the floor.

'There you are Teresa. Would you come into my office, please?'

Terri nodded and followed her boss's behind like a bad smell.

'Now, what exactly did happen with the BIE logo approval last week?'

Terri's right buttock was halfway into a chair when she realised she wasn't expected to sit down. Pulling herself into an upright position she went on the attack.

'Is it my fault that the Chairman left the Directors' meeting early for a TV appearance and didn't get to see the logo?'

'Good point,' said Harold, 'but not good enough.' He unscrewed his Parker pen and laid it on the blotter. 'As I understand it the matter was never discussed at the meeting . . .

'Bastard, thought Terri, he's been talking to Anne Blakemore on the top floor.

'. . . and therefore no one got to see it, or more to the point, approve it.'

'Harold are you asking me or telling me?' she countered, knowing there was nowhere to hide.

'Teresa, I suggest you sit down and give me something useful for when I meet the CEO this afternoon.'

She dropped into the vacant chair and looked at the floor for inspiration, willing her deceased spiritualist grannie to drop some metaphysical excuse into her head from whichever cloud she happened to be floating on.

'Teresa, I'm waiting.'

Happy Hands Harold, as he was known in the office, could be so supercilious when he had the advantage, and Terri began to feel angry.

'Look, accidents happen. We were on a tight schedule. The print room were getting fed up with us after we had postponed the print run three times, cocking up their machine schedules, and the sales team were screaming for something, anything, to send out to customers overseas. I added the logo approval to the Directors' agenda at the last minute, thinking it would be passed without question. How was I to know that Cyril Trowbridge has a thing about elliptical maps of the world?'

'Well, he does, and we have just spent ten percent of our annual marketing budget on a pile of brochures destined for the shredder. Heads will roll over this, Teresa, and mine won't be one of them.' Harold's finger was inches from her nose.

Too damn' right it won't, you greasy old toad, she thought. Bugger it, I'm off to the Caribbean with or without a head, and as far as I'm concerned the Chairman can stick the logo up his jacksy! The thought was not ideal considering her job was on the line. She took a deep breath and tried for some lateral thinking.

'All I can suggest is that the Chairman designs his own logo on the back of a fag packet and the graphics department turn it into ten thousand stickers, which the sales team can use to cover up the old one. That way we get to use the brochures, the marketing budget remains intact, and Cyril Trowbridge can go back to the House of Lords a happy man.' Terri sat back, her sarcastic words hanging in the air, while images of the local Job Centre came springing to mind.

Harold's podgy hand was pulling out his desk drawer when he appeared to hesitate. She sensed she'd struck gold dust and tried not to smile, mentally applauding her Grannie for planting the idea in her head.

'Umm,' Harold said. 'Ummm.' It was like watching the workings of a Rolex timepiece whirling.

'Leave it with me, Terri.' He closed the drawer and sprang from his seat like a five-year-old on his way to the ice-cream van.

It didn't take rocket science for Terri to realise that she had just handed Harold Crompton a way of coming out of the debacle smelling of roses, while she was left carrying the can.

'We'll talk about this again later,' he said. 'Now, back to the grindstone, old girl. Time is money and all that.' He opened the door and ushered her out into the open-plan office before she had time to register that he had not only insulted her but had left his sweaty palm print on her posterior.

'What is it about your backside, Terri Gillingham?' she mumbled, as she walked back to her desk, anger rising with each step.

Her computer screen lit up like Times Square as she jabbed the space bar in frustration and clicked on '*Mail*'. She knew that reporting her boss for being a patronising, male chauvinist pig, with wandering hands was probably not a good idea under the circumstances, but Terri was in no mood to compromise.

'If my head rolls, Harold, so does yours!' she whispered, and started to type.

To: Mr F Bolton, Director, Human Resources
Copy: Mrs Audrey Laws, Unite Union Representative
From: Teresa Gillingham – Marketing Co-ordinator, BIE Division
Dear Sir,
I wish to report that I have just been sexually harassed by Mr Harold Crompton, Head of BIE Marketing, whilst attending a private meeting in his office . . .

Chapter Six

Evie

Aquamarine seas, pelicans on the wing and the sound of Bob Marley serenading her under a palm tree filled Evie's mind as she massaged Fred Picton's shoulder-blades, her abundant boobs rubbing back and forth across his bald patch as her hands made deep indents into his skin.

The action was proving a tad uncomfortable for Fred as he lay on his stomach, face pressed into the hollow of the massage table in one of the treatment rooms at the Belgrove Park Health Spa in Surrey. His 'Top to Toe' spa day was an unexpected seventieth birthday gift from his wife, Audrey, and one that he would have thoroughly enjoyed, had his member not been trying to bore a hole in the leatherette padding. At an opportune moment he came up for air and found Evie's white-clad nipples tickling his eyebrows. He groaned with delight, adjusted his lower torso and sank back into his hollow, wondering what he would do when it was time to turn over.

Pouring warm oil onto Fred's spine, Evie pushed her palms up his loose buttocks and along his spinal column, coming to rest against his neck where she paused, then made circular movements with her thumbs as she retreated back to his coccyx and pressed hard. As each vertebra came under her thumb pads she imagined tiny seashells pressing into the soles of her feet, warm sand tickling her toes and coral speckles reflected in the crystal-clear shallows of the Caribbean.

She sighed and moved to one side, spreading Fred's legs apart as her oiled fingers dug into the muscles of his inner thighs, kneading the white skin automatically while her head remained miles away, swimming naked under a blanket of tropical stars, the Caribbean Sea lapping around her tanned body like liquid velvet.

Fred's eyes were watering, both from muscle pain and the fact that his masseuse's little finger was brushing up against his left testicle. Somewhere amidst these erotic sensations he could only assume that Audrey had never checked what sort of an establishment Belgrove Park Health Spa was. He hoped his wife would never find out.

With her hands grinding into his fleshy hips Evie dreamt of a bronzed Adonis in tropical whites kneeling at her steamer chair, feeding her papaya from a platter of tropical fruit. She imagined leaning forward to kiss his cute dimple and licked her lips.

By now Fred was up for anything, the aroma of almond essence invading his nostrils, the soft music lulling him into an unthinking state and his masseuse's hot breath hovering above his navy tattoo turning him into a geriatric Rambo. The blokes at the golf club would never believe him, he thought, and closed his eyes, letting the rhythm of the massage produce an effect like Viagra on his libido. He was about to make a suggestive comment when a knock on the treatment room door jolted them both out of their reveries. Evie sprang back from her client's raised buttocks as if electrocuted.

'Sorry to interrupt, Evie,' whispered the blonde head halfway around the door, 'but you have a phone call and the caller says it's urgent.'

Evie grabbed the dislodged fluffy white towel and draped it over Fred's nether regions, patted him gently on the shoulder and nodded sideways to Isabel to take over before making a rapid exit. Outside she leant against the rose-coloured corridor wall, one hand pressed firmly across her mouth, and tried to ground herself.

'For God's sake, Evangelina, what d'you think you were doing?' She cringed at the possible outcome with Fred had Isabel not interrupted them. 'Get a grip, you idiot. Anyone would think you were desperate.' She eased herself off the wall and headed for the spa reception area, her cheeks matching the colour of the wallpaper. She came around the bend to find Sylvia, the reflexologist, holding out the telephone handset. Evie nodded, took the phone and said hello.

'Hi, it's Terri. We appear to have the green light.'

Evie stopped herself from returning to thoughts of her dimpled Adonis. 'You mean, the cruise is on?'

'Yes, isn't it great? I don't know what George said to Adrian Falks, but I have just received a text asking me which dates we prefer. That's why I'm ringing. I need to give him an answer before close of business today. Can you make the last two weeks in July?'

Evie sashayed around the reception desk and grabbed the clipboard from the top drawer. 'I think so, just give me a minute to check the staff roster.' Her eyes scanned the work sheet and she punched the air. 'Yes . . . yes, I can. Sylvia is

down for leave for the first week, but I know she will swap
with me when I tell her I'm off to the Caribbean. She normally
only goes to her mum's in Margate anyway.'

'Great. The rest of the A-team are free those weeks so put
the dates in your diary and get ready to rumble.'

'What, even Sam?'

'Yes, even Sam. Apparently CJ has had a change of plan this
year and is whale-watching off Prince Rupert Sound. Sam is
spitting bullets and determined to teach him a lesson.'

'Well, here's to the Caribbean and the A-team afloat. I hope
the Grenadines can stand it.'

'I'll second that,' said Terri. 'By the way, sorry to have rung
you at work but it was urgent. Were you in the middle of
something vital?'

'Nooo,' said Evie, picturing Fred's buttocks. 'Nothing vital.
Talk later. Bye.'

She was just writing a 'post-it' note to the reflexologist
when her fellow masseuse, Isabel, came flying round the
corner, her hair dishevelled and her attire in disarray. Evie
watched, open-mouthed, as she bounced off the wall and
disappeared into the ladies' toilet, the seam of her overall torn.

'Oops,' whispered Evie to herself and crept quietly out
through the French doors, making a detour through the spa's
grounds to the staff room, feeling guilty for having
inadvertently raised her client's expectations. The Belgrove
Park Health Spa's rules were very clear on the matter of client
fraternisation and poor Fred Picton would not be getting
another 'Top to Toe' any time soon.

Deloitte Villas had a drab, rain-soaked appearance as Terri carried a bottle of Pinot Grigio into the lounge of number 45 and filled two glasses.

'When are you going to get yourself a decent settee?'

Terri looked across to see George shuffling her hips around on the Chesterfield trying to find a comfortable spot. 'When I get to the end of the month and actually have a surplus in my bank account.'

'What are the chances?' George asked, stretching for her wine glass.

'None,' replied her friend, doing likewise. 'Now, what did you say to Adrian Falks that made him cave in without a fight?'

'I pointed out that our gay status,' her mouth puckered, 'was in no way a barrier to being given the holiday, and said that if he felt uncomfortable about it, I would be happy to contact *True Life Movies* and offer the services of Prestige Travel to them instead. I even pointed out that as we were in the middle of Fulham and not in the wilds of Yorkshire, Prestige Travel was the ideal company for their needs. It all went down like a lead balloon.'

'I can imagine. Crisp?' Terri pushed the bowl of Kettle Chips under George's nose.

George took a handful then paused. 'The photo shoot seemed to be a problem, though.'

'Photo shoot. What photo shoot?'

'Apparently, the TV station do a follow-up piece after the holiday. I imagine it's to prove to the viewers that these competitions really do happen.'

'And they need some happy family shots with the kids frolicking in the surf.'

'Got it in one.'

Obviously, the A-team would not pass muster, thought Terri. 'So, what did you say?'

George stood up, lifted the cushion, gave it some Muhammad Ali treatment and settled once more. 'I told him we didn't do publicity and suggested he trawl the advertising agents for a set of actors. He seemed relieved and quite taken by this idea, so I left him to it and got on with my day. You really do need to find another settee, Terri, this one has seen one too many late-night fumbles. All the webbing has gone.'

'I wish,' Terri replied, recollecting that the last time that settee had seen any intimate action was before Live Aid. The doorbell interrupted her thoughts, so she headed for the front door.

'What exotic take-away cuisine are you offering me tonight, Ms Gillingham?' George called over her shoulder, sliding to the floor where she landed in a heap.

'Chicken Korma with pilau rice,' Terri shouted, moving down the hallway, 'and don't just sit there, go and get the plates, they're in the oven warming.'

A strong smell of curry permeated the house as Terri surfaced at two in the morning with *Movies4Men* blasting in her eardrums. She wandered around aimlessly clearing the glasses and plates from the coffee table and wafting the front door back and forth as she pinched her nose. Staggering up the stairs, she flopped on the bed and kicked off her shoes, rolled into the duvet and doused the light.

An odd image filled Terri's vision as her body relaxed. Happy Hands Harold was mounting snooty Anne Blakemore on the dilapidated Chesterfield while her Grannie floated overhead aiming poisoned darts at his naked backside.

'Go for it, Gran,' Terri muttered, and promptly fell asleep.

Chapter Seven

Gatwick Airport

Terri drummed her fingers on the driver's headrest as the A-team sat on the M23 in a traffic jam, waiting to reach Junction 9 with rain lashing the roof of the hired people carrier.

'Not a good way to start,' Sam complained from the front.

Terri chewed her lip and ignored the comment. Ever since Sam had been told she was flying steerage instead of her usual first class, she'd done nothing but whinge.

'If we don't get to the South Terminal in the next twenty minutes we won't be starting at all,' muttered George in the back seat.

Terri nodded, everything crossed including her eyebrows.

'No sweat, ladies,' said the driver, 'I'll have you there on time. Never returned a passenger to his pick-up point yet, and I don't intend to start now.'

'Perhaps we should ring the airline and tell them we're on our way,' suggested Evie.

'No point,' remarked Sam. 'Caribbean Island Airway's staff probably only speak Creole.'

'OK, that's enough.' Terri sounded like Joyce Grenville. 'Let's just chill.'

The driver swung off the motorway and down numerous back-doubles, pulling up outside North Terminal with minutes to spare. The concourse was like Wembley Stadium on Cup Final Day as they disembarked in the drop-off zone and Sam took the lead, dragging her large Louis Vuitton luggage behind her, leaving Terri to bring up the rear having paid off the taxi using some of the £1,000 cash allowance from *True Life Movies*. At this rate, she thought, as they elbowed their way to the check-in desk, the cash will have run out before we hit the airside lounge.

The check-in queue stretched to Brighton. A seething mass of humanity stood clinging to baggage trollies, kids of every age group and hue sniffling or screaming their heads off as they snaked their way to the front. The A-team looked at each other and collectively groaned.

'It was never like this in our day,' moaned George as a child slapped a sticky hand across her arm from the opposite lane.

'Normally, it's never like this for me when I travel with CJ.' Sam's jaw stuck out so far you could have eaten off it.

'Leave it to me,' said Evie, abandoning her case and strolling over to the rep standing to one side, clipboard in hand.

Minutes later the A-team were out of the queue, over to a spare check-in desk and on their way to departures before they could say Beagle Air.

'How did you do that?' asked George, handing her boarding pass to an official at the gate.

'Easy-peasy,' Evie replied, pulling her handbag from under her jacket. 'I told him I was heavily pregnant and might empty my bladder all over the concourse floor if I didn't get to a toilet soon.'

'You've been taking lessons from one of my staff,' said George, moving towards the baggage X-ray machine.

'From where I was standing,' said Sam, 'the chap spent most of the conversation peering down your cleavage with eyes as big as doorstops.'

Evie giggled. 'He did say that the father of my child was a very lucky man.' She bent down to remove her shoes and gave the elderly official standing by the luggage belt an eyeful.

'I'd say at your age it's more like the Immaculate Conception,' Terri quipped, struggling to get her belt free of her trousers. 'Why do we have to go through all this anyway?' She slammed the belt into the plastic tray with her watch, passport, shoes, jacket and handbag. 'I might as well be naked.' The woman standing waiting for her on the other side of the metal-detector arch looked like a Sumo Wrestler.

'Perhaps we should start the Naked Travellers Club,' shouted George from the other end of the baggage belt. 'We could charge one hundred pounds a pop and issue white towelling dressing gown with the club's logo on the pocket. Members could then travel in comfort and give all the men a thrill as they exposed themselves for inspection.'

'Not a pretty sight,' replied Terri, thinking of her own reflection in the bedroom mirror.

'If Evie exposed herself the bloody machine would blow up,' commented Sam as the Sumo wrestler caressed her ribcage.

'To say nothing of those wrap-around legs of yours, Sam.' Evie submitted herself to an over-zealous body search as the chap at the monitor struggled to keep his face straight.

'Right, A-team, follow me,' Sam announced, piling everyone into the lift by Curry's/PC World and delivering them to the VIP Lounge on the upper concourse where she flashed a card under the nose of a wet behind the ears, uniformed male and waltzed through like the Queen of the Nile.

'Ugh, I hate airports,' groaned Terri, as she collapsed into a soft chair and kicked off her mules.

George helped herself to a *Daily Telegraph*, a platter of smoked salmon canapés and four glasses of pink fizz and carried them over on a tray. They each took a champagne flute and waited for George to do the honours.

'To CJ,' she announced holding her glass aloft. 'Long may he hump Sam.'

'To CJ,' Evie and Terri echoed.

'Oh, for God's sake, you lot, keep your voices down!'

'Good morning, ladies and gentlemen. This is your captain speaking. I would like to welcome you on board this Caribbean Island Airways flight to St Lucia and Antigua. Our flight time to St Lucia will be eight hours and thirty-five minutes and we will be flying at . . .'

'The speed of sound,' muttered George sarcastically, chipping away at the peeling bulkhead by the window.

'. . . thirty-six thousand feet and anticipate arriving in Hewanorra Airport at. . .'

'Did he say Holy Nora airport?' asked Evie, poking her head between the seats.

Terri shrugged hearing only one word in three.

'. . . so sit back and enjoy the flight while Roxanne and her team pander to your every need.'

'Oooh,' tittered Evie as she sat back in her seat. 'Fred Picton ought to be here.'

'Who's Fred Picton?' asked Sam sitting alongside.

'Oh, just someone I'm acquainted with.'

Two heads spun round, noses meeting in the gap between the seats.

'Give with the details, Shapiro.

She tapped the edge of her nose. 'Need to know basis, girls, and you don't need to know.'

Sam squeezed her way into the rear starboard toilet and concertinaed the door into place. The compartment stank of urine and stale soap. Memories, she thought, and lowered herself on to the plastic loo seat. She searched around for toilet paper but the recess was empty, as was the tissue box and hand towel compartment. 'Great,' she grunted.

'Excuse me,' she said as she pulled the galley curtain to one side, revealing one of the cabin crew having a quick puff. Sam did a double take as the cigarette magically disappeared into the coffee pot. She was not amused. 'Are you supposed to smoke onboard these days?

'Er . . . Can I help you?'

'Yes, dear, you certainly can. There's not a shred of toilet paper in that loo.' She pointed to the door as an obese passenger struggled to get inside. 'And if you don't want me to report you to your Number One, I suggest you get a complimentary Gin and Tonic to seat 15B pretty sharpish.

'A G&T. Seat 15B. Certainly. Straight away.'

'On second thoughts, make that four.' Sam wandered back up the aisle chuckling to herself, recalling a similar occasion when she had been caught by a Beagle Air passenger glugging brandy, straight from a miniature bottle. 'That misdemeanour cost me a half-bottle of Johnny Walker Red Label.'

'What?' asked Evie, looking up from a double-page P&O world-cruise advertisement.

'I've just caught the Number Three smoking.'

'Great. Drinks all round?' enquired Evie.

'How did you guess?'

Terri watched the captain saunter down the aisle, a ripple of excitement in the air as he nodded and chatted to various passengers, the braiding on his epaulettes glittering under the cabin lighting. Captain Jim Taylor immediately sprang to mind.

Why is it men take on a Richard Gere persona when they're in uniform? she thought. As with this particular specimen, Jim Taylor had been tall, sun-tanned and oozing authority, playing the cabin like the consummate professional he was. A hot flush spread up her neck as she remembered that he had also played with her. She shrugged. I was only eighteen after all, she argued inwardly, and he did have big hands.

'Good afternoon, ladies. I trust you're enjoying your flight.'

Terri nodded, her cheeks burning and tried to remind herself that this one was young enough to be her son.

'Have you flown with Caribbean Island Airways before?'

'No,' she cooed. 'Our first time, actually.'

'First and last,' mumbled Sam from the seat behind.

'We used to fly the skies as crew on Beagle Air, years ago.' God, Gillingham, she thought, you sound inane.

'Really. My father was a pilot with Beagle Air. You probably know him.'

'It isn't Captain Jim Taylor, by any chance?' asked Evie, muddying troubled waters.

The pilot looked at her and his expression melted. 'No . . . no, Captain Paul Chambers, actually. I'm named after him.'

George was now practically imploding in her seat.

'You must give me your names and I'll tell him I've met you.'

Terri was about to reveal all when a sharp pain pierced her right ribcage and Sam came to George's rescue. 'I don't think so, Captain. I don't think your father was there in our time. How long have we got to go before landing?'

Captain Chambers made a big thing of looking at his watch and turned his eyes to the ceiling, pretending to calculate flight vectors, wind speed and jet streams for the benefit of the lady sitting in seat 16C. 'Another hour and twenty-five minutes,' he finally announced, his loud voice carrying six rows.

'As if he didn't know that before leaving the cockpit,' muttered George from her foetal position.

'Like father, like son,' Terri whispered.

'Don't remind me.'

George and Captain Paul Chambers Senior had had a vitriolic relationship all through the A-team's flying days. He had been Beagle Air's Chief Training Captain at the time and took a shine to Georgina from the first day she appeared in the training school. On more than one occasion he had tried to get his hand up her skirt but George, hot from a convent education, was having none of it.

He was an ex-Second World War pilot with male chauvinist tendencies, so her constant rejections dented his very inflated ego and he decided to get his own back.

At the time, Beagle Air were operating Douglas DC3s with two pilots, one stewardess and forty-eight passengers and, like the other fresh-faced members of the A-team, George was painfully naive. On her first solo flight after qualifying, Paul Chambers made his move.

'Now, let's see what you remember about retracting the rear wheel.'

Georgina looked vacant.

'Please tell me you know how to retract the rear wheel after take-off and lock it down again before landing?'

George hadn't a clue what he was talking about. All she knew was that there was a small wheel under the tailplane that kept the fuselage from touching the ground.

'Good God, what have you been doing for the past three weeks in the training school? I'll certainly have words with the Chief Training Stewardess when we get back.'

George felt her world spiralling down into her new Bally court shoes before she'd even had time to scuff the soles.

'Well, I suppose I'll have to show you myself. It's really quite simple.' Captain Chambers huffed his way to the rear of the cabin, dug around in the stowage area behind some sludge green webbing and extracted a large metal pole with two horizontal U-bends on the shaft and a bayonet fitting at one end. With this in hand, he walked into the cabin and dropped the bayonet end into a small hole in the floor of the aisle.

'Now, you turn the pole fifty-two times clockwise to bring the wheel up, and fifty-two times anti-clockwise to put it down.' He looked up. 'Do you understand?'

By now George would have believed that Sean Connery was an Irish leprechaun. 'I'd better write that down,' she said, rushing to her manual and grabbing a pen.

'And don't forget to tell the captain when you do your cockpit briefing.' He paused waiting for George to catch up.

'Er, briefing?'

'Yes, dear. The briefing. *"Passengers strapped in, cabin stowed,* **wheel up.***"* Or *"Passengers strapped in, cabin stowed,* **wheel down.***"* Have you got that?'

Not only had George got it, she proceeded to wind away, day in, day out, for three months, with only her confused passengers to act as witnesses. It all came to a head one day when the Chief Training Stewardess climbed aboard to do a line check on Georgina and could not believe her eyes.

'What the hell did you think you were doing?' she asked, in the Queen Bee's office after the flight.

'I was raising and lowering the rear wheel as I was taught,' said Georgina, puffing out her chest.

'Taught!' yelled the Chief Training Stewardess. 'Taught by whom?'

'Captain Chambers, Miss.'

'Captain Chambers? But that's ridiculous, Georgina. The rear wheel on a DC3 is static. You couldn't shift it even with a sledgehammer. I'm afraid you've been the victim of one of Paul Chamber's stupid pranks.'

The penny suddenly dropped and, with upper arm muscles the size of coconuts, Georgina turned into a ball-buster looking for revenge.

Some months later, on a cold, snowy February evening, she was flying back from Edinburgh with Captain Paul Chambers at the controls and it was touch and go whether he could land the Dakota in Gatwick due to inclement weather and poor visibility.

On approach in a snowstorm, the captain battled with his joystick, trying to keep the aircraft level, sweat beading his forehead, visibility down to three hundred yards and the passengers bouncing around in their seats from the turbulence. Just as he got a visual on the runway Georgina shot into the flight deck and shouted, 'ABORT! ABORT!'

The nose came up, the aircraft shot into the clouds and the passengers grabbed onto their arm rests for dear life. After struggling to get the aircraft back onto a level horizon at five thousand feet Captain Chambers turned to his stewardess.

'What the hell's the problem, Georgina?'

'Sorry, Captain,' she yelled over the noise of the engines. 'I forgot to lower the rear wheel!!!'

(You may be wondering what the metal pole was actually for? Well, it was for the First Officer to manually wind down the flaps if the aircraft suffered hydraulic failure. As for the hole in the floor . . . By shining a torch down it, the First Officer could check that the engine's oxygen bottle gauges were in the green zone.)

The story went viral around Gatwick Airport and Captain Paul Chambers Senior never forgave Georgina for making him look like a pillock amongst his contemporaries.

As for his son, standing behind Terri's left shoulder, she had to agree with George. It was probably better to let sleeping dogs lie.

Chapter Eight

St Lucia

Hewanorra baggage hall roasted like the inside of a pizza oven as the A-team stood waiting for their luggage.

'What happens now?' asked Sam, standing under a colonial roof fan, dabbing her neck with a hankie.

Terri reached in her bag and pulled out the Global Adventure Holidays folder. She rummaged inside. 'We're, er . . . Oh, here we are. We're to meet the Blue Lagoon Caribbean Cruise rep by the information desk in the Arrivals Hall,' she read aloud. 'He will have a taxi waiting to transport us to the Bay Gardens Hotel in Rodney Bay.'

'Where's that?'

'Haven't a clue. Anyway, we stay there tonight then move aboard tomorrow after breakfast.'

'*We are sailing, we are sailing,*' crooned Evie, her hands in the air swaying from side to side.

'Singing is not one of your better talents, Shapiro,' complained George as she elbowed her way to the carousel which staggered into life with a grunt. 'Quit the Rod Stewart impression and help me with the luggage.'

'Does it have a swimming pool?' asked Sam, refusing to move off her spot.

'Of course it does,' Terri answered, pulling the two baggage trolleys apart with unnecessary force.

'Then lead me to it. I need some aqua-therapy.'

'What you need and what you'll get are two very different things, Samantha Hutchins, if you don't get your arse over here right now.' George was having trouble heaving the Louis Vuitton off the moving belt and Evie nearly had a hernia lifting it onto a trolley.

'What have you got in here, Sam? The crown jewels.'

'That's for me to know, Evie, and you to guess.' Sam condescended to wander over.

'Here, grab this,' demanded George, dropping Terri's wheelie bag on her toe.

'Christ, George, watch what you're doing.' Sam was now hopping around on one leg as Terri lifted her case on top. 'And don't scratch my Louis Vuitton, it's worth a fortune.'

'So is my Tesco's best,' argued Terri, holding onto George's waistband as she stretched for Evie's silver-grey Samsonite.

'This is worse than the Harrods January sales,' complained Sam, 'and to cap it all, I've just broken a nail.'

'Oh, do stop whinging, woman, and push that trolley through Customs.

The A-team were still waiting at the information desk long after the last of the Caribbean Island Airways passengers had climbed aboard their charter bus and waved them farewell. Evie sat balancing precariously on the top of her case while George, Sam and Terri cross-examined the duty officer.

'What do you mean, you've never heard of them?' George was in travel agent mode, doing a good job of ruining the duty officer's day.

Rum Punch

'They're a large cruise company,' said Terri. 'Blue Lagoon Caribbean Cruises. You must have heard of them.' The duty officer shook his head.

'Try speaking in patois,' suggested Sam.

'Don't be ridiculous, Samantha, St Lucia was a British colony. Everyone speaks English here.'

'I happen to have been educated at Peckham Comprehensive,' said the staff member, 'and I can assure you, I have never, ever heard of Blue Lagoon Caribbean Cruises either here or anywhere else.'

'I say, girls, perhaps this is him,' suggested Evie, pointing to the entrance.

They all turned to see a thin Rastafarian wearing a Carib tee-shirt and a green, yellow and red knitted tea-cosy hat over his dreadlocks.

The three others shrugged, turned back to the duty officer and continued giving him grief when a lilting Caribbean voice stopped them in their tracks.

'Well, 'ello dere, ladies. Welcome to Saint Lucia and 'ave a nice day.'

They slowly turned to face their worst fears.

A mass of white teeth shone out of a beaming mouth. 'I be Moses, ladies. Your Blue Lagoon Cruise rep.'

Sam looked him up and down slowly and shook her head. 'No,' she said. 'No, you're not.'

'Yes, lady, yes I am,' he confirmed, 'and I 'ave de transport waitin' outside.'

Terri could hear Sam's teeth grate together as she glared in her direction.

'What do you want me to do, Sam? We either go with the flow or get back on the flight to Gatwick. Now what's it to be?' By now Moses was busily pushing both trolleys towards the exit.

'I, for one, have no intention of getting back on that aeroplane,' announced George. 'One Captain Chambers in a life-time is quite enough for me.' She followed in the Rastafarian's footsteps, dragging Evie with her, while Terri looked at Sam with her shoulders up around her ears.

Samantha fizzed like a shaken Schweppes tonic bottle. 'Very well, but the hotel had better not be a beach hut or I'm checking into the local Hilton and *you're* getting the bill.' She turned towards the exit and clipped her way across the concourse on four-inch heels.

'Grannie, help?' begged Terri as she made a backward wave to the duty officer and stepped out into the scorching car park.

The Bay Gardens Hotel was like a glimpse of heaven when the clapped-out Dormobile with its bone-shaking suspension turned into the wide gateway and deposited its passengers at a grand, porticoed entrance. Terri staggered out of the vehicle, convinced that her vertebrae had fused together, and nodded to the uniformed concierge before entering the air-conditioned marble reception area behind the others and collapsed onto a leather settee by a water feature surrounded by tropical flowers. She closed her eyes, thankful that the Bay Gardens was not a wooden hut and tried to erase the experience of the previous two hours from her memory.

The journey from Hewanorra Airport had been a nightmare. The dilapidated transport had snaked along hairpin roads at top speed and thumped in and out of potholes, bouncing along while white-sand beaches, dense rain forests and giant Atlantic rollers flashed by. It was like something out of *Top Gear,* mused Terri, as exhaust fumes contaminated the interior every time the Dormobile faced west, and she spent the whole trip holding up the roof lining above her seat.

Moses rode shotgun in the front, chatting to the driver, chewing tobacco and singing away to 'Natty Dread'. As they approached the north-west of the island, he pointed out the Governor's Residence on their left before hanging on for dear life as the Dormobile careered down the hill into the back streets of Castries and along the harbour front, where a white, slab-sided cruise liner was tied to the dock.

'Look!' shouted Evie, stating the obvious. A huge, floating block of flats towered above them as the vehicle passed by the open market, swerved to the left and followed the coast road out of town towards a place signposted Gros Islet. Somewhere along that road they had turned into the hotel entrance.

Terri's teeth were still rattling as she opened her eyes and saw a beautiful girl in multi-coloured sarong and matching turban standing over her holding a tray of drinks. Terri blinked, thinking the girl was a mirage, and then she spoke.

'Good afternoon, ladies, and welcome to de Bay Gardens Hotel.' She handed each of her guests a fruit cocktail, glasses dripping with condensation and exploding with fresh pineapple, cherries and mint.

It went down like nectar. The A-team oozed gratitude.

'May I take your passports so that I can complete de formalities?' Her smile washed away the traumas of the day and, for the first time in twelve hours, the group settled into an aura of contented apathy. Terri hoped it would go on for ever. Needless to say, it didn't.

'Excuse me. Ms Gillingham, may I have a word?' The manager was calling Terri from across the lounge, four passports open in his hand.

'This is where Plan A hits the buffers,' announced Sam playing with her cocktail stick. 'Anyone can see I'm too old to be your daughter.

Terri groaned, her energy level at rock bottom.

'Leave him to me,' announced George, her joints cracking as she rose. Terri closed her eyes once more, thankful that George still had some fight left in her. Surely, she thought, we can't fail now, having got this far? However, she wasn't convinced. Failing had been embedded in her DNA since birth.

Evie decided to give a running commentary from behind the Carmen Miranda table decoration. 'George keeps trying to interrupt . . . but the manager is having none of it . . . Now George's right hand is raised, palm out, and she's shaking her head . . . Crikey, she's nodding frantically and beckoning us over to join her.'

'You go, Terri,' said Sam. 'I feel ridiculous in my four-inch heels, pretending to be your off-spring.'

'Thanks a bunch, Sam. I don't remember you refusing to go along with this charade back in May.'

'In May, Teresa, I had other things on my mind.'

Evie and Terri approached the reception desk like criminals about to be arrested.

'Girls, I'd like to introduce you to Mr Kosmo King from the Dominican Republic. He's the manager of the Bay Gardens.'

Their smiles lacked enthusiasm.

'Kosmo,' George nodded in his direction, 'is distraught because the hotel is unable to accommodate us under the circumstances.'

Terri's dental bridge slipped.

'The hotel is over booked and there are no double-bed rooms left. I have pointed out that we are unhappy with this state of affairs, Terri, as we specifically requested a double bed back in London and that we will certainly be complaining to Global Adventure Holidays on our return. However, I fear we must accept the two twin-bedded rooms on offer as we appear to have no choice in the matter.' Evie couldn't look at her. 'To compensate us for this inconvenience, Kosmo insists that dinner and our bar bill will be on the house.' Kosmo King looked like the famous nodding bulldog from Admiral Insurance. 'Would this meet with your approval, darling?' George turned to her friends, her expression stony, and winked. Terri nearly wet herself.

Swimming under the stars was an experience like no other. Evie kept telling the others that she had dreamt of doing this every day since the Beagle Air reunion at the Dog and Duck, while Terri floated on her back with a Planter's Punch attached to her right hand, watching a satellite track slowly across the tropical heavens.

'Well, girls,' she said as Sam pressed the Jacuzzi button and frothy water encircled her in pale blue lighting, 'this is definitely better than bracing Skegness.'

'Oh, I don't know,' replied George, sipping her champagne cocktail while reclining in a blow-up plastic armchair in the centre of the pool, 'I'm told the North Sea can be very invigorating at this time of year. Assuming you can find it at low tide.'

Chapter Nine

Rodney Bay

The A-team were packed and ready to go on their cruise when Moses turned up with his decrepit Dormobile at ten-thirty the following morning. Kosmo King was standing to attention under the portico as a myriad of cases were loaded into the van by the concierge. Feeling rested, replete and a tad hungover, Terri ran her thumb across her waistline, checking the communal money belt was secure under her sundress, amused that the kitty was still very much intact thanks to the generosity of the Bay Gardens' management.

She was dreaming of five-course dinners, Las Vegas cabaret shows and dancing the night away in the arms of some handsome deck officer as the Dormobile turned onto the main road heading away from Castries. Three minutes later it turned into Rodney Bay Marina and pulled up alongside a shower block.

'Perhaps the cruise ship is anchored off,' suggested Evie.

Terri nodded, lips squeezed together, fingers crossed. 'I bet there's a crew of matelots in white mufti waiting for us at the dock with the ship's tender,' she said confidently.

'Ever the optimist,' muttered Sam as she dragged her case past a row of shops, rondavel-shaped bar, a swimming pool and the administration block before coming to rest facing a huge marina full of yachts.

Moses, nodding enthusiastically, beckoned the A-team on as he headed down pontoon 'B' purposefully, his tea-cosy hat bobbing up and down. They followed like lemmings, scanning the boats crammed together down both sides of the concrete walkway looking for the Blue Lagoon shore party.

Nearing the end, Moses turned, stretched out his arm and beamed with delight. 'Well, dis is it, ladies. Blue Lagoon Caribbean Cruise's very own tirty-eight-foot catamaran, *Rum Punch*!'

Four mouths uniformly dropped open at the sight of what looked like a twin-hulled, oversized dinghy. Each stared at the vessel in horror, then turned on Moses. His smile froze, his nose twitched and, like a meerkat in panic mode, he leapt onto the boarding platform, shot up the steps, ran down the side of the superstructure and threw his head back ninety degrees, shouting: 'Shadrach, man! Your passengers, dey be waitin'.'

Four pairs of eyes followed his gaze, travelling vertically up the mast, past two metal struts attached to supporting wires and onwards to the very top where a figure sat suspended from a rope, its legs dangling through what could only be described as a dark blue nappy. It waved.

'If you think I'm spending two weeks on this bathtub with Tarzan, Terri, then you can think again,' announced Sam, her index finger pointed skywards as she shielded her eyes from the sun.

Evie stepped back two paces to get a better look. 'Are you sure it's Tarzan, Sam?'

'Well, as sure as hell, it couldn't be Jane,' mused George, rubbing the back of her neck. 'Not with dreadlocks and muscular legs like that.' She scanned the deck. 'I wonder where the cabaret room is.'

'Somewhere between the Starlight Bar and the cinema,' replied Terri, her words freezing the air, her Gillingham temper to the fore. She leapt onto the steps and grabbed Moses by his throat and pushed him up against the cabin window.

'Bring me down, eh?' shouted the figure from above. No one was listening.

'Explain yourself,' Terri demanded, 'and it better be good or you're going to meet your maker, sonny.'

'Eh, Moses man, bring me down.'

By now, Moses's eyes were bulging, and Terri was about to spend the balance of her two score years and ten in a St Lucian jail for GBH when George appeared at her side.

'Let him go, Terri. Murdering the messenger is not going to help, now is it?' The Rastafarian's eyeballs oscillated between them, his pupils dilating. 'Moses, bring Tarz . . . that bloke up there, down,' she instructed as she peeled her friends fingers from his Adam's apple and pushed her away.

'You be one unhappy missy,' Moses choked as he unwound a rope from a cylinder jutting out from the mast at hip-level and paid it out slowly.

'And you be one little shit for referring to this dump as a cruise liner,' Terri yelled from behind George's shoulder.

'Just what I bin tinkin',' announced a deep masculine voice as a pair of size thirteen feet landed on the deck. 'Moses, de missy 'ere, she be right. You be one little shit. Now get de udder ladies aboard and make dem comfortable while I makes us all a long cool drink. De ladies, dey look a bit on de frazzled side to me.'

The A-team sat around a table on the stern deck in stony silence while the skipper busied himself in the galley, throwing handfuls of ice cubes into high ball glasses, flooding each with four fingers of Mount Gay rum, a mix of fruit juices and a dash of Grenadine, completing the process with a flourish of grated nutmeg. He stretched across the windowsill and handed a glass to each female then stood in the doorway, shoulder against the frame, arms and legs crossed.

'Now den, ladies, what I wants to know is dis. What yous all be doin' 'ere on *Rum Punch*?'

'My thoughts exactly,' countered Terri, glaring across at Moses in the saloon as she gulped down what she thought was the best rum punch cocktail she'd ever tasted. 'If we knew the answer to that, we definitely wouldn't be here.'

'Well den, missy. I suggest you starts at de beginnin' and we goes from dere, eh?'

A pregnant pause ensued as Mount Gay rum went to work on frayed nerves. No one seemed eager to start so the host commenced proceedings.

'Cat got de tongue, ladies? Well, I's better make de introductions. I'm Shadrach Jonathon William Bligh.' He bowed. 'Shadrach to me friends, and I be de owner and captain of dis fine vessel.'

The new arrivals all acknowledged him with a nod.

'Now, dis is what I knows. Today, I bin expectin' a couple wid two teenage kids wantin' a two-week cruise in de

Grenadines. What I gets instead is four fine ladies from de city, all wearin' high-heeled shoes and fancy togs and pullin' enough baggage to sink de damn' navy! So, which one of yous fine ladies is goin to tell me what you bin and gone and done wid my family from Engaland, 'cos my eyes ain't deceivin' me, and yous are definitely not dem.'

Sam, George and Evie remained mute. Obviously, thought Terri, the other members of the A-team had decided that this was her prize, her idea and her cock-up, and she should be the one to sort out the mess.

Great, she concluded, searching for the right place to start. 'Actually, Captain Bligh, that is exactly who we are.' His eyebrows rose. 'My name's Teresa Gillingham. This is Evangalina Shapiro, this is Samantha Hutchins, and at the other end of the table, Georgina Stanhope. We have been close friends for years and our being here all started back in May this year when I won a Caribbean holiday for four on a TV channel called *True Life Movies*. . .'

Terri was on her second rum punch by the time she reached the bit where they arrived at the Bay Gardens Hotel and by now her eyes were crossing and she was getting cantankerous.

'So, here we be . . . I mean, here we are, Captain, expecting to spend our two-week vacation cruising in style on a seventy-thousand-tonne ship of the line, with associated baggage,' her head nodded to a mass of cases and bags sweltering on the pontoon, 'not sailing into the sunset like the proverbial Owl and Pussy Cat on a bloody thirty-eight-foot pea-green boat.'

Evie kicked her under the table, the Mount Gay now threatening to take control of Terri's tongue.

'Who said we was seventy-tousand-tonnes?' The captain flicked the top off a bottle of Carib beer with his thumb nail and took a swig.

'Oh, I don't know,' Terri said irritably, trying desperately to remember. 'The bird on the television. Adrian Falks from Global Adventure Holidays. My dead grannie. What does it matter? The fact is we were expecting a cruise. Got it? A CRUISE.'

'And dat's just what yous got,' he replied.

Teresa emptied the dregs from her highball glass, playing for time and refusing to acknowledge the credibility of his statement.

George, meanwhile, decided to clarify matters. 'Did you actually ever see any reference to a cruise ship, Terri?'

Their party leader gritted her teeth and reluctantly shook her head.

'So, this cruise of ours could have been on the *QEII* or on a rubber dinghy?'

She nodded again.

Sam was drumming her fingernails on the tabletop. 'What exactly did *True Life Movies* portray in that trailer of theirs?'

Terri's lungs deflated. 'Oh, you know the sort of thing. Exotic tropical locations, palm fringed beaches, girls in skimpy bikinis . . .'

'And maybe the odd catamaran?' asked Evie.

Terri lowered her eyes and nodded again.

'Great,' said George, collapsing back into her seat. 'Would somebody like to tell me what happens now?'

'I'd say dat you be in one whole creek o' shit widdout a paddle,' said Shadrach Bligh pointing the Carib bottle directly at Terri. 'Let's get dis real straight now. Firstly, yous is not a lesbian?'

'No.'

'And your friend dere,' he pointed at George, 'she not be a lesbian eider?'

'No.'

'And de English couple wid de two kids?'

'They never existed.'

'Den, from where I'm sittin', ladies, we all be in de shit.' He scratched his forehead and stared at his size thirteens looking for inspiration. 'Have any of yous sailed before?'

The A-team looked as if they were watching a tennis match at Wimbledon.

Oh, Lordie, Lordie.' He gazed at the stratosphere. 'So, yous never been to sea?'

'Only on a cruise lin . . .' offered Sam before being cut short by Evie's knee.

'Well den, ladies. De way I sees it, yous have two choices. You can go back to England and kiss goodbye to a vacation in dis wonderful tropical paradise while I sits around Rodney Bay twiddlin' me tumbs for two weeks, or I can takes yous sailin' under de stars like de Owl and de Pussy Cat in dis white, eighteen-tonne catamaran.

'But I might be as sick as a parrot,' complained Sam.

'Very true, missy, but you could be just as sick on dat big cruise liner sittin' in Castries harbour right now, because we both be floatin' on de same sea.'

Sam opened her mouth to contradict, then hesitated.

'Look, Captain,' said George, cutting in. 'Sam has a point. How can we possibly decide when we don't know the first thing about sailing?' Georgina was always the practical one. 'Is there any way we can try it and then decide?'

'Well now, let me tink.' Captain Shadrach Jonathan William Bligh pulled a stool from the saloon and sat down at the table. 'Hows about dis for a plan? You gets yourselves outta dose fancy clothes you're wearin' and into sometin' sensible for a day's sailin', and *Rum Punch* and me, we will cruise you along de coast to Marigot Bay for dinner. If yous enjoy it, Moses can bring all de luggage across by road. If not, he can bring yous back to Rodney Bay and no harm done.' He sat back, his hands locked behind his head, looking more like Black Beard than Captain Bligh.

'We'll need time to think it over,' replied George.

'No problem, missy. Moses and me, we be in de marina bar awaitin' your decision.' He pushed his stool under the table and shook hands with them all, Terri's finger bones cracking under the pressure. 'Nice meetin' you, ladies, and no hard feelin's if you decide to go home.' In two strides he was by the helm then he hesitated, turned and looked the women up and down. 'Just a couple o' points before I go. In de first place, *Rum Punch*, she don't look anytin' like a bathtub and as far as I know, Tarzan never knew nuttin' about sailin'.'

Sam went the colour of her cocktail.

With that he was down the steps across the boarding ladder and off along the pontoon, Moses under his tea cosy in hot pursuit.

'Well,' said Terri, after the others had completed a thorough inspection of the yacht, 'what's it to be? Are we going to take up this chap's offer or do we email Adrian Falks and tell him to get us home?'

'Count me in,' announced Evie collecting the glasses and putting them in the sink. 'It can't be any worse than flying to Glasgow on a Beagle Air Dakota in November.'

'And George is a dab-hand with the wheel,' said Sam, sitting at the controls, her fingers curled around the large chrome helm.

'Very funny, Miss Hutchins. Don't expect me to rush over with a sick bag when you puke all over the electronics,' countered George testing her weight on the trampoline netting up front. 'Anyway, what's changed your tune? You were like Cruella de Vil earlier.'

'She's suddenly taken a fancy to dreadlocks,' said Evie, her head appearing from a forward hatch. 'I have to say, the beds are a decent size.'

'Assuming you don't have to share.' George was obviously not happy.

'OK, that's enough,' demanded Terri, asserting her authority. 'Where we sleep will be up for discussion if and when we decide to remain onboard. Right now, I suggest we take a vote on today's cruise down to this place, Marigot Bay, and if we don't hurry up it'll be too late to go anywhere.'

'Fine,' agreed George, returning to the stern. 'But, tell me one thing. Who gets the casting vote later tonight? The Owl or the Pussy Cat?'

Chapter Ten

Marigot Bay

The anchor splashed into Marigot Bay and Shadrach Bligh paid out some chain, letting *Rum Punch* settle peacefully into wind on the mirror-flat water. It had taken just two short hours to cruise along St Lucia's north-west coastline, the twin hulls keeping the yacht in a stable condition throughout. The A-team were now lying on the trampoline netting sunbathing, another *Rum Punch* in evidence while strains of Bob Marley streamed through the various hatches and air vents.

The skipper took a beer from the fridge and sat at the helm watching them, wondering how he would find another charter fee at short notice if his passengers decided to call it quits. The thought clouded his day and all he could do was trust to his luck and the effects of his cocktails.

Three hours earlier, he had been playing pool with Moses when the women finally appeared in the bar at Rodney Bay. Gone were the high-heeled shoes and flowing dresses, replaced by rubber flip-flops, purchased at the marina shop, skimpy shorts and designer crop tops. He had to admit, they all looked pretty damn' good from where he was sitting.

'I guess, ladies, you've decided to go a-cruisin',' was all he said as he threw some EC dollars on the bar counter and nodded to Moses, his clenched stomach muscles relaxing for the first time since mid-morning.

Fifteen minutes later *Rum Punch* eased away from her berth and Moses threw the ropes aboard then stood waving from the dockside, his legs surrounded by luggage.

The catamaran motored through the 'Cut' separating the marina from the bay and Shadrach thanked his lucky stars that the sea was like glass. If he was to save his charter fee he had to get these women to Marigot Bay in one piece and without any of them losing their breakfast over the side.

'Ladies,' he called back over his shoulder, 'why don't yous stretch your legs on the foredeck and get some o' dat Caribbean sunshine while I get de fenders stowed and haul up de mainsail?'

He watched the one they called Terri grab her camera and gingerly make her way towards the front, her knuckles turning white as she clung to the guardrail for support. It seemed to take forever.

'If you feelin' adventurous, missy, you can sit on de seat right out at de end of de pontoon. It's a great place for gettin' pictures of de dolphins.'

'What dolphins?' she yelled.

'Dose dolphins,' said Shadrach, pointing over the starboard gunnel.

Terri rushed across the netting to the other pontoon all fear forgotten as a pod of porpoises leapt from the water and chased *Rum Punch* across the bay. 'WOW!' she shouted. 'Come and see these, girls, they're racing along the side like torpedoes.' By now she was sitting astride the starboard seat, her legs dangling either side, her camera snapping for all it was worth. The one they called Evie made it to the port seat while the other two watched the acrobatic display from the starboard guardrail, broad smiles on all their faces.

'Now, dat's what I call a happy crew,' muttered Shadrach as the sun's reflection sparkled on the chrome stanchions and *Rum Punch*, under full sail, headed for the point.

The rest had been a breeze. Sailing one mile offshore they had creamed along at seven knots leaving the town of Castries to port, the dock masked by a *Celebrity* cruise liner, and continued south towards their destination.

The tall one called Sam suddenly appeared at Shadrach's elbow and coughed. He didn't turn round, his eyes concentrating on another yacht about to cross his path from port. 'Yes, missy, what yous be wantin?'

'I . . . I just wanted to apologise for my remarks back there.' She nodded her head in the direction of the stern. 'I was out of order.'

Shadrach swung the helm to starboard as *Rum Punch* took avoiding action causing Sam to swivel sideways and fall onto the rear deck. 'Bloody Frog,' he shouted into the wind.'

'What?' asked Sam on all fours.

'Dat yacht. It's French and de bleedin' skipper don't know his elbow from his arse!'

'His arse from his elbow,' corrected Sam, clambering up the saloon bulkhead. Once upright she clung to the helm seat for dear life. 'As I was saying, I'm sorry, I was having a bad day.' She examined the fingers of her left hand where another two nails had broken. 'Shit!'

'Dat's all right, missy. No 'ard feelin's. What's your name again?'

'Samantha.' Her right buttock ached and she wondered how she was going to explain the big bruise on it to CJ. 'You can call me Sam.'

'Right on, Samanta, but take some advice from de captain. If yous gonna sail, yous better cut dem finganails.' He winked at her and returned to screaming at the French yacht and making rude hand signals as they turned back on course, gathered speed and headed for Marigot Point.

Well, so far so good, thought Shadrach as he waved to a West Indian standing below a copse of palm trees, his legs surrounded by dive bottles. After anudder rum punch and a fine meal at De Shack, dese beauties will be putty in me hands. He kept his fingers firmly crossed.

Walking to the rear, he unwound the ropes holding *Rum Punch's* dinghy to the davit arms extending out beyond the stern and stood amidships yanking on both ropes until they were freed from their jammers. He then lowered the small boat slowly towards the water. Terri stood watching the procedure with interest.

'Can I help?' she offered.

'Sure,' replied Shadrach, jumping into the dinghy and unclipping the two retaining straps. 'Take dis strap and clip it to de ring on de davit.' He pointed to a D-ring on the outer end of one of the stainless-steel arms and Terri leant out to reach it.

'Be careful, missy, you don't want to wet those skimpy shorts now, eh?'

Terri wobbled alarmingly, lost her footing and hung onto the arm like a chimpanzee practising pole dancing. 'Call me Terri,' she stuttered as her feet scrambled for purchase.

'Here, let me,' said Shadrach, grabbing her ankle and placing her left foot back on deck.

'Thanks, Captain. I guess there's a knack to this.'

'De name's Shadrach. Now hang on with de udder hand and try again.' His lips were super-glued together as Terri clung to the pole with both hands and leant out once more.

'Dere you go,' he said as the clip snapped into place. 'Now de udder side.'

'What in God's name are you doing, Terri?' exclaimed George, appearing as Terri's body canted at a thirty-degree angle, her toes threatening to walk on water.

'Pilates,' she muttered, stretching for all she was worth.

'It looks more like one of those positions from the *Karma Sutra* to me,' replied George, holding onto the back of Terri's shorts.

'If we're going to sail *Rum Punch* for the next two weeks we might as well try and be useful,' said Terri, returning to an upright position.

Shadrach's ears were on high alert. 'Now, ladies. I'm off ashore to dat dere buildin.' He pointed to a single-storey wooden hut on the shoreline, its timber decking extending out over the water. 'Dat be De Shack, a great place to eat de best jerk chicken in de Caribbean, so I goes to book us a table.'

The outboard motor swayed above his head from its hoist as Terri and George, like two Bisto Kids, sniffed the air, their noses picking up a faint whiff of barbecue sauce from the direction of The Shack.

'I won't be long. Enjoy a swim while I's gone.' Shadrach locked the outboard onto the dinghy's stern, pulled the cord and the four-stroke engine sprang to life.

'We've left our swimsuits in our cases in Rodney Bay,' shouted Terri above the din.

'Den go naked and swim under de hull,' shouted Shadrach as he pulled the motor-arm across his chest and arced away from the yacht.

'You must be bloody joking,' yelled George, watching his wake.

'Don't be such a prude, George, this isn't Fulham High Street.' Evie, a red bath towel tucked around her body, descended the steps, placed her left foot on the swim ladder, flipped the towel over the handrail, exposed her buttocks to the West Indian adjusting his dive tanks across the inlet, and slipped into the aquamarine bay. 'Come on, girls, it's fabulous in here.'

Sam appeared with three more towels. 'In for a penny, in for a pound,' she said, her shorts hitting the deck. 'Christ, if CJ could see me now!'

Three minutes later the A-team were all swimming naked between the yacht's twin hulls, safely hidden from prying eyes as sunlight cascaded off the catamaran's undersides. They were giggling like three-year olds, Mount Gay rum putting a rosy tint on proceedings.

'You couldn't do this on a cruise liner,' argued Evie holding her nose and disappearing below the ripples.

'What cruise liner?' crooned Terri, floating on her back, her eyes closed, the wavelets tickling her nipples.

'That bloody big ship you mistook for this catamaran, Teresa Gillingham!' said George swinging off the anchor chain.

Shadrach lifted the telephone handset from the side wall of The Shack and dialled Rodney Bay Marina. As he waited for the phone to connect he looked across at *Rum Punch* and saw the women mount the swim ladder one by one, sparkling water shimmering off their limbs, each tenting a towel to protect their modesty.

'Yoh! Moses man, Shadrach callin'. Yous can bring de cases over to De Shack. Dem ladies, dey looks as if dey be stayin'.'

He nodded as Moses made some retort.

'Dey bin swimmin' in de altogedder, chirpin' like parakeets. I got a feelin' in me water dat I bin and cracked it.'

He paused again. 'No, forget de big rubber doughnut. We ain't got room for dat and de baggage. And bring anudder twelve bottles o'rum, man.' He watched the women dancing around the foredeck, arms flapping in the air as 'No Woman, No Cry' blasted from the cabin. 'I tink I gonna need it. Dem women, dey drink like bleedin' fish!'

Fire burned the western horizon as dusk crept across Marigot Bay and up the eastern hillside. Terri sat on the edge of The Shack's deck, her toes dangling in the charcoal-coloured water, body replete from a finger-licking Creole meal, breath ninety-percent proof.

Behind her, George, Sam and Evie were examining a nautical chart as Shadrach pointed out their route through the Grenadines, soft steel drum music throbbing in the background.

'First ting in de mornin',' said Shadrach, 'we need to do some emergency drillin'.'

'Shouldn't we have done that before we left Rodney Bay,' asked George, and hiccupped.

'Jesus, Georgina, don't you ever let up?' That was Sam.

'You be right on de button, Georgie,' cut in Shadrach, 'but I judged yous to be in no mood for emergencies dis mornin'.'

'You'd be right there, Captain.' That was Evie. 'However, you're looking at four highly qualified ex-air-stewardesses from the nineteen seventies and we're all dab hands with a fire axe.'

'Well, missy . . .,' coughed Shadrach.

'Evie.'

'. . . Evie, I be hopin de fire axe won't be called for on dis trip.'

'Shame,' replied Evie. 'I've always wanted to smash my way through a bulkhead.'

'Den I'll see what I can do for yous. Now, I tink it's time to go. Moses, he bin loadin de baggage onto *Rum Punch* during dinner and yous need to unpack before retirin'.'

Terri wondered where they were going to put it all. The stowage on the catamaran was limited to say the least.

'What about sleeping arrangements?' George again. 'I have no intention of sharing a cabin with Terri.'

'Dat's OK, ladies. One of yous can 'ave my cabin.'

'But where will you sleep?' Evie should have worked for Oxfam.

'On de roof,' announced Shadrach nonchalantly. 'Me, I prefer to kip under de stars, but whoever uses de port head will 'ave to share it wid me.'

'What's a head?' asked Sam drowsily.

'You'll get all de lingo tomorrow, Sam. Right now I 'ave to get you back on board widout any of yous fallin' in de drink.'

Fat chance thought Terri seeing double.

The A-team staggered to their feet and rolled towards the dock using Shadrach as a support post. With arms and legs entangled they flopped into the dinghy, causing it to rock violently. George appeared to be knitting with the rope at the bow while Terri leant horizontally out across the water to give Shadrach room to yank the outboard into life before he squeezed his posterior between her and the engine and proceeded to steer them gently out into the bay.

Oooh! she thought, feeling his hot thigh against her hip. That's cosy.

As the dinghy was swallowed up by the night, all that could be heard on shore was Evie reciting Edward Lear at the top of her voice.

The owl and the pussy cat went to sea

In a beautiful pea-green boat.

They took some honey and plenty of money

Wrapped up in a five-pound note . . .

Burp!

Rum Punch

They sailed away, for a year and a day,
To the land where the palm trees grow. . . '
'That's not right,' said George.
'Tis so.' Hiccup.
. . .The owl sang to a small guitar,
What a lovely pussy you are, you are,
What a lovely pussy you are . . .

Chapter Eleven

Incompetent Crew

Shadrach rolled off the cabin roof, slid down the saloon window and dived into the Caribbean, the sun catching the soles of his feet as it kissed the ridge above the bay. It was seven o'clock in the morning and he assumed his passengers would be fast asleep. He did not know ex-air-stewardesses.

As he surfaced and shook a spray of water droplets from his dreadlocks he saw four pairs of eyes peering at him from behind an expanse of Plexiglass.

What dey be doin' awake? he thought, and dived once more, moving in squid-like fashion towards the swim ladder.

'I assume you'll want this,' shouted Terri, chucking a towel across the stern deck onto the top step and walking back into the saloon. 'And hurry up,' she chided over her shoulder. 'You wanted an early start and we've been waiting since six.'

Shadrach cupped his manhood with both hands, grabbed the towel by his teeth and swivelled on his coccyx.

Bleedin' women, he thought, and with split-second timing had his dignity restored and walked into the cabin to a chorus of: 'Nice butt.'

'Less of de cheek,' he demanded, heading for the internal stairs.

'Exactly,' emphasised Evie. 'By the way, our bathroom's free. Sam and I abluted before dawn.'

Shadrach scratched at his rough stubble and lathered his chin with shaving foam while his reflection posed him a question.

'Jesus, man, how de hell are you gonna keep control of dese crazy women?'

'Wid difficulty,' replied Shadrach, scraping a razor down one cheek.

'Den do it fast, eh? Dem hostesses, dey hunt in packs, man, and if yous not careful, yous gonna be de prey.'

'No chance.' His toothbrush threatened the mirror. 'Me, I'm de skipper of dis ship and what I says goes.'

'Ummm,' was all he got by way of reply.

'Right den, ladies,' he announced appearing on the stairs, clothed and wiping his face with a hand towel. 'Emergency drillin'!'

The A-team sat side-by-side on the saloon settee, a picture of aging innocence with blood-shot eyes.

'First, de ship's lingo. Now, de galley is de galley, not de kitchen.' He pointed at the sink. 'Got it?'

Four heads nodded.

'Good. Now, de back is de stern wid de stern deck and de front is de bow wid de foredeck.'

More nods. Shadrach could not be sure if they was taking the rise.

'De dinghy is de Rib.'

'It looks nothing like a rib,' said Sam, feeling her ribcage.

'No, Samanta, Rib is short for Rigid Inflatable Boat. R.I.B. OK?'

'If you say so.'

'Now, de wheel is de helm, de cupboards, dey be called lockers, and de windows, dey be known as hatches. . .'

Evie cut in, rising to her feet, her arms outstretched. '. . . of which four are emergency exits, one at the bow, one at the stern and two under the pontoons.'

'. . . Keel-aulin', Miss Evie, is still practised in dese 'ere parts.' Shadrack's Captain Bligh stare spoke volumes.

She lowered her butt onto the seat, right fingers touching her temple. 'Aye, aye, Captain.'

'Now, where was I? Oh, yes. De toilets. So, de toilet is called de head and . . . '

'Why?' interrupted Sam, manicuring her nails, her long legs stretching out across the cabin.

''Cos in de old days, dat's where de sailors went to . . . er . . .' Shadrach hesitated trying to think of a suitable word.

'Shit?' enquired George.

He closed his eyes and gritted his teeth. 'Right.'

'Why not call it the bottom then?' Sam thought her quip rather clever for such an early hour.

Shadrach could feel his authority slipping. ''Cos, de . . .'

'Shit?' assisted George.

'. . . went trew de hole at de head of de ship and de waves, dey washed it off de bow.'

'Makes sense,' said Terri. 'So, the front is the head and the toilet is the head. Have I got that right?'

'No.' Shadrach crunched his upper lip with his bottom teeth. 'De front is now de bow and de toilet is now de head.'

'Sounds like a typical male cock-up to me,' concluded George.

'Do you tink we could get on?' asked Shadrach, the whites of his eyes showing.

The A-team smiled, rather like hyenas before ripping a carcass to pieces, but they remained silent.

'We 'ave tree fire extinguishers in de main body of de yacht. One at de bottom of each staircase,' he pointed to either side of the saloon as his audience exchanged glances, 'and one on de galley bulkhead alongside a fire blanket. De extinguishers, dey all be . . . '

'BCF extinguishers,' piped up Terri to his left.

'BromoChlorodiFluoromethane,' interjected George.

'They can be used on all fires including electrical fires because of the chemical content,' added Evie.

'However,' put in Sam, 'the area must be ventilated as soon as possible after use as the fumes are toxic.'

Shadrach had, by now, repaired to the chart-table seat, one leg crossed over the other, his elbows leaning against the desk, head on one side.

'Well, that's what they taught us at Beagle Air anyway,' said Sam, shrugging.

Terri continued. 'You should aim the jet as close to the base of the fire as possible. . .'

'DAT'S ENOUGH!' Shadrach's palm smacked the table-top and pens shot into the air.

Terri clamped her mouth shut and looked at her skipper who appeared to be praying. He sighed deeply and leant over to open a locker door. 'Right, movin' on.' He pulled a life jacket from its stowage and four faces lit up like beacons, mouths opening in unison.

'Don't even tink about it!' he ordered, throwing the jacket at Terri. 'Now, try dis on for size.'

'I can't get my buckles to meet,' announced Evie.

Shadrach turned from the galley sink, a mug of coffee in his hand, to see her straining with the stainless-steel connecting buckles, her breasts refusing to give way.

'Here, let me try,' said Terri, grabbing both sides of the jacket and failing miserably to pull them together. 'It's no good, Evie, you'll just have to have a boob reduction or else push your tits out of the way.'

Evie tried the latter technique as Shadrach's eyes watered.

'Done it,' she announced, standing to attention in front of her skipper, her nipples trying to bury themselves under each armpit.

'Christ,' groaned Sam, trying to join both ends of a plastic toggle at the front of her jacket, the adjoining blue webbing strap cutting into her private parts from the rear. 'This is worse than a prostitute's thong.'

'I wouldn't know, Sam,' came George's muffled retort, her head trapped between her thighs as she tried to grab her own blue webbing strap, which was swinging like a pendulum beyond her buttocks.

'Give me a Beagle Air life jacket any day. How the hell do you inflate this,' grumbled Terri searching for a red toggle.

'De life jacket inflates automatically on contact wid water,' muttered Shadrach, losing the plot.

'I wish my boobs would do that,' quipped Terri, following his back as he left the saloon.

All togged up in red and blue life jackets the A-team made it onto the foredeck, Sam now puce in the face.

'I's goin' to demonstrate how to tie de fender to de rail.' Shadrach made exaggerated movements with the fender rope tying it securely to the guardrail. 'Are yous familiar wid de clove hitch?'

'Dib, dib, dib,' muttered George from the rear.

'What d'you say, Georgie?'

'Nuttin', Skipper,' mimicked George as Terri rammed her in the arm.

'OK, Evie, now you try it.'

Evie took the fender from Shadrach's hand, heaved it over the guardrail and promptly dropped it in the sea.

Shadrach was bereft of words.

'I was never very strong,' announced Evie, adjusting her nipples back into position.

'No worries, Evie, I'll get it,' said Terri, climbing over the guardrail and leaping off the side.

'Nooo!' shouted Shadrach as Terri disappeared below the waterline then reappeared, fender rope in hand as a loud 'Whoosh!' rent the air and she shot out of the water like a cruise missile.

'Whoops,' said Evie, glancing sheepishly sideways at Shadrach.

'Oh, Lordie, Lordie. What de hell do I do now?' he groaned.

'Look for new crew?' suggested George as Sam struggled to pull her webbing strap away from her crutch and Evie's bikini elastic snapped under pressure, her breasts springing back into place, nipples erect.

'Terri, try the back stroke,' shouted George, leaning out over the rail. Evie dashed past on her way to her cabin and Shadrach sank to his knees, head in hands.

'It's all right for you,' spluttered Terri, fighting to make headway. 'You haven't just had your ribs macerated.'

'Well, no one asked you to imitate Esther Williams.'

'I have one thing to say to you, Georgina Stanhope. It begins with "P" and it ends in "off"!'

Teresa was back on the starboard pontoon seat, her camera around her neck trying to keep a low profile as *Rum Punch* turned out of Marigot Bay at ten o'clock that morning and headed south. Having accidentally inflated her life jacket she was in the doghouse, the offending item now consigned to the forward locker along with the cases until a new gas cylinder could be sourced.

Shadrach turned the catamaran into wind and raised the mainsail, the wind whipping around its edges as the boom bounced around its mounting on the mast. Terri felt it crash sideways as the yacht turned back on course then watched the front sail uncurl. The huge expanse of white canvas billowed and bowed towards her, the wind taking up the slack, then straightened as Shadrach's toned arm muscles wound it tight.

Their eyes met as Terri looked back to watch him work, his message clearly received and understood. He was daring her to fall off.

After the events of the morning the atmosphere on board was slightly strained. Sam lay on her stomach on the trampoline netting reading the latest Jilly Cooper, a large blue bruise discolouring one tanned hip. Her nails were stubs of their former taloned selves and her hair was scraped back in a ponytail under a NYPD baseball cap which she had found in her cabin. What CJ would have said if he could have seen her was beyond Terri. This new, dishevelled Sam was a far cry from the sexy mistress of Beauchamp Villas.

The thought brought Terri back to her former life in Paternoster Square, Happy Hands Harold and her email to the Human Resources Director. Her complaint had made the Unite union rep's day. Mrs Audrey Laws, all guns blazing, had stormed into the CEO's office and immediately demanded an explanation for the Marketing Manager's nefarious sexual indiscretions. This opened the flood gates for complaints of a like nature from other female members of staff and resulted in Harold's immediate removal to the basement to run the 'male only' print shop while a Human Resources investigation got underway.

It became the only topic of conversation around the British Electricity Board's head office for days while Terri remained at her post, peeling ten thousand sticky labels from their backing paper and placing one over each of the offending logos.

Keeping a low profile was becoming an art form for Teresa. Anne Blakemore on the top floor was avoiding her like the plague when she found out what all the fuss was about and Harold's replacement was so celibate he should have been a nun, his opinion of women in the workplace verging on the

Dickensian. Mulling all this over, Terri decided she was not looking forward to returning to Paternoster Square at the end of the holiday.

'FISH! FISH!' yelled George from the stern.

Terri turned to see George bent double over the starboard stern rail, the yacht's fishing rod held to her chest, the end bowed towards the waves vibrating like a violin string and the line whizzing away from the reel at breakneck speed. Terri leapt from her seat and rushed to the rear, camera at the ready as Shadrach turned the yacht into wind and *Rum Punch* slowed immediately. With the noise of sails flapping wildly, George slowly wound and unwound the reel as Shadrach shouted instructions to her whilst re-winding the foresail back into a roll.

'The gaff,' he ordered, pointing to the underside of the stern canopy.

Evie gingerly removed a long pole with a pointed shepherd's hook from its restraints and handed it over as a silver head appeared above the waves, a large pink lure attached to its mouth.

'Ugh,' remarked Sam, and returned to her book as a long metallic body thrashed to and fro. George, muttering expletives under her breath, slowly hauled it towards the yacht.

'Dat's a yellow fin tuna,' announced Shadrach, and descended the starboard steps, gaff in hand, to hook the monster by the gills, heaving it into the yacht's Rib where it continued to fight for life as his passengers watched in abject horror.

Throwing the gaff to the deck, Shadrach flicked the lid of a cockpit locker and moved towards the Rib while unscrewing the cap of a plastic bottle. He then poured neat rum into the tuna's red gills. Tossing the bottle to Terri, who just managed to catch it, he removed the lure from the fish's lip, grabbed the helm and brought *Rum Punch* back on course, the wind once more billowing her mainsail.

'Where did you learn to do that, George?' Terri asked as the tuna went to meet its maker in a haze of alcoholic bliss.

'My dad was a dab hand with the rod,' she replied, locking the reel and placing the rod back in its holder. 'I've been trout fishing with him for years, although this is a bloody sight bigger than a trout.' Her head shot round. 'You did get it on film, didn't you?'

'In the can,' Terri acknowledged, patting her digital Sony.

'As I said,' commented Evie placing the gaff back where it belonged, 'you couldn't do this on a cruise liner.'

'True, but what do we do with it now?'

'We eat it, you idiot, what do you think we do with it?' George pushed past the other two and headed for the galley. 'Where's the filleting knife, Skip?'

With the tuna gutted, boned, filleted and bagged, George packed it in the freezer, leaving the offcuts in the fridge.

The mood had lightened considerably after her impression of Ernest Hemingway and the catamaran went on its way without further incident, Shadrach humming to himself at the helm and his clients lying on the foredeck, sunbathing and enjoying the scenery.

'Where are we going?' asked Terri.

'Jalousie Bay,' answered Sam.

'To see the Pitons,' added Evie.

'What are they?

'Two bloody big spits of rock either side of Jalousie Bay, Terri. They're St Lucia's greatest landmark.'

She shrugged.

'Well, it's a good job that wasn't the question on *True Life Movies*,' remarked George, 'or we wouldn't be here.'

'Oh, it wouldn't have been,' Terri said, shaking her head and missing the point. 'That's far too difficult for *True Life Movie's* viewers.'

'Exactly my point.'

'Stuff off!'

'Now, now, girls,' said Evie, trying to keep the peace. 'George, why are there bits of raw fish in the fridge?'

'Because she's going to use it as bait when she tries to hook a new fella,' explained Sam.

Two of George's fingers V-signed the air. 'Our skipper, Evie, is going to make ceviche with it.'

'Ummm,' crooned Evie. 'Marinated in rum, it should be delicious.'

What's ceviche? thought Terri, keeping her mouth firmly closed.

'Gosh,' mused Sam. 'I haven't had ceviche since CJ and I were staying at the Four Seasons Hotel in San Francisco last year.' She was such a name dropper.

'Well, Lordie, Lordie,' replied George, ramming her sunglasses on her nose and pulling her sunhat over her eyes. 'It seems to me, dat CJ fella, he ain't doin' right by yous at all, Missy Samie. No, siree, he ain't doin' right by yous at all!'

'Up yours, Georgina.'

Chapter Twelve

'Bang between the Pitons'

Two massive pointed rocks rose out of the sea, one to either side of *Rum Punch*, dwarfing the catamaran as she lay peacefully at anchor in the bay with her bows pointing towards the beach. George was busy teaching Evie how to do a clove hitch with a piece of string on the foredeck guardrail and Sam was on her fourth lap swimming round the yacht as Terri sat on the trampoline netting with Shadrach's binoculars glued to her face, scanning the rain forest-covered hillside.

'Gosh, this is beautiful,' she exclaimed. 'The bird life's fantastic and their colours are amazing.'

'No, Evie. For the third time, the rope end goes under the loop.'

'Perhaps if I tried it left-handed it would make more sense?'

'There seems to be a hotel on top of the ridge,' Terri continued. 'I can see wooden buildings poking out above the tree-tops.'

'Dat's de Ladera Dasheen 'otel,' said Shadrach sitting on top of the saloon, Carib beer in hand. 'Very expensive and ecologically friendly.'

'Can we go up there for a Happy Hour cocktail?' called Sam from the water. 'CJ would be green with envy.'

'Nope.'

'Why not?' Evie asked, her fingers trapped in the string.

"Cos yous be goin' over dere for dinner.' Shadrach pointed to a strip of beach over on the right backed by thick shrubs.

Terri was now focusing on the mass of dense greenery as two pelicans floated by in the shallows. 'Well, I guess a beach barbecue in this setting is just as exotic.'

'De barbecue ain't on de beach, Terri. Yous are goin' to Bang between de Pitons.'

'Sounds pornographic,' remarked Evie, sucking her fingers.

'CJ definitely won't like that.' Water splashed around the Plimsoll line.

'Who's CJ?' Shadrach looked at Terri.

'Samantha's man who does,' chipped in George.

'And he does it in great style,' Terri added. 'She happens to live in a very exclusive pad in Knightsbridge.'

He frowned.

'London,' she corrected. 'As upmarket as that hotel on the ridge.'

'So, dis CJ, he be Sam's husband, eh?'

'Husband, yes. Sam's, no.'

'Oh.' Shadrach scratched his chin.

'Would you lot stop talking about me as if I wasn't here.'

Teresa leant over the port rail and saw Sam treading water. 'I say, girls. Miss Hutchins is trying to communicate with us from the basement.'

'Then tell her we can't hear her and it's rude to listen in on other people's conversations.' Evie was having another attempt with the string. 'George, I think I've got it. My God, I have, I've got it.'

'You sound like Eliza Doolittle.' Terri returned to the binoculars.

'Dey made dat film in Marigot Bay,' said Shadrach.

'What, *My Fair Lady*?'

'No.' He was making no sense. '*Dr Doolittle.*'

'Really?'

'Yep. Dey set up dere cameras where de Marigot Beach Resort and Dive Centre stands today.'

'Crikey, I could have been an extra,' said Evie attempting her new talent on a fender rope.

'In your dreams,' said George. 'Which end of the *pushmi-pullyu* animal would you have been?'

'The front end, of course.' The fender was hanging from the rail, rigidly attached with a clove hitch as Evie burst into the chorus of 'If I Could Talk to the Animals.'

No one was sure if Shadrach's applause was for Evie's singing or her knot tying. Either way she bowed and deposited her petite frame next to Terri.

'So, what exactly is Bang between the Pitons?'

'Well, dat's a long story,' said Shadrach.

'Another beer?' enquired George.'

'I tort you'd never ask, Georgie.'

'Make that one beer and one Campari and Soda,' ordered Sam appearing on the foredeck, her gold bikini exposing more than it hid.

'Mine's a rum punch,' said Evie.

'Make that two.'

'Bloody hell. It's like being back at Beagle Air.'

'What's dis Beagle Air you keeps referring to?' asked Shadrach, handing over his empty beer bottle.

'Don't ask,' said George and headed for the galley.

The A-team waited in silence while Shadrach explained. Apparently, Bang between the Pitons was owned by Colin Tennant, 3rd Baron Glenconner, and a close friend of Princess Margaret. Sam was all ears.

'He moved from Mustique a few years ago, bought up a load of old wooden shacks, shipped dem to dis beach and created a typical Creole village in de clearin'. Dem shacks, dey now be shops, bar, restaurant, and private accommodation. De tourists, dey come from all over de island for de eatin', drinkin' and dancin'.'

'Will he be there tonight?' Sam's eyes sparkled.

'Offering roast suckling pig and the odd spliff?' George handed out the drinks.

'I say nuttin', Georgie.'

'Georgina Stanhope, you shouldn't believe all you read in the gutter press.'

'Well, you obviously do, Sam, or you wouldn't be hyperventilating like some oxygen-starved goldfish.'

'I'm just thinking how miffed CJ will be when he sees a photograph of me fraternising with Lord Glenconner!'

'I better not forget my camera then,' quipped Terri and felt Mount Gay rum anaesthetize her throat.

Shadrach was sitting at the chart table writing up the ship's log when the whirring of the water pump changed, causing him to look up. He walked down the port stairs and flicked a switch on the electricity panel.

'Jesus! De bleedin' water tank is empty.'

He banged on the port head door just as Sam peered around the edge, her hair dripping and shampoo in her ears.

'The water's stopped,' she announced, lips pursed.

''Cos you've used it all. How long yous bin in dat shower?'

'Fifteen minutes.'

'FIFTEEN MINUTES!' Shadrach's voice rose from bass to falsetto. 'Where de hell do you tink you are, Niagara Falls?'

'There's no need to be rude.'

He took a deep breath. 'Sam, dis is a tirty-eight-foot catamaran, not de bleedin' Queen Mary. You has just used up four days' worth of fresh water and dere ain't anywheres to uplift more till we reach Bequia, fifty-five nautical miles away.'

'Well, how was I supposed to know? You should have told us that when you did the emergency briefing. Right now, I need to rinse my hair.'

'Den do it in de sea,' said Shadrach, returning to the chart-table.

'I can't rinse my hair in salt water!' screamed Sam.

Shadrach had his hands over his ears. 'Den stay in de head until we reach Bequia.'

Terri was sitting on the saloon settee watching the skipper through her face mirror propped against the saloon window, keeping her back to the galley, her mascara brush hovering over her lashes. He sharpened the filleting knife and thinly sliced the offcuts of tuna, laying them out on a platter. He stretched across to the fruit bowl and grabbed a fresh lime, rolled it up and down the chopping board with his palm, cut it in two then clenched half in each of his fists, allowing lime juice to trickle through his fingers onto the slivers of fish. The drained peel and pips were consigned to the rubbish bin and, with a flourish of the black pepper grinder, the ceviche was done.

So that's how you make it, Terri thought, accidentally poking the end of the brush into her eye. 'Ow!'

Shadrach shot round and saw her blinking mascara down her cheek.

'Tissue,' she sniffed, flapping her arm in the air, her eye closed, tears pouring out of the duct.

'Here.'

A whiff of raw fish and lime juice invaded Terri's senses as she rammed the tissue against her eyeball. 'Thanks.' As she blinked, she caught sight in the mirror of the disaster which was now her face. 'Oh, hell. I look like a panda.' She staggered to the starboard head and began the make-up routine all over again.

By the time she returned, garnished glasses of Pina-colada were lining the galley work top alongside the silver platter. 'Oh, I say, they look good.'

Shadrach wiped his hands on a dishcloth and handed her a drink.

'Where did you learn to do all this?' Terri took the glass and nodded to the drinks and ceviche.

'Used to run a bar,' he said, and placed the remaining items on the stern deck table.

She was about to question him further when Evie appeared from her cabin looking like Gina Lollobrigida. 'Wow, don't you look the business?'

Her white leather slacks moulded perfectly to her lower torso and her white seersucker off-the-shoulder blouse was adorned with a mass of coloured beads at neck, waist and wrist. She did a twirl in the centre of the saloon, glided out onto the deck and helped herself to some raw tuna.

Terri looked down at her cream cheesecloth strappy dress from Primark and felt like the poor relation. By the time George and Sam appeared she was ready to hide in the forward locker but no one else seemed to notice so she lifted her chin, stabbed a sliver of fish onto a cocktail stick and sampled the ceviche. It was delicious.

'Right den, ladies, are yous ready to go Bang between the Pitons.'

'Lead me to it,' enthused Evie.

'Are all de hatches closed and locked?' Terri frowned, rushed back down to her cabin and shut her hatch, flicking the locking mechanism into place.

Pocketing his keys, Shadrach jumped into the waiting dinghy and held out his arm to Evie.

'Christ, this thing stinks of fish,' said George as she settled onto the rubber pontoon, holding her nose.'

'You have washed it, haven't you?' asked Sam, her foot hesitating on the bottom step.'

'Sure have, missy. Now pass me dem shoes and climb in wid your feet bare.'

Terri brought up the rear and seconds later the dinghy's umbilical cord slid from *Rum Punch's* cleat and they were on their way.

'What's happened to all the stars?' asked Evie looking up. Everyone followed suit as a flash of lightening answered her question.

Shadrach revved the engine and the Rib shot across the bay as the first drop of rain landed on Terri's nose. 'Oh, no.'

Without warning, the wind picked up, the sea whipped itself into a frenzy and the heavens opened. Terri placed her hands over her head in an attempt to shelter from the deluge as George screamed, jets of water smashing into her at the bow. Shadrach shouted for them to hang on as a thunderclap ripped through the air and another flash of lightning lit up the bay.

'Jesus Christ!' yelled Sam as her head was scarified with needlepoint precision. Terri clung to Shadrach's shorts as if her life depended on it.

The dinghy smacked against the low wooden dock and George grabbed a rusty ring at her side nearly dislocating her shoulder as it continued its forward momentum. Shadrach cut the engine and leant out to make purchase with the wooden edging and the dinghy finally came to rest against the pontoon, close to the beach.

Two strong hands lifted Terri bodily out of the boat. She ran straight for the shore looking for shelter. Evie came next, her white leather trousers cascading water onto her feet, followed by Sam trailing her jewelled sling-backs, her hair dripping. George didn't even bother to run. She was soaked from head to toe, her pale blue kaftan streaked with sand.

'Are you ladies OK?' asked Shadrach, his muscular body lit up from behind by another lightning bolt.

Terri looked down to check all her body parts were intact and did a double take. Her best Primark cheesecloth had become completely transparent and nothing was now left to the imagination. Shadrach's eyes were out on stalks as Terri shot behind Sam, using her as a modesty screen, and tried to work out what to do next.

'I can't meet Lord Glenconner looking like this,' complained Sam, unwinding her silk scarf, which threatened to choke her.

'Well, at least you got to rinse your hair,' muttered George through chattering teeth.

'Here, Terri, take dis.' Shadrach handed two large banana leaves to Sam who shoved them behind her back.

Terri could see George shivering close by and felt her own feet squelching inside her pumps. 'What am I supposed to do with two banana leaves, Shadrach? Dance my way into the restaurant like one of the Windmill Girls?'

'Well, it's that or expose your stretchmarks to the great and good of St Lucia,' said Sam. 'Is your camera OK?'

'Christ knows. Right now, that's the least of my worries.'

'Your camera's fine,' said Evie, holding up a plastic Ziploc bag containing Terri's Sony digital. 'Now, let's all surround Terri. No not you, Shadrach. And try to find the ladies' loo.'

As quickly as the rain came, it stopped, peace pervading the night as Terri shuffled along a dirt track surrounded by her bedraggled guard of honour towards a pastel-painted shack, the

banana leaves fore and aft and a cacophony of tree frogs
announcing their arrival. Once inside the toilet shack they took
stock. It wasn't a pretty sight.

'You wouldn't be able to do this on a cruise liner,' stuttered
George, up close and personal with the hot-air hand blower.

'As my grannie used to say, George, put it all down to
experience.' Terri was busy winding toilet paper around her
chest and down her knickers trying to hide her relevant bits
then let the dress fall back over the top. 'How do I look?'

'Like one of those blow-up first-aid dolls at the Beagle Air
Training Centre,' replied Evie.

'Thanks a bunch,' she groaned as her right nipple popped
out from between two layers of loo paper.

'Never mind, Terri, at least you've made one skipper's day,'
remarked Sam.

'And,' Terri muttered shoving her nipple back in place,
'let's face it, girls . . . I couldn't do that on a cruise liner, now
could I?' She looked over to her dishevelled pals and they all
fell about laughing.

As it happened the restaurant was in the open air, the tables
under canopied gazebos. George spent the first half hour
drying out by a huge barbecue beyond the dance floor while
Evie was being chatted up by some Australian hunk. Sam
stood, scanning the diners for signs of Colin Tennant and Terri
sat in the shadows keeping a low profile, again. Their esteemed
skipper had returned to *Rum Punch* leaving George with the
VHF handheld and instructions to call him when they were
ready to return.

The food came and went, the booze flowed freely and the steel band had everyone on the dance floor except Terri. She sat in the shadows recalling Shadrach's expression when the lightning had exposed her curves. Surely, he can't find me attractive? she thought. Not with all my extra bits.

'*Why not?*' demanded Grannie from her cloud. '*Anyone would think you were a wrinkled old prune.*'

'There's no need to exaggerate,' argued Terri, sipping her Mojito. 'But let's face it, Gran, I'm not the lithe young thing I used to be?'

'*Nor is Jane Fonda, dear, but you don't see her sitting in a corner hiding her light under a bushel.*'

Terri grunted.

'*Don't grunt, dear, it's not lady-like. Now, stop feeling sorry for yourself and start flaunting your bits.*'

'I already have,' muttered Terri, as she spotted Evie tangoing with the Aussie who was the skipper from a big yacht anchored next to *Rum Punch*, while Sam had Colin Tennant by the waist as he led a conga-line around the dance floor.

Time for the camera, Terri decided, closing her ears to her Grannie and finishing off her third cocktail. She cosied up to the conga-line and waited for Colin Tennant to reappear. Eight shots later she had images of Sam and Lord Glenconner locked in a body hug, his Fedora on Sam's head and his walking stick acting as a pole for Georgina to limbo beneath. Evie's beads were in a jumble as she introduced her friends to Dale, and then they all collapsed on their chairs as another rain-storm buffeted the gazebo canopy.

'*Time to go home*,' sang Evie as the A-team wandered back to their shelter by the beach, stars now filling the sky.

'Did you get the pictures, Terri?'

'Yes, Sam, though I don't think any of them will make the front page of *HELLO!* magazine like the ones of Colin Tennant with the royals, hanging above the bar.'

'What a poser,' said George, calling Shadrach on Channel 8.

'If you've got it, flaunt it,' remarked Evie.

'And you certainly flaunted it, Miss Stanhope. How come you're so good at limbo dancing?' Terri sat on the dock, removing the damp loo paper from her armpits.

'Sign of my misspent youth.'

'Well, you'll pay for it tomorrow when you can't get out of bed, sunshine.'

Terri stared into the pitch-black bay as an outboard motor coughed into life and felt her stomach quiver as Shadrach appeared out of the darkness, his broad hand controlling the tiller. Well, she thought, standing up, maybe Captain Bligh likes his women with a bit of padding and stuck her chest out provocatively.

George nudged Evie and winked.

It was three o'clock in the morning by the time Terri staggered into her cabin, Mojitos clouding her vision. 'I should removed my make-up,' she mumbled, but the double-bed looked too inviting and she didn't think she could make it to the head without falling over. She slid her strappy dress off her shoulders, let it and her knickers pool around her ankles and stretched out on the bed linen taking up a Marilyn Monroe pose. Two seconds later she was on her feet and screaming like a banshee, rainwater soaking her back.

'Shadrach Jonathan William Bligh, get your ass down here. Now!'

Chapter Thirteen

A Date with Jack Sparrow

Shadrach was stretching a blue bin bag over the hatch of Terri's cabin and sticking it down with duct tape when the tender from the eighty-three-foot Jongert ketch, lying to starboard of *Rum Punch,* appeared at the stern.

'Oi, mate, I've got ya water.'

Shadrach stood up and wandered down the catamaran's side, wondering what an Aussie was doing with four twenty-litre canisters lashed to the inside of his tender.

'Is Evangaleena awake, bro?'

The port rear hatch opened and Evie's head appeared above the deck. 'Yes, Dale, I'm here.' She pulled herself up and waved.

Shadrach was feeling less than civil having been given a dressing down by Terri in the middle of the night, her anger exacerbated by too much alcohol and the fact that it wasn't the first time she had been saturated that evening. The failed seal around the plexiglass hatch was worrying and had kept him awake until dawn. If one seal had failed then the others might fail too and replacement hatches were well beyond his means.

'Morning, Shadrach,' said Evie as she moved past him and jumped onto the bottom step where the Aussie was securing his tender, stepped aboard and received a bear hug.

'Dale, meet Shadrach, our skipper.' She turned to him. 'Shadrach, this is Dale. He's the skipper of that yacht over there and he's going to let us have some fresh water from their tanks.' She pointed to the Jongert and beamed.

Shadrach noted the huge Cayman Islands flag fluttering from a varnished wooden flagpole, the bottom corner just tipping the waterline. 'Nice.'

'OK, mate, give us a hand will ya? Evangaleena, once we've done a couple of runs I'll take you back across to *Southern Cross* for some grub.'

'Right, I'll go and get some clothes on.'

'If you must, doll, but from where I'm standin', you look just dandy.'

Shadrach coughed, scratched his nose and waited for Evie to depart in her sarong before heaving the canisters aboard and carrying them to the freshwater filler cap. Dale made two more runs and as the balance of two hundred and forty litres of much-needed water was deposited inside the water tank, Evie appeared back on deck.

''Bye, Shadrach, won't be long. Tell the others I'll see them after breakfast.'

'We leave at nine,' he shouted, and watched the Aussie lift her into the tender, wrap an arm around her waist and carry her off like one of the Sabine women. Evie raised her hand in the air, acknowledging Shadrach's words. He felt affronted but didn't know why. Maybe it was the size of *Southern Cross*, or that he felt raw from being a mere charter skipper. Either way he swore under his breath and went back to duct taping the bin liner over Terri's hatch.

She woke in a blue haze lying on some padded cushions with a bath towel wrapped across her mid-riff. At first she couldn't think where she was then heard a ripping sound from above and saw a kneecap pressing down on the middle of her now blue hatch. She looked around, trying to get her bearings, then saw her M&S bikini briefs hanging limply from a wall lamp. Turning over, she promptly fell off the cushions onto the plywood bed base and hit her elbow on the wooden surround.

'Jesus, this is worse than my Chesterfield,' she mumbled and crawled back onto the upholstered foam, looked at her watch and groaned. It was after eight and *Rum Punch* was supposed to be leaving at nine to cross the St Lucia Channel to the island of St Vincent.

Terri didn't think she could cope standing on two feet let alone tackle an inter-island passage so she closed her eyes and hoped no one would notice that she was missing. Someone did. Shadrach was on the other side of her cabin door lightly knocking. Terri tried to ignore it by hiding her head under a cushion, but it persisted, getting louder as the seconds ticked by. Finally, the handle moved and a nose appeared in the crack between the door and its frame.

'Terri?'

'What.'

'Do yous want some coffee?'

'No, now go away.'

The door quietly closed and Terri immediately felt guilty. It was not all Shadrach's fault, she thought, coming up for air. The rain had been torrential and window seals were notorious for leaking when you least wanted them to. Look at your clapped out Mini, she mused, that leaks like a sieve.

Well, that's all very well, countered her rational mind, but this is a boat not a set of wheels and leaks have been known to sink ships.

Terri struggled to the end of the bed and placed her feet on the floor. 'Steady as you go, girl.' She was vertical, hanging onto her knickers for support and waiting for the cabin to stop rotating. Her best Primark was screwed up on the top of the wardrobe between her iPod and a copy of Louis de Bernières' *Captain Corelli's Mandolin,* its pages turning yellow at the edges from contact with damp cheesecloth.

She found a clean pair of pants and a sarong and made it to the bottom of the stairs as George came out of the head.

'We have fresh water, Terri, if you want to clean your teeth.'

Her tongue slid around the inside of her mouth and sludge came to mind.

'No, thanks. Not now. What I need is a strong coffee fix.'

An ebony hand stretched down the three stairs, a steaming mug leading the way. Terri took it, sank onto the bottom step and let the caffeine go to work on her hang-over.

'Where's Evie?' George ask from her cabin door.

Terri thought George was talking to her and shook her head. A bad move, and she groaned.

'She be breakfastin' wid Dale on *Sudden Cross.*'

'Who's Dale and why's he cross?' whispered George into Terri's left ear.

She shrugged, her brain still in sleep mode.

'We'll be leavin' in tirty minutes, ladies, so eider breakfast before we leaves or starve until we arrive in St Vincent. More coffee, Terri?'

Staggering up the stairs, Terri handed her mug to Shadrach as she passed by and collapsed onto the stern deck bench seat.

'I see Terri is her usual perky self.' Sam was sitting at the other end of the bench, peeling a banana. 'Do you want some fruit?'

The replenished mug slid below Terri's nose and she managed a thumbs down signal.

'She's having trouble with words this morning,' advised George, buttering some bread and liberally smothering it in jam.

'Then there's no point in asking her why her mattress and bedding are lying on the foredeck, steaming in the sun.'

'My hatch leaked,' Terri managed to say, holding the mug in both hands to stop it shaking.

'Oh, so you didn't sleep with Captain Bligh last night then?'

Pain violated Terri's eyeballs as her head shot up and George choked on her jam butty. 'No, I bloody well didn't.'

'Really?'

'Cooee, I'm home.' Evie breezed up the steps, a paper bag under her arm, and stepped into the galley. 'I thought you might like some fresh croissants for breakfast, compliments of *Southern Cross*.'

She put them on a plate and placed them on the table. The aroma hit Terri's nose, her stomach heaved and she was across the saloon, down the stairs and had her head in the toilet pan when Sam's next words reached her from above.

'Don't worry, Evie, Terri's just suffering from morning sickness. She got laid last night out on the foredeck, by you know who!'

'For goodness' sake, Sam, keep your voice down or he'll hear you.'

Too late, George, thought Terri, and retched into the bowl.

While Terri lay prostrate in Sam's cabin with a wet flannel over her eyes, the rest of the A-team waved goodbye to the Pitons and prepared for their first real passage.

Within the hour the catamaran had left the protection of St Lucia's west coast and reinforced Trade Winds whistling across the St Vincent Passage punched into her sails and sent her skimming across the waves like a crab on speed, heading for the top end of St Vincent, forty nautical miles away.

Sitting in the stern watching St Lucia sink below the horizon, George and Sam listened to Evie waxing lyrical about Dale and the interior of *Southern Cross*.

'It was fabulous. The saloon was all cherrywood with ornate marquetry on the dining table and it had a galley to die for. As for the master cabin, well . . .'

'Don't tell us, Evie. Leave something to the imagination.'

'Nothing to tell, George. Dale was the epitome of good manners.'

'That's a contradiction in terms, Evie. Aussies don't do manners.'

'He's not an Aussie, Sam, he's from Christchurch, New Zealand.'

'I thought they only fancied sheep.'

'Ladies, get your life jackets and put dem on,' shouted Shadrach from the helm. 'De wind, she be pickin' up.'

They went below like drunken sailors on shore leave and returned, each carrying a survival jacket.

'Now, what was I saying?' said Evie, parting her breasts like Moses dividing the Red Sea and fastening her jacket. 'Oh, yes. Dale showed me a copy of the local St Vincent newspaper, which he'd picked up on his way north. You'll never believe this but in a place called Walli . . .Walloba . . .'

'Wallilabou,' called back Shadrach.

'Yes, that's the place. Well, some Hollywood film company is making a film called *Pirates of the Caribbean* and they're looking for extras from within the cruising community. Dale thinks I would be perfect.'

Sam took one look at the webbing strap attached to the rear of her own jacket, recalled being cut in half and stuffed it out of view. 'Who's in it?'

'Guess?'

'Popeye,' suggested George, bent double.

'Here, let me help,' said Sam, grabbing George's blue webbing strap and thrusting it between her legs.

'Johnny Depp!'

'Bloody hell,' exclaimed George, hanging onto the saloon bulkhead as the starboard pontoon lifted out of the water. 'Now, that's one guy who definitely makes my toes curl. Shadrach, do we go anywhere near this Wally place?'

'No, Georgie, but I tink de crews will all be stayin in Cumberland Bay and dat is where we be headin'.'

'Great!' shouted Evie. 'I've always wanted to be in films.'

'Then don't audition wearing that life jacket or they'll think you're deformed.'

'Would someone check on Terri?' requested Shadrach, imagining Evie's voluptuous figure being squeezed into an eighteenth-century corset. He rearranged his shorts and concentrated on keeping *Rum Punch* on course.

Terri staggered on deck feeling grim just as the others were climbing into the dinghy on their way ashore. She could have joined them but the last thing she needed was some wardrobe mistress dressing her up like Moll Flanders and a casting director shouting at her through a megaphone. Terri had decided to take a rain check.

With the yacht to herself, she untied her sarong and slipped naked into Cumberland Bay, letting the warm Caribbean water soothe away the stresses of the previous night. Floating on her back, her eyes closed, she let the afternoon sun blush her cheeks and drifted away, doing erotic things with Johnny Depp, when a sixth sense told her she wasn't alone. Opening one eye, she caught sight of something in the water. Trying to remain calm, Terri legged it back to the swim-ladder then peeked below the waterline.

A shark's head was moving straight towards her along the catamaran's keel, its dorsal fin swaying as it weaved through the sea. 'Fuckin' hell!'

She cleared the water like a Harrier jump jet on afterburn and landed on the port pontoon fully exposed.

'I say!' An old geezer who sounded like Leslie Phillips was hovering at the stern getting an eyeful.

'Watch out,' Terri shouted, covering her nakedness with a sarong, 'there's a shark under our boat.' The lecherous features turned a whiter shade of pale, the body flipped over and its wrinkled buttocks sliced through the water, breaking the men's one-hundred-metre Olympic free-style record. Pervert, thought Terri, and went below.

'I tell you, there was a shark under *Rum Punch*. If you don't believe me go and look for yourselves.' Terri's mates all stared at her with disbelief written across their features.

Shadrach slid backwards off the dinghy and disappeared. Terri's heart was doing a drum roll as she waited, imagining blood discolouring the aquamarine water around the yacht. He was gone for ages and she could feel her knees knocking together, the others peering at the water from the tender.

'Does anyone know what we do if Shadrach dies?' she asked, being a tad intense.

'Would we have to pick up the body parts for identification?' asked Evie.

'God, I hope not,' announced Sam, gripping the outboard motor for support. 'I knew this wasn't a good idea. We would have been much safer on a cruise liner.'

'If we had been on a cruise liner you wouldn't be about to star in *Pirates of the Caribbean*,' said George.

'Do we know who Shadrach's next of kin is?' continued Evie.

'No. Perhaps Moses will know what to do. We could ring him in Rodney Bay Marina and give him the bad news.'

Terri was back praying to Grannie and writing Shadrach's obituary when his head appeared alongside the dinghy, his white teeth blinding her vision. He rose from the water and rested his butt on the bottom step, all his limbs intact.

'Has it gone?' Terri asked, relief making her sound stupid.

Shadrach looked up, beckoned her with his finger and slipped back into the water. 'Terri, follow me.'

In short measure they were all submerged under the catamaran, watching a three-foot black and white striped fish with a flat head, swimming up and down the length of the yacht.

'Dat ain't no shark, Terri,' announced Shadrach as their heads popped up above the waterline, 'dat be a Remora. De suckers on its head are for clingin' to de underside of whales and udder big mammals so dey can hitch a ride up and down de Caribbean chain, eating scraps from de mammal's mouth. If der be no mammals around, dey stick to de bottom of boats, like young Geordie here.'

'Lazy little devil,' said George, reaching out to touch her near name sake.

'Why do you call him Geordie?' asked Terri.

'Wearin' dat black and white strip, he gotta be a Newcastle United supporter. No taste, o' course. Dere's only one team worth supportin' and dat's West 'am.'

'And you would know, coming from the West Indies.'

'Can we feed him?' asked Evie in her RSPCA role.

'Sure ting. He loves fish scraps.'

'How long has he been free-wheeling on *Rum Punch*?' Terri was intrigued.

Shadrach mounted the step ladder and shook saltwater from his dreadlocks. 'I'd say about tree weeks now.'

'Then why didn't we see him when we were under the yacht in Marigot Bay?' asked Sam.

'He has a way wid de ladies, Samanta, and de ladies, dey just loves our Geordie. He tinks nuttin' of cruising de anchorage lookin' for food, and de waitress at De Shack . . . she feeds him real good. '

'Typical football supporter,' declared George, towelling herself down. 'All mouth and trousers.'

'Anyone for a cocktail?' asked Shadrach, trying to change the subject.

'Just sparkling water for me,' answered Terri, dripping across the stern deck, the thought of more alcohol turning her stomach. 'So, girls, give with the news. How comfortable was the Wallilabou casting couch?'

'Lumpy,' said Evie, busy cutting up fresh limes, 'but productive. Sam and I are to be whores for the day. . .'

'No comment,' muttered George.

'And George will be doing a Nell Gwyn impression with a basket of pineapples in Port Royal.'

'What about the skipper?' asked Terri, nodding over her shoulder.

'Shadrach has landed the best part. He's to be a crew member on the *Black Pearl.*'

'The *Black Pearl?*' she queried.

'Captain Jack Sparrow's pirate ship. Anyway, we have to be on set at four-thirty in the morning so, if I'm to look my best for Johnny Depp, I'll need an early night. What's for dinner, Captain?

'Seared tuna,' came Shadrach's reply. He was pulling fish steaks from inside a freezer drawer.

Terri dropped ice cubes into her water glass. 'Then our football supporter will be in for a real treat.'

'To say nothing of young Geordie below the hull,' muttered a voice from the foredeck.

'Samantha Hutchins, will you zip it? Now, has anyone seen my bedding?'

Chapter Fourteen

Wallilabou

Dawn was clipping the tree-tops on the ridge above Wallilabou as Terri made her way through the hive of activity that was the *Pirates of the Caribbean* film set. Cameramen were fiddling with a lighting rig on a wooden jetty; a guy was up a steel gantry opposite two huge wooden derricks on stone plinths, his head glued to a camera eyepiece; Terri was nearly trampled by a conga-line of hefty canvas bales, which were being stacked in front of a row of stone houses, and a group of extras in red military uniforms were being marched up and down the quay with muskets over their shoulders. Out in the bay, a large square-rigger bobbed at anchor, and inshore a solo wooden mast kept rising and falling in the shallows as divers circled the base, disappearing periodically to check the workings below the waterline.

Feeling like a spare part, Terri wandered down the beach and sat on a rocky outcrop surveying the scene, jealousy oozing from every pore at not being part of the action.

They had arrived in Wallilabou from Cumberland Bay in another dust-covered Dormobile, or 'dollar-bus' as the locals call them, with the moon still low over the horizon and fireflies flashing phosphorescent signals amongst the undergrowth. Sam told the security guard that Terri was one of the whores and bustled her through the chicken-wire fencing before he could argue then abandoned her as she headed for the wardrobe department with George and Evie. Seeing an empty clipboard, Terri grabbed it, tried to look efficient and merged with the gofers. Someone went by carrying a paper cup of coffee which smelt so good she backtracked along his route and discovered a refreshment van close to the perimeter fence.

Armed with a bacon and egg baguette and a large cappuccino, compliments of the film's producers, she meandered back onto the waterfront, egg yolk dribbling down her chin and felt it was time to make herself scarce.

With the sea lapping against the rocks at Terri's feet, she merged with the shadows of the rain forest and thought back to the last time she had been with a film crew.

It was at Beagle Air in 1972. Terri had come on duty, ready for a day flight to Malaga. With the seat pockets full of sick bags, the galley victualled and the bar boxes loaded, she waited with her number two, Stephanie, for the passengers to board. The Traffic Officer mentioned something about them being film crew but Terri took no notice, more interested in the fact that she only had a First Officer in the cockpit, the Captain being conspicuous by his absence.

Minutes ticked by, the passengers settled into their seats and a general air of excitement gathered around the hat racks. Finally, the terminal building departure door flew open and Captain Barney Crawford filled the entrance, his four gold stripes glinting in the morning sun, a black eyepatch over one eye and a white stick angled to the ground. Terri was instantly suspicious. He proceeded to tap his way across the tarmac in full view of the passengers on the port side, clattered his way up the aircraft's rear steps and arrived in the galley shouting, 'Teresa, am I there yet?' then tapped his way through the full length of the cabin and disappeared into the cockpit.

Murder was on her mind as she tried to persuade seventy-eight nervous passengers that this was actually a joke.

Things then went from bad to worse when, checking the cabin before take-off, Terri approached what she thought was a man in seat 11C from the rear.

'Excuse me, sir,' she said, gently tapping him on the shoulder, 'would you please fasten your seat belt?' When their eyes met she was staring into the tight-lipped face of Glenda Jackson, the UK's most famous dramatic actress of that time. Leaping back, her cheeks on fire, Terri mumbled an apology and speedily advanced to Row 10 wondering why on earth the actress was sporting such a short haircut.

'I've just accused Elizabeth I of being a man,' she said to the flight deck crew, following her pre-take-off check. 'How am I supposed to get back to the rear galley without being sent to the Tower?'

'Try using my white stick,' suggested Barney, turning the Viscount onto the taxiway. Terri's middle finger indicated her mood and she backed down the cabin pretending to check that the starboard hat rack was secure. She reached the rear galley with her head intact.

The rest of the flight was no better. Whilst loading the trolley with duty-free booze and cigarettes in the galley, a chap came to stand by the rear door. Seconds later, he was asking Terri in an American drawl if she was staying in Malaga for the night. Terri smiled, very used to suggestive chat-up lines, and was about to churn out the usual '*Sorry, sir, but there are some services we ONLY offer to our first-class passengers*', when Stephanie arrived, all dewy-eyed, and asked for his autograph.

Terri sank below the trolley trying to look busy as he took Stephanie's pen and pad, asked for her name, scribbled his signature across a blank surface and then enquired if they could recommend a good traditional restaurant in Malaga where he could get a paella.

'Who was that?' she whispered as he returned to his seat.

'What d'you mean, who was that?' Terri could practically see Steph's tonsils as the number two gaped at her. 'That, you Neanderthal, was George Segal.'

Terri was about to ask who the hell George Segal was when his head popped around the galley bulkhead once more and asked for another whisky and dry.

'You get it,' she instructed Steph as the actor winked at her. She quickly returned to loading half bottles of Gordon's Gin onto the trolley and waited for her blushes to fade.

Every time Terri saw a replay of *A Touch of Class* on the TV, with Glenda Jackson wearing a Cathy McGowan wig and being chased around a bedroom by George Segal, she turned the colour of cochineal and wondered what might have happened if she had returned that wink. Now, if that had been Sam, she thought . . .

Shadrach was walking along the beach in Terri's direction, his jaunty stride bringing her back to the present. The dawn light picked out his features, the first of the sun's rays catching the polished, colourful glass beads hanging from the dreadlocks either side of his cheeks and from two Chinese pigtails hanging from under a stick-on beard. Terri chuckled. He had a dirty red bandana round his head, a gun belt slung across his chest over a fitted dress coat, knee-length leather boots with exaggerated turnovers and a moth-eaten tri-corn hat in his hand. As he came closer she thought she could pick out charcoal black rings around his eyes. He appeared to be talking to himself.

'Hey, Shadrach,' she called out, 'have you missed your vocation?'

His eyes searched the shadows then locked onto Terri sitting on the rock and came over. There were only two problems with this. Firstly, it wasn't Shadrach, and secondly, Terri knew the A-team were never going to believe her. Pity Jack Sparrow is married, she thought as the object of her erotic dreams plonked his butt alongside her on the rock and began engaging Terri in polite conversation.

'Who's Shadrach?'

'My skipper in real life and one of. . .' what the hell was the name of his ship? '. . . the *Black Pearl's* crew.' Not bad, Terri, she thought, for someone with sudden onset senile dementia.

'One of the extras, then?'

Terri nodded, desperately trying to expunge the image of this icon climbing naked into her virtual Jacuzzi.

'What vessel does he have in real life?'

'A sixty-foot catamaran,' she replied, the lie nonchalantly tripping off her tongue.

'Where are you heading?'

'Grenada. What about you?' Definitely senile dementia.

'Davy Jones's locker,' came the reply. Johnny Depp raised one eyebrow as they looked at each other and they both burst out laughing.

The shoot went on all day and Terri watched with fascination as the director put everyone through their paces over and over again. When there was a lull in proceedings she helped herself to more delicious edibles on offer at the refreshment van then returned to her perch at the end of the bay. She never did see Shadrach dressed as a pirate and only glimpsed Sam once in her whore's outfit, towering head, shoulders and uplifted boobs above everyone else.

The moon had made another appearance by the time they all climbed back into the dollar bus and headed for Cumberland Bay, her friends waxing lyrical about seeing Keira Knightley or Orlando Bloom from afar while Terri kept her own counsel and a straight face.

'What's the matter with you, Gillingham?' asked George, dragging a bag of pineapples behind her onto the stern deck of *Rum Punch* as the first drop of rain landed on the saloon roof. 'You haven't said a word all evening.'

'Oh, I was just reliving my conversation with Johnny Depp down on the beach earlier today.'

'Like hell you were,' said Sam following her into the saloon. 'Just like the time you were convinced George Segal fancied you when all he wanted was a paella.'

'Sticks and stones, Sam. Sticks and stones.'

Terri walked into her cabin and leant back on the closed door. Tonight, she thought, I'm going to dream for England.

Reaching into her pocket, she pulled out a blood-orange glass bead which had fallen into the sand from Jack Sparrow's beard and placed it under her pillow as torrential rain shot-blasted the blue bin liner above her hatch.

'I couldn't have done this on a cruise liner,' she whispered to the dry seal as she doused the light and went back to her imaginary Jacuzzi.

Chapter Fifteen

Man Overboard!

It was day five and *Rum Punch* was on her way south, the A-team experimenting with sail trim. George was on the helm, Terri on the main sheet, Sam dealing with the genoa and Evie standing by with the winch handle.

'Turn tirty degrees to starboard,' ordered Shadrach from behind George's shoulder.

'Tirty degrees to starboard it is, Cap'n'

'Ease de main, Terri. Same wid de genoa, Sam. Steady as she goes, George. Now feel her pick up speed.'

Rum Punch raced through the flat water, her two pontoons riding in symmetry across the surface.

'Wow!' shouted Evie, 'this is better than skiing.'

'Right crew, George is now gonna bring us up as close to de wind as she can manage widout stallin, then she'll tack. Get ready to bring de boom amidships, Terri, and release the genoa sheet as we go round, Sam, while Evie pulls it onto the port side.'

George watched the compass as the wind came onto her nose and the bows crossed the centre line.

'Right, Evie,' shouted Shadrack above the sound of flogging sails, 'winch like de devil until de genoa is as tight as a baby's arse and well done, Georgie, you be a natural.' His hand smacked against her back. 'Dat's enough, Evie. Now all of yous, reverse the process before we runs into dem rocks straight ahead.'

George took one look at the sea boiling above a reef some way off and threw the helm to starboard. *Rum Punch*'s bow shot round, the port pontoon left the water and Evie dropped the winch handle over the side as she tried to cling onto the guardrail.

'Man overboard!' shouted Terri as she and Sam dumped air from the sails and *Rum Punch* steadied on a beam-reach, the winch handle bobbing up and down in the water off their port quarter.

'Keep your eye on it, Evie,' shouted Shadrach as he elbowed George out of her seat, gunned the engines, and turned through the wind. 'Terri, release the mainsail halyard, *now*.' He pushed the auto button on the helm, as the mainsail concertinaed in a heap over the boom, then opened the jammer holding the furling line. 'Sam, keep de line tight until I tells you to release.' He pulled on the furler for all he was worth and the genoa spun inwards like a top, curling around the forestay. 'OK, Sam, now let it out real slow.'

'Said the actress to the bishop.'

'What?'

'Nothing,' said Sam, and paid out the line until the genoa was fully stowed.

'Can you still see it?' Shadrach bellowed.

'I think I can,' replied Evie, half out of the boat, her arm pointing behind them.

'Right, crew, let's go get it.'

'What's the big deal?' remarked Sam, tidying away her rope. 'It's only a winch handle and it can't be worth much.'

'It happens to be de only one we have,' muttered Shadrach. 'Shout out if you spot it, Evie.'

'Wilco, Cap'n,' she replied, bouncing up and down on the trampoline netting.

'I assume it floats,' yelled George, standing on the saloon roof holding the binoculars aloft.

'Yep. It's plastic wid a hollow handle, but all you'll see is de orange end.'

'Then I've got it,' she announced, pointing the binoculars at a small orange dot. 'About two hundred metres on the starboard side.'

Rum Punch's engines throttled back and the catamaran came to a stop upwind of the handle, rising and dipping in the waves. 'Off you go then, missy, you lost it, you get it back,' Shadrach told Evie.

She ran to the stern, removed the gaff from its stowage, disappeared down the steps and hooked the offending item as it drifted past. As she reappeared on deck to a round of applause, George remained glued to the horizon.

'Skipper, I think I can see something glinting in the waves out there.' She pointed to the west and everyone turned to see what she was talking about.

'I can't see anything,' grunted Sam, taking the winch handle from Evie and running it under the galley tap.

'Perhaps it a whale's water-spout.'

'Don't be daft, Evie, whales aren't around the Caribbean at this time of year.'

'And you would know,' came the retort as Shadrach jumped up alongside George and took the binoculars. Evie and Terri continued to gaze at the expanse of deep blue water to the west but saw nothing unusual.

Only the soft lapping of the sea against the hull could be heard as Shadrach scanned the horizon. Back and forth he went, with George trying to give directions.

'It was black and orange, and very small.'

On his third attempt he paused, went rigid then all hell broke loose.

'Keep de binoculars on dat spot . . . and whatever you do, don't lose 'em.' He pointed due west, handed the binoculars to George and jumped down to the helm. 'Terri, wet some towels and stack 'em on de stern. Evie, first-aid box, bring it here. Sam, make up some ice packs from de freezer.'

'But . . .'

'Don't argue, missy. Do it!'

'Have we got enough water?' shouted Terri from the head.

'Yous better pray we have.' Shadrach's eyes were peeled, his brain focused on getting *Rum Punch* as fast as possible out to sea, the A-team forgotten.

Evie unzipped a green first-aid bag and rummaged through it by Shadrach's feet. 'I can only find a box of plasters, some athlete's foot spray and eight packs of condoms in here,' she said, looking up.

Shadrach's eyes dropped to the deck and he gritted his teeth. 'Where did you find that?'

'In our head.'

'Not that one, Evie. The ship's first-aid box, under the chart-table.'

'Oh, right.' Evie rapidly gathered the contents together and retreated into the saloon where Sam was smacking a large lump of ice with an ice pick.

'What d'you think is going on?' Sam asked.

'Search me, but whatever it is, it doesn't involve sex or a triathlon.'

George kept losing the image in the lenses and her breathing became erratic. The only time previously she had been involved in a waterborne rescue was in the Crawley swimming baths, when she had been expected to upend a six-man life raft while the Beagle Air Chief Training Stewardess watched from the side-lines. She had failed miserably, ending up with the inflatable over her head, and two beefy lifeguards had to come to her rescue. This was different, this was real.

Don't panic, Georgina, said her inner voice. Deep breaths and try again. She searched the ever-moving area between sea and sky as *Rum Punch* pitched in a rolling gait, causing her stomach to heave in sympathy, convinced she had lost sight of it. Then, as she rose on a following sea, there it was: a black head in orange jacket.

Rum Punch dipped then rose again and the figure was there once more, its left arm supporting another body. 'Shadrach, there are two of them, but only one's wearing a life jacket.'

'Figures,' he replied above the wind.

'What's happened to them?'

'Probably capsized fishin' and lost dere pirogue.'

'But if I hadn't spotted them?' She didn't dare take her eyes off the pair.

'Dey'd be fish food.' Shadrach was doing everything he could to push the catamaran through the water at breakneck speed while the others stood in a clump on the foredeck, shoulders rigid. 'Come down now, Georgie, I can see dem from here.'

The A-team went into emergency mode, each following instructions without question. The mainsail was stowed, their life jackets donned and lifelines attached, the rear deck cleared of clutter as they mentally ran through their first aid training.

'Now,' said Shadrach, 'dis ain't gonna be easy in dis sea. I want yous all hooked on. No one's to go overboard.' He glared at Terri.

'Aren't you going to wear a life jacket?' asked Evie.

'No.'

'But . . .'

'Now listen to me. I intends to drop de dinghy in de water. Terri, you make de dinghy line secure wid plenty of scope and pull us in when I say. Georgie, you come wid me, and Sam, be on de starboard steps ready to help haul de lads aboard.'

Sam nodded, holding her safety-line's carbine hook ready in her left hand.

'Be careful, missy, we be dealin' wid possible concussion or worse, and de yacht, she'll buck like a bronco. Evie, stand behind Sam and make sure she don't fall in. You two. . .'

George and Terri snapped to attention.

'. . .when we gets back between de pontoons, go on deck and help de udders.'

Terri crossed her fingers behind her back. She swallowed hard and watched the two bobbing heads draw ever closer. Thank God they're not rugby prop-forwards, she thought, and focused on her role.

Shadrach picked up the VHF handset. 'May Day, May Day, May Day. Dis is de catamaran, *Rum Punch*, *Rum Punch*, *Rum Punch*. Our position be . . .'

The elder boy stared through salt-encrusted eyes, his jacket barely inflated, his hand clawed around the smaller one's waistband, the floppy head resting on his shoulder, eyes closed.

'Probably brothers,' Shadrach shouted as he prised the elder boy's fingers apart and curled them onto the dinghy's rope handle while simultaneously grabbing the youngster under his armpits and pulling him aboard, using George as ballast on the opposite pontoon.

A wave nearly capsized the dinghy and the older boy's fingers lost purchase on the rope; his head slid beneath the life jacket and he dropped out of view, his jacket floating free. George screamed. Shadrach looked back, threw himself over the side and disappeared into the deep. George shot into the centre of the dinghy and gently dragged the youngster's body along the floor of the Rib, turning him into a foetal position in the bow. Then she peered over the side and waited. Seconds ticked by with nothing but heaving sea filling her vision before Shadrach surfaced, a head cradled between his strong hands, and back-kicked towards the dinghy.

Lying flat across the rubber boat her arms and shoulders over the side George locked her elbows below the unconscious boy's armpits, just as Shadrach had done earlier, and waited for instructions.

'Right, Georgie. I'll push, you pull. On de count of tree . . . but wait for de wave. Now, one, two, tree!'

George's knees pistoned under her stomach as she took the strain, a dark curly head and sunburnt shoulders rising from the water and flopping across the pontoon. She pulled her right arm free and grabbed the belt of his shorts then pulled again, hearing something tear as adrenalin powered through her muscles and the dead weight of the boy's body flattened her against the floor. George closed her eyes and let tears of relief dilute the sea-spray.

'Come on, Shadrach, come on!' shouted Terri from the port step willing him to jump aboard the dinghy, but the rope handle remained tantalisingly out of his reach as the Rib leapt about, almost burying him. Terri's blood pressure roared in her ears.

Evie, standing at the starboard guardrail, had a long mooring rope curled in her hands. She hurled it in Shadrach's direction, the outer end tied in a loop, the inner end attached to a cleat at her feet. The rope flew through the air like a lasso and landed by Shadrach's head. He was through the loop and screaming at Terri to pull the dinghy in as Evie hauled him through the water and back aboard.

With the dinghy securely tied fore and aft, the casualties were gingerly eased onto the starboard steps as Sam's feet appeared and disappeared in the heaving waves, then carefully lifted onto the deck and laid on the cool wet towels, their limbs flaccid.

Sam immediately took control, checking for signs of life in an orderly fashion.

'Terri, give that one mouth to mouth. Evie, get me a mirror.'

Shadrach should have been in charge but instinct told him that the women knew what they were doing so he held back, placing his arm around Georgina's shoulders as she stood by the helm, every muscle in spasm.

Terri was on automatic pilot, undoing the older boy's waistband, clearing his airways, pushing his head back and pinching his nose then covering his mouth with hers and blowing air into his lungs. Her mouth disengaged and she filled her lungs while counting. Four seconds later she did it again and by the third breath the boy convulsed. She pushed his head sideways and water spewed from his lips. Checking his pulse, she nodded to Sam and rolled him into the recovery position before placing an ice pack in a cold towel and draping it over his head.

'Evie,' whispered Sam, 'I can't find a pulse here. I need you to help me do CPR, *now*.'

The St Vincent Coastguard vessel arrived alongside as Sam's fingers clasped the youngster's wrist and her expression lightened. 'I've got it!' she said. 'Weak but regular.'

'Tank de Lord,' praised Shadrach, his palms together and pointing to heaven. 'You be a marvel, Samanta.'

Sam rubbed her arm across her forehead and sat back on her heels. 'Not really, Skip. I trained as a nurse before Beagle Air.'

'Well, dat don't explain Evie's talents wid de rope.'

Evie chose not to comment, her hands rubbing life back into her patient's fingers.

George was about to answer for her but looked to Terri first for approval. Terri rubbed her nose, looked down at Evie then back up at George and nodded. 'It's not the first time she's done that, Shadrach. Evie grew up in a circus and when she was a little girl she used to ride bare-back, dressed as a cowgirl.'

The Coastguard crew were full of praise after inspecting the survivors and their chief offered the A-team a lift back to Kingstown to freshen up. They refused, preferring to remain aboard *Rum Punch*, Sam watching like a mother hen as the teenagers were transferred to the Coastguard vessel, insisting on boarding to check that they were suitably comfortable for their return to dry land. Shadrach followed and remained with the chief for some time.

'Where you be heading, Cap'ain?' asked the chief as they appeared back on deck.

'Bequia,' confirmed Shadrach. Their hands locked together. 'Admiralty Bay.'

'Den 'ave a good trip and don't worry about de boys. We'll take good care o' dem.'

Shadrach nodded, jumped aboard *Rum Punch* and waved as two powerful engines burst into life and the Coastguard vessel powered through the waves, heading for St Vincent's capital.

'Was you really in a circus, Evie?' asked Shadrach on his way back to the helm.

'I grew up in one. My dad was the ringmaster at Circus Americano in Italy.'

'Well, I never!'

'Where were you born, Skip?' asked George, knees under her chin, eyes peering out of salt-encrusted lashes.

'Uh . . . Jamaica . . . Montego Bay. Me dad, he was a fisherboy like dose two.' His head nodded towards Kingstown.

'What happened to them, Shadrach?' Terri was rubbing antiseptic cream onto rope burns running across her palms.

Shadrach walked over, took her hands in his and examined the deep red welts. She looked up, enjoying the feel of his fingers on her tender skin and waited for his response.

'De elder brudder said dey were out fishin' when de squall hit last night. Dere pirogue turned over in big seas and sank, leavin' dem to drift wid de current.' His index finger was gently massaging her left palm.

'So, if George hadn't seen them through the binoculars, they would have been lost at sea.'

'Dat's right, Terri.

'Fat lot of good one rotting life jacket would have done them,' pointed out Evie.

'It was dat or nuttin'.'

'George, are you alright?' Sam followed Georgina out of the saloon at a run. Seconds later part of the sea on *Rum Punch*'s port side turned a sludgy shade of yellow.

Chapter Sixteen

Aftermath

No one felt much like lunch or enjoying the beautiful views of St Vincent's western coastline as an air of anti-climax took hold. After the events of the morning and the excitement of the previous day the A-team wandered off to their cabins for a siesta, drifting in and out of sleep while *Rum Punch* carried them south across the Bequia Channel.

Sam's thoughts turned to CJ, wondering how he was getting on in Alaska, and she was shocked to realise that she really didn't care. Before leaving the UK she had insisted that he email her regularly from the ship but, being unsure if that was possible, CJ had instead paid for regular messages to be published in the personal column of *The Times*, such as:

To Kitten, missing you, Tiger xxx

She turned onto her stomach and rested her chin in her hands. Since Hewanorra Airport baggage hall she hadn't seen a *Times* and, after everything that had happened subsequently, CJ and Knightsbridge now seemed to be on a parallel planet.

The two fisherboys came to mind and she smiled, reliving that moment of joy when a weak pulse fluttered under her fingers and she knew she had saved a life. It had been years since she had thought of anyone else's welfare, the fact highlighting how self-centred she had become under CJ's influence.

Compared to her sanitised life in London with Harrods Food Hall across the street and her unlimited credit card to hand, those youngsters risked life and limb on a daily basis to catch a few fish to feed their families.

It's a lottery, she decided. If you're born in the Home Counties, your fish comes scaled, gutted and filleted, but if you're born in the Grenadines, you either go and catch your own or starve. Yet, she thought, the kids she had seen on St Lucia and St Vincent were always laughing, playing cricket on the beach with a stick and ball or getting a clip round the ear from their mammas when they misbehaved and a big hug when they didn't.

Sam hadn't seen her parents for ten years, their objection to her status as a kept woman driving a wedge between them. It had never before occurred to her that they might miss her or that they might just have a point. She rolled back onto her side and stared at CJ's photograph by her bed.

'I've been living in a five-star bubble, servicing your libido for years, CJ, on the basis that you loved me. But you don't, do you? I'm your very expensive bit on the side, nothing more. I've given up having kids, relationships with my family or a social life, all for you. What have you ever given up for me?'

She closed her eyes and imagined her future and didn't like what she saw. The respect in everyone's eyes that afternoon when she had pulled the smaller boy back from the brink of death had felt good and she realised she wanted more. It was time to change things, she decided, with or without CJ's consent, and she was determined to put her plans into action once she returned home. The first thing she was going to do was call her parents. She wondered what reaction she would get when her father answered the phone.

Evie was dreaming of Dale and sailing into the sunset with him on *Southern Cross*. They were alone on the foredeck, the wind in her hair, his arm around her waist, his Antipodean drawl whispering '*Evangaleena*' into her ear.

It had been years since anyone had called her Evangelina in that loving way. Her dad had called her his little princess. Her mum, Sweetpea. Only her little brother had used her name.

'*Evangelina, Evangelina, look at me. Aren't I clever?*'

She smiled in her sleep, her eyes oscillating under her eyelids as she watched him pendulum through the air way above her head, so proud to see him upside down, his little legs straddling the thin bar, his arms held out wide. He was eight years old, full of confidence and her greatest fan.

Then he fell and she never heard him speak her name again.

She woke with a start, her cheeks wet, heartbeat on overdrive. Rescuing the fisherboys had brought it all back in vivid detail. She could remember people crowding around the small broken body, her mum running into the Big Top screaming and one of the clowns pulling Evie away from the scene as someone shouted for an ambulance. The pain and the loss had been unbearable. She could still feel her father gripping her shoulder at the grave side as a red rose left her hand and landed on the lid of the white coffin. She was twelve years old and something had died deep inside her that day.

Her dad had used a twelve-bore shot gun to kill his pain. Her mum returned to Cornwall, a widow with Evie in tow, and died of breast cancer three years later. Evie had ended up in a foster home, learning to fend for herself while she grew into a Latin beauty, much to the delight of the interview panel at Beagle Air who snapped her up the minute she walked through the door. She was gregarious, adventurous and popular, but no-one had ever been allowed to get close except the A-team, who had watched over her like family and knew that, behind her happy façade, a little girl with a broken heart was trying to get out.

She blew her nose, shook out her erratic curls and thumped the mattress. 'Enough, Evangelina. You're on holiday and those two brothers are alive and in safe hands.' She flopped back onto her pillows and made a determined effort to get back to her dream of Dale and the *Southern Cross*, her pulse steadying as her skin warmed under his practised touch.

George couldn't sleep. She tossed and turned, sat up, lay down, rearranged her pillows and counted sheep but it was to no avail, something was on her mind and it needed attention. She drummed her fingers against her thigh and recalled Shadrach stepping back on board after his tête-à-tête with the Coastguard chief, looking furtive. Picking up a notepad and pen, she began to write a list.

<u>Shadrach Jonathon William Bligh.</u>
Born - Montego Bay, Jamaica
Age- 45ish???
Smoker - No
Wife - Never mentioned.

Kids - Never mentioned.

Father - Fisherman as youth. Then what?

Mother - Never mentioned

Siblings - Never mentioned

Past employment - Ran a bar/ Blue Lagoon Caribbean Cruises???

Talents - Sailing, Repairs, Food, Drinks, Rescues & pulling women???

Finances - Questionable

Hobbies - West Ham supporter!!!

Rum Punch

Type - 38ft Lagoon Catamaran

Age - 1990's??

Owner/Skipper - Shadrach J W Bligh?

Condition - average to poor

Equipment - lacking

Staff - Moses!!!

Conclusion

Must have something to hide.

Possible drug running or worse, using charter trips for cover?

(*Must check lockers, etc.*)

Bloody good sailor!

All round nice guy.

Attributes - big hands!

George studied the list and chewed the inside of her cheek.

'*Pirates of the Caribbean* has obviously gone to your head, Georgina Stanhope.'

She threw the notepad into a drawer and closed her eyes, wondering if Terri had been telling the truth when she said she had met Johnny Depp, then rejected the idea as being ridiculous and finally fell asleep.

In the blue-hued cabin, Terri lay under a wet towel trying to stay cool. Her hands burnt, her stomach churned and guilt ate at her conscience.

She wasn't sure she had done the right thing, giving George the nod to reveal Evie's past, and it niggled her. Evie had sworn them to secrecy years before, insisting that no one needed to know either about the circus or her family but, today, Terri had been convinced that divulging that secret to Shadrach had been the right thing to do.

As for Sam, thought Terri, that had been a St Paul on the road to Damascus moment. To watch her hold the life of a youngster in her hands and save him from a premature death had been extraordinary; her transformation from self-centred, spoilt mistress to a caring, compassionate paramedic was a joy to behold and Terri hoped the effect would last.

George's herculean efforts in the dinghy only added to the mix, emphasising Terri's own meagre talents and plunging her ever deeper into despair.

'I'm a failure,' she announced. 'I'm good to neither man nor beast. No wonder I never found my Mr Right. Who wants a useless, over-the-hill, ex-trolley dolly with a drink problem?'

The last thought hit her smack between the eyes. She jettisoned the towel and peered into the bulkhead mirror. Her reflection was cruel. Too many curries and bottles of cheap red wine had left their mark and time was not on Terri's side.

'That's it,' she announced to her reflection. 'From now on it's only one drink a day. You can also start getting familiar with your cooker again and that gym membership that lapsed will just have to be reinstated.'

'*Famous last words*,' jeered her grannie as Terri disappeared back under the wet towel.

'Sod off, gran. This time, I mean it.'

Rum Punch cleared Bequia Head and made tracks for Northwest Point. Shadrach sat at the helm feeling the catamaran's rudders biting into the Caribbean; his dreadlocks were tied at the nape of his neck and his broad hands gripped the wheel.

It had been a crazy five days since leaving Rodney Bay with his passengers and he was punch drunk on events. Sam had turned from a cantankerous bitch into Mother Teresa, Georgie had proved she was a match for any America's Cup foredeck crew, Evie could charm the hind legs off a donkey and remain freezer-cool in an emergency, and Terri chose to portray herself as a victim while exerting total control over the others. They were a force to be reckoned with and he wasn't sure he was up to the task.

Thankfully, they didn't know *Rum Punch* was limping down the Grenadines with a busted chart plotter, suspect batteries, the dinghy in constant need of air and one of the engines spewing black smoke. Nor that he was ducking and diving to make ends meet with a bank balance well into the red.

Rescuing two local lads out fishing was all very well, but if the press got hold of the story, his boat and her crew would become front-page news throughout the Lesser Antilles, when all he really wanted was to stay below the radar. He crossed his fingers and checked his course. Only a short while to go, he thought, and he could pick up a mooring buoy in Admiralty Bay, take on fresh water, barter for some food and get a decent night's sleep, squalls permitting.

He raised his head and laughed off his mood. 'One tings for sure, Shadrach Jonathon William Bligh, life at sea ain't ever dull!'

Chapter Seventeen

Bequia

Terri heard a powerful outboard motor close by and came up on deck to investigate. Shadrach was waving to another Rastafarian sitting on the edge of his colourful pirogue, hand on the tiller, heading at speed towards the catamaran's side.

'Hey, mon. Yous wantin' a boowee?'

Shadrach gave a thumbs up and 'African'. . . the name written on the side of his boat . . . did a one-eighty-degree turn and led the way into a huge anchorage peppered with yachts.

'What's a boowee?' she asked as she watched him slow by a huge orange ball, hook a trailing line out of the water and hold it in the air.

'Dat is,' replied Shadrach. 'Here, take de helm and keep de speed low while I go forward.'

Terri leapt into the seat and grabbed the wheel with both hands, keeping her eyes locked on the boat boy, hoping her skipper would get back quickly before she ran the local chap over.

'Engines in neutral,' shouted Shadrach as George leant across and centred the throttles. The catamaran went ahead on forward momentum only, a line was thrown to 'African' and seconds later *Rum Punch* was tied to the ball with a long rope.

'Cut the engines.'

George pulled on a toggle and turned a key. A soft breeze ruffled Terri's hair as the catamaran settled back on her mooring line and the two Rastafarians went head-to-head in conversation.

'How did you know what to do?' Terri asked George, nodding at the engine panel.

'I've watched Shadrach.'

'Well, so have I, but it never registered with me.' Terri was feeling inadequate again. She looked around Admiralty Bay with its palm-fringed beaches, brightly painted wooden buildings and aquamarine waters, and recalled her afternoon's decisions.

'Right, Teresa Gillingham,' she whispered under her breath, 'no time like the present to start.' She cast her sarong aside, stood on the starboard deck clad in a rather fetching M&S swimming costume and dived into the sea, coming nose to nose with young Geordie's flat head as she swam below the yacht. 'Evening, Geordie,' she bubbled and rose to the surface between the twin hulls before beginning a fifty-lap circuit of *Rum Punch*.

Evie's reflection met her on her twenty-third lap. 'Happy Hour, Terri!' she called.

'Not for me, thanks.'

Evie's reflection did a double take. 'What did you say?'

'No, thanks.'

'Hey, girls, Terri has just refused an alcoholic drink.' Terri kicked ahead.

'She must be sickening for something.'

'No I'm not,' she yelled as she passed the stern for the twenty-fourth time. 'I'm cutting back.' She closed her ears to the hilarity emanating from the stern deck and powered into a crawl.

By the time she staggered up the rear steps, the back of her swimming costume lodged in the crack of her bottom, and her lungs on fire, a large flatbed vessel with Daffodil Marine plastered along the side was hooked onto *Rum Punch*'s hull. Sam threw Terri a towel and she wandered forward to see what was going on. Shadrach appeared to be taking on fresh water. Great, she thought, I can have a shower and wash my hair. 'George, what have you done with my shampoo?'

'You'll find it in my cabin.'

Evie's Cuba Libre looked so inviting. . . Terri closed her eyes and marched past the stern table purposefully.

Picking up the shampoo bottle from the dressing table, Terri noticed a notepad lodged in the top drawer with Shadrach's name written across the top of the page. Pulling the drawer open a little wider, she scanned the scribbles with growing interest. Seconds later she stepped into the head with George's list imprinted on her brain, her attraction to the skipper getting a reality check.

George was probably right, she thought as cold clear water cascaded from the shower head, shampoo bubbles running down her neck. She often is when it comes to men, Terri concluded, and stretched for the bath towel, throwing it over her head. If Shadrach Bligh is dealing in drugs, the idea caused her to shiver, then it's as well I learnt about it now before making a complete fool of myself. She stepped out of the cubicle rubbing her skin vigorously to dry off.

'Face it, Teresa, just because he has a great physique, a fabulous smile and charisma oozing from every pore doesn't mean he's genuine.' She examined her left hand, brushed her lips across the palm and rubbed more antiseptic cream into her rope burns. Anyway, she argued, West Ham are rubbish!

George's questions now needed answers and Terri, as the party leader, was on a mission, determined to root out the truth, starting with a round-table discussion with the A-team the next time they were alone. She walked outside and flopped down on the bench seat, swathed in towelling.

'Ready for a Cuba Libre now, Terri?' Sam held up a bottle of white rum and a can of Coke, dripping condensation.

'No, thanks. I'll have a fizzy water instead.'

Sam put the bottle and can down, placed a freezing palm on Terri's forehead and checked her pulse. 'Well, it's not sunstroke,' she announced, and went back to the galley.

'You were right the first time, Sam,' commented George. 'She must be pregnant!'

'Either that or she's found religion.'

'If you must know, I've turned over a new leaf.' Terri thought she sounded like Mary Whitehouse. 'Only one drink a day from now on and fifty laps of the yacht every morning.'

'Is it catching?' asked Evie, downing her drink.

'Christ, I hope not,' said George. 'What would we do with all that rum?'

Terri was counting the kitty when George walked into her cabin, rubbing her wet hair.

'Are we solvent?'

'With your joint earnings from Wallilabou, we're rolling in cash.'

'Oh good, 'cos I've been asking Shadrach where we should eat tonight and he's suggested the Frangipani Beach Hotel. I'll get him to book us a table.'

Terri stashed the EC dollars in her money belt. 'Can you ask him if there's a cyber café in Port Elizabeth? I need to check on something.'

'Me too. I dread to think what's been happening at Prestige Travel since I left.'

'No doubt Sam will want to check in with CJ as well.'

'Leave it to me. Eight-thirty OK for you?'

'Sure. And, George, make sure I don't drink tonight.'

'You're really serious about this, aren't you?'

Terri held up her hands, fingers crossed. 'About time, wouldn't you say?'

George stuck her thumb in the air and turned away as Terri stuffed the money belt under her mattress.

When she came on deck the other members of the A-team were already there, dressed to kill and watching Shadrach blowing up the dinghy.

'Do we have a problem?' asked Terri, peering over the stern.

'No. Dinghies always lose pressure when de sun goes down.' He refused to look at her while he spoke and Terri made a mental note to check on that fact as well. He unscrewed the nozzle from the air valve and pushed the foot pump under the bow. 'OK, ladies, ready when you is.'

One by one they climbed aboard and the dinghy glided across the bay on flat water, the sky a canopy of stars.

'A bit different from Jalousie Bay,' said George as they approached the wooden jetty and jumped ashore. 'Let's hope the Frangipani has a more extensive menu than Bang between the Pitons.'

'Aren't you joining us, Shadrach?' Terri was staring at the top of his head.

'No. I tought I'd eat some o' dat tuna in de freezer. Make more room.' He pulled on the engine cord, the outboard sprang to life and he was off back to *Rum Punch* without a backward glance.

'Who's got the handheld?' asked Terri, dragging her eyes back to shore.

'George.'

'Right, let's go eat.'

Finishing a charcoal-grilled sirloin steak, Terri placed her knife and fork on her empty plate and sat back. 'That was wicked,' she said, sipping fizzy water while the others sampled the house red.

'I've been told that we can access the internet in the local newspaper office at the back of the village,' said George. 'They open at nine in the morning.'

'Great. Let's have breakfast ashore,' enthused Evie, 'then do some emailing.'

'Good idea. Anyone for dessert?' Terri turned to attract the waitress's attention.

'I fancy Key Lime pie.' Evie undid the button on her leather trousers.

'Not for me,' said Sam. 'I'm stuffed.

The waitress took their plates, and the order, then winked.

'Strange,' said Terri, focusing on the staff member's abundant hips as she waddled back to the kitchen. 'That waitress just winked at me.'

'Perhaps she fancies you.'

'Don't be ridiculous George . . .'

The lights went out, the music stopped, the kitchen door flew open and a huge cake studded with spluttering sparklers levitated across the restaurant and landed centre table in front of Sam. When the lights came back on a tall, well-dressed West Indian, microphone in one hand, a bottle of Veuve Cliquot in the other, stood at Terri's shoulder and addressed the diners.

'Ladies and gentlemen, it gives me enormous pleasure to inform you that these ladies here rescued two of our boys from drowning today after their fishing boat capsized during de night.' Sam was almost under the table with embarrassment and the others writhed in their seats. 'The boys had been in the water for twelve hours and were not breathing when they were brought aboard, but these angels of mercy gave them the kiss of life and saved their souls!'

The diners were on their feet, applause nearly bursting the A-team's eardrums and the steel band went into a rendition of 'When the Saints Come Marching In'.

Lightbulbs flashed, the waitress crushed Terri's ribs in a bear hug and Evie was hoisted aloft on a sea of arms, as Sam and George shook hands with the world and its mother.

When Terri was finally released, she turned to find the Frangipani's Master of Ceremonies bowing low.

'James Fitz-Allen Mitchell, at your service, ma'am,' he announced clasping her hands in his. 'I would like to say how honoured I am to welcome you to the Frangipani, Miss'. . .

'Gillingham. Teresa Gillingham. I . . .'

His hands came up, cutting short her words. 'Miss Gillingham, the whole of Bequia . . . no, St Vincent and all the Grenadines. . . are in your debt today for saving Jo-Jo and Samuel from a watery grave.'

'But, we. . .'

'Please, don't be modest. And if there's anything we can do to make your stay special, all you have to do is ask.'

'Mr Mitchell. . .'

'Sir James,' whispered the waitress in Terri's left ear.

She coughed and started again. 'Sir James, this is all very overwhelming. We did what anyone else would have done under the circumstances, and without our skipper these two boys would still be out there.'

'Nonsense! I've read the Coastguard's report. You and your friends helped pluck them from the sea and kept them alive until help came.'

Terri didn't know what to say.

'Tomorrow we're having a big Bequian jump-up in your honour and I know Jo-Jo and Samuels' folks will be forever in your debt.'

The cake was cut, the champagne cork popped and everyone in or near the Frangipani joined in the excitement. There was no need for George to use the handheld VHF to call Shadrach. They were carried back to *Rum Punch* in a flotilla of pirogues, the boat-boys singing their praises right through the anchorage as they went by.

Shadrach stayed out of sight until his passengers were deposited back on board then sat by the chart-table twiddling a pencil as Evie recounted the events of the night.

'Who is this Sir James?' Terri asked.

Shadrach sighed, raised his head and looked at each of them in turn. 'Only de Prime Minister of St Vincent and de Grenadines.'

Fizzy water went up Terri's nose.

'He also happens to be de owner of de Frangipani.'

Chapter Eighteen

The 'Jump-Up'

Young Geordie was enjoying the rest of the leftovers from Shadrach's tuna under the starboard keel as Terri lapped her way around *Rum Punch*'s waterline at seven the following morning. Her head felt clearer and she had an appetite the size of Yogi Bear's.

The water taxi turned up at eight. Shadrach was left with the dinghy, and the A-team headed to the Frangipani for breakfast. They were munching through hot croissants with ginger marmalade, filter coffee and freshly squeezed orange juice, on the hotel's terrace thirty minutes later when a cruise liner eased into Admiralty Bay and dropped its anchor.

'It does look like a block of flats, doesn't it?' muttered Sam, orange bits forming a moustache on her upper lip.

'With two thousand passengers on board, I'm told that if you play deck games you trample a third of them to death,' added Evie.

'That's not all,' said George, helping herself to more coffee. 'If you're in the second sitting for breakfast you have to sunbathe standing up 'cos all the steamer chairs are taken.'

Terri couldn't help smiling. 'You lot seem to have changed your tune.'

'Maybe *Rum Punch* is growing on us.'

'Then I'll email Adrian Falks at Global Adventure Holidays and let him know his lesbian family are having a ball.'

'Fine, just don't mention the jump-up. He'll think it's something kinky.'

Terri called for the bill, EC dollars at the ready, only to be told it was on the house. 'At this rate, we'll be going home with more cash than we came with,' she said as they wandered along the waterfront heading for the local newspaper office.

'The barman told me last night that Jo-Jo and Samuel will be discharged from the hospital in St Vincent today. The Coastguard will be delivering them back here later this afternoon.' Sam strode out ahead, stopping every five yards to shake hands with another local.

'Shouldn't we do something for them?' asked Evie.

'Like what?' George was having her back slapped by a large German in Bermuda shorts and a gaudy tropical shirt.

'How about a decent lifejacket for each of them?' Sam turned at Terri's suggestion, nodded her head and waited for the others to catch up.

'Great idea. I'll go down to the dive shop after we've finished here and see what they have for sale.'

'Better still,' said Evie, 'why don't we ask all the yachties in the bay to donate any spare lifejackets they have on board?'

'And any spare flares,' enthused George.

The A-team was on a roll. 'Who's volunteering to go and see the captain of the cruise liner out there?' Terri asked as they turned onto a dirt road following the map she'd scrawled onto her palm. 'He can probably donate enough life jackets to supply every fisherman this side of St Lucia.'

'Lead me to him,' announced Evie, eyes sparkling in the sunlight as she mounted the steps of the newspaper office and opened the door.

For the next half an hour all that could be heard were fingers tapping on keyboards and an electric fan whirling overhead. While the others checked in with their previous lives, Evie went to work on the editor, gleaning what information she could about the cruise liner's captain. She then waved to the others and disappeared.

Sam, meanwhile, peered at her screen and read CJ's email from three days earlier.

Hi lover,

Managing to use the ship's computer while the family are off photographing the pods of Finbacks, Hump-backs and a glacier. Not my scene. Missing you like crazy and can't wait to get back to London.

Hope you're not too bored without me. Will make it up to you, promise!

Much love

CJ

x

'Typical,' she muttered under her breath, 'it would never occur to you that I might be having fun in your absence.' She placed her index finger on the delete button and zapped the message from her inbox.

George was equally tetchy, tutting as she read Ralph's email.

Hi, Boss,

Just to let you know Fran's waters broke all over the office floor on Tuesday and she was rushed to the maternity unit by local ambulance. (Took them twenty minutes to arrive

here by which time Fran was yelling the place down.)
Customers decided to return another day so don't expect to
see them anytime soon.
Having difficulty handling office alone. Can I call in agency
staff to help?
Ralph

'Bloody hell!'

Terri and Sam looked up from their keyboards, noted
George's white lips and returned to their own screens. She
clicked 'Reply'.

Dear Ralph,
What state is the floor in? Possible insurance claim.
Ring Janet at 'Holidays Are Us' in Richmond and see if they can spare
someone to help out.
Typical of Fran to have the sprog early. She's never been reliable. Better get
Interflora to send some flowers. Don't overdo it. Ten quid should be
sufficient . . .

George paused, huffed loudly then continued.

. . . OK, fifteen quid. Take it from petty cash.
Not sure when I can email again. If Richmond can't help, ring my dad,
he's always good for a few days stand-in, but DON'T LET HIM
NEAR THE COMPUTERS!!!
Georgina

Terri had received a long epistle from her department secretary
at work listing the problems she was having with the
replacement boss, complaining that she had too much work to

do in Terri's absence and updating her on Happy Hands Harold.

Audrey Laws from Unite had persuaded the Human Resources Director to retire Harold on medical grounds, citing his inability to keep his hands to himself. Harold had subsequently departed on a full pension and the female staff had all sighed with relief.

Meanwhile, the new manager had been going through Terri's filing cabinet in her absence, retaining the file on the BIE brochure and logo, apparently intending to discuss the matter with her on her return. Anne Blakemore had sent down a memo from the top floor castigating Marketing for sending out brochures with sticky labels. The Sales Department had complained that they were constantly peeling at the edges and the Chairman wasn't happy.

Terri leant her elbows on the keyboard and cupped her chin in her hands.

We've just pulled two boys, half dead, out of the sea and the Chairman has nothing more serious to worry about than his blasted stickers, she thought. Well, sod him. She signed out of Hotmail and typed the words Blue Lagoon Caribbean Cruises into her search engine.

As she went to pay minutes later the editor shook his head.

'Ladies, you gone an' made de front page of dis newspaper, and we've increased our print run by fifteen percent! I wouldn't dream o' chargin' you for de internet.' He held up a copy of *Caribbean Compass* hot off the press, the A-team's startled faces filling the cover page. 'Here, take a copy wid you.'

'Not the best shot I've ever seen,' commented Sam as they made their way back to the waterfront.

'Don't knock it, missy,' mimicked George, squeezing past a boat load of American cruise passengers at the jetty, their ship-to-shore orange and white tenders lined up along the dock. 'Dis be our fifteen minutes o' fame, so yous enjoy it, Samanta . . . Oh, hello, yes, thank you . . . Yes, that's right . . . No, they're fine, the Coastguard has them . . . Yes, they were very lucky that we spotted them.'

By the time the trio reached the dive shop their hands were sore from all that hand shaking, their backs were stinging, and they had a good idea what politicians had to put up with out on the hustings.

Shadrach was faring no better. *Rum Punch* had spent the morning being assailed by a constant stream of dinghies, their owners all wanting to know exactly what had happened during the rescue and donating all manner of spare pyrotechnics, lifejackets and the odd XXL wet suit. By the time the A-team arrived back on board, the stern deck looked like a yachties' boat jumble and Shadrach seemed to be lost for words.

'I guess Evie's been busy,' said Sam, climbing over a pile of jackets to reach the saloon.

'Where is she?' asked George. Shadrach didn't respond.

Another dinghy arrived at the rear steps full of cruisers and Terri decided distance was the best policy, quickly returning to the waterline to meet and greet.

With typical A-team precision, the haul was quickly catalogued, sorted, stacked and tied together, then shipped ashore to the Frangipani's lock-up for the Right Honourable James Mitchell to distribute as he felt fit.

Evie reappeared an hour later, sporting the cruise liner's corporate t-shirt, baseball hat and linen beach bag. 'Phew, I'm hot!' she sighed.

'How did it go?' Terri was leaning over the dinghy, nose close to the water.

'What are you doing?'

'Shhh, keep your voice down. I'm checking for leaks.'

'Does Shadrach know?'

'Not unless you tell him. He's in the head taking a shower and we're not the flavour of the month. I've called an A-team head-to-head on the foredeck after he goes ashore.'

'Fine. What response did I get from my VHF announcement on the morning cruiser net?'

'Sam will tell you, she has the inventory.' Terri leaned further out, her nose underwater. 'Ah, there you are, you little bubbles.'

They sat on the trampoline netting, Terri in charge.

'Firstly, well done you.'

Evie saluted as the cruise ship gave a long blast on its horn. They all looked up. 'It must be round-up time for the cruise passengers,' she said and looked at her watch. 'They've had all of four hours to see Bequia.'

'How did you wangle two VHF handheld radios out of the captain?'

'I fluttered my eyelashes, Sam, and told him he would be mentioned in despatches. Sadly, he didn't have any suitable lifejackets.'

'Well, bloody good work, Shapiro. I wish I had your talent with men.'

'Oh, that's not all, George. He's going to have a whip-round on board, but I won't know the result of that until later. Now, what's on your mind, Terri?'

She bit her upper lip. 'George and I think Shadrach's not all he's cracked up to be.'

George produced her list. 'It's like this . . .' She went through her suspicions point by point. 'This morning, Terri did a check on the internet and came up with some interesting results.'

All eyes were on her.

'I looked up Blue Lagoon Caribbean Cruises. They're based in Grenada and have eight catamarans for charter, all listed by name and size. The odd thing is, *Rum Punch* isn't one of them. Then I searched the site for Captain Shadrach Jonathon William Bligh and came up with zilch.'

'Well, that's not a surprise. If you Googled me you wouldn't get anything either.'

'Don't be so sure, Sam. You may well be infamous around Knightsbridge.'

'Stick to the point, girls, we haven't got long. The thing is, the skippers of the other catamarans are listed. Don't you think that's strange?'

'I guess,' agreed Evie.

'And I've just found a small leak in the dinghy. Shadrach was bluffing when he said they lose pressure at night. What with that, a yacht with only one winch handle and a leaking fore-hatch stuck down with tape, George and I think our skipper is struggling to makes ends meet and has something to hide.'

'Don't forget, he was up the mast when we arrived in Rodney Bay doing some repairs.' Evie was in Agatha Christie mode now. 'What was all that about?'

'Search me,' said George but I think we should try and get to the bottom of this. He could be dabbling in drugs to pay his way, using us for cover.'

'Jesus!' Evie turned white under her tan.

'Appearing on the front page of the *Caribbean Compass* won't have helped either,' added Sam. 'No wonder he's in a bad mood. If he's trying to keep a low profile round these parts, we've just put paid to that.'

Terri nodded. 'Have you noticed how he's stayed in the background since we arrived here?'

George had her finger raised. 'I suggest we search the yacht from mast to keel.'

'Crikey, it's like "Swallows and Amazons",' said Evie, jumping up. 'When will Shadrach be back?'

'In about an hour. He's gone to check us in and stock up on fruit and veg at the open market.'

With Sam's height, tight spaces below deck were a problem for her so she acted as look-out while Evie took the port side, George the starboard, and Terri examined the engine bays and deck lockers. With one eye on the shore Sam then rummaged through the chart-table drawers, George lifted the floorboards and Evie checked the galley cupboards.

'What do we do with the drugs if we find them?' she asked the others.

'Throw them overboard,' suggested George. 'Young Geordie's probably partial to a bit of weed and its subsequent effect sure beats Newcastle Brown Ale.'

'How would you know, Georgina Stanhope?'

'That's for me to know and you to . . .'

'OK, OK!'

Butter wouldn't have melted in their mouths when Shadrach walked into the saloon an hour later. He dumped the shopping on the galley work surface and slipped his wallet into the chart-table drawer.

'Need any help?' asked Terri.

'Sure,' he said nodding at the galley. 'De shoppin' needs stowin'.' He dropped the dinghy keys on the desk and turned to them. 'I've just seen Jo-Jo's dad. De boys are expected back at five-tirty and he asked if we'd be on shore to greet 'em. We all bin invited to dere place in Belmont for dinner.'

'Will the press be there?' George scrutinised Shadrach's expression.

He didn't flinch. 'Yep, and Sir James, de local po'lice, de Coastguard Service, and Uncle Tom Cobley and all.' He grabbed a bottle of beer from the fridge and strolled outside.

The A-team exchanged glances. Terri eyeballed Evie and flicked her head towards the door, then went to work stowing the supplies.

Evie sauntered onto the foredeck and jumped up alongside Shadrach on the saloon roof. His eyes remained fixed on the boat ahead, the beer bottle frothing at the rim.

'Don't you miss your family, Skip?' No response. 'I mean, with you being on *Rum Punch* all the time?'

Shadrach slowly turned his head towards her. 'Not really, Evie. I ain't seen my folks in years.'

'What about your wife and kids, don't they miss you?'

He chuckled and downed more Carib. 'I guess dey would if dey existed, but sadly dey don't.'

'So, a free agent then. Guess that explains the condoms.'

His sunglasses dropped down his nose as his eyeballs slid sideways.

'Sorry, it just came out.' Evie giggled, her laughter infectious.

'What about your folks?'

She dug her thumbs into the coach roof and took a deep breath. 'My brother died when he was eight, falling off a trapeze. My dad followed shortly after with a broken heart and my mum got breast cancer three years later.' There, she'd said it.

Shadrach's smile went out. 'I'm real sorry, Evie.'

'That's OK, we all have our crosses to bear.'

He took another swig of beer, Evie waiting patiently for his next comment. 'My folks moved to England back in de fifties. Me dad worked for London Transport on de underground and me mam was a clippie on de buses. Dey were poor but me younger brudder, he did good. Made my folks real proud. Got 'imself a scholarship to de grammar school.'

'And you?'

'Not de brainy type. Got mixed up wid de wrong set and ended up in de Juvenile Court. Nearly killed me mam.'

Evie crossed her fingers under her knees. 'Did you do time?'

'No, just a caution, but I become de black sheep of de family and left Kennington as soon as I reached sixteen.'

'Same as me,' said Evie, bringing the spotlight back onto herself. 'I was fostered out in Cornwall. Couldn't stand it so packed my bags and left. Got a job in a Bristol nightclub and never looked back.'

'How d'you get to know de others?'

'Saw an advertisement for Beagle Air in a national newspaper and thought flying sounded exotic. Borrowed a dress from one of the showgirls, jumped on a train and got the job.'

Shadrach looked her up and down. 'Dat I can understand.'

'What did you do?'

'I went to sea. Started on freighters as a deckhand den got an offer to join a sailin' ship bound for Australia. Sailin's bin in me blood ever since.'

'What happened to your brother?'

Shadrach's eyes clouded. 'Meshach. He became a fancy lawyer, defendin' de rights of folks around de East End. Lives in a fancy apartment up town. Wife, two kids. De apple of me mam's and dad's eyes.'

'And you?'

'What do you tink?' He finished his beer.

'Poor relation?'

'Got it in one.' He looked at his watch. 'Time to get ready.'
He jumped down from the roof. 'Must blow up de dinghy
before we leaves.'

'Right.' Evie walked into the saloon, gave a thumbs up to
Terri and went below.

Sir James met the dinghy as it tied up at the jetty and led the A-
team into the Frangipani, his arm slung around Shadrach's
shoulders. A small, wiry West Indian man with grey hair was
standing by the reception desk. He was dressed in faded cotton
trousers with frayed bottoms and a Caribbean shirt featuring
palm fronds and coconuts, his toes escaping from battered
brown sandals. Towering beside him swathed in amarillo yellow
and burnt paprika cotton was an Amazon of a woman, her
matching cotton turban almost touching the ceiling light, her
bust resembling a Goodyear tyre, and a piano keyboard of a
smile lighting up her face. Without waiting for an introduction
she strode forward and wrapped Sam in a blanket embrace,
praising the Lord for bringing her to these shores, while the
others stood back and waited with trepidation.

Hugs completed, the A-team, devoid of breath, were
ushered into the packed restaurant where the day's booty was
spread out across the tables and chairs, the two new life jackets
and VHF handheld radios standing in pride of place at the
centre.

'Miss Gillingham,' said Sir James loudly as silence enveloped the room. 'I have received a fax from the cruise liner captain whose passengers enjoyed the beauty of Bequia here today.' He looked around his audience for approval. 'I will read you what he says.' He pulled a piece of paper from his jacket pocket.

Terri smiled and clutched Evie's arm.

'*We received a visit from Miss Evangelina Shapiro today.*' He looked across at *Rum Punch*'s crew and saw George's finger pointing above Evie's head. He gave her a Morgan Freeman smile and continued. '*On hearing about the plight of the fishermen of Bequia, I asked my passengers and crew to give generously to a fund to help improve the lives of these brave young men.*' Sir James paused to allow the tension to build.

'One hell of a showman,' whispered Sam into Shadrach's ear.

'*I'm pleased to inform you that a money transfer for fifteen thousand US dollars will be deposited in an account of your choosing once we reach Grenada and we ask you to use this gift in the spirit in which it is given. God bless you all. Captain Brian Conway Jnr.*'

A collective intake of breath thinned the air then a blast of sound reached the rafters. The women cried, the men hollered and stamped their feet and Evie leapt into Shadrach's arms. He twirled her around and around while yelling in her ear what a star she was, his dreadlocks flying out behind him.

Terri's smile stopped short of her eyes as she watched the pair while Sam and George stood either side of Sir James, clapping for all they were worth.

Suddenly someone shouted that the Coastguard were coming and everyone rushed outside, leaving a gap in the middle of the crowd for Jo-Jo's and Samuel's parents to move to the front. Sir James was quickly by their side escorting them down the jetty as the St Vincent and Grenadine's Coastguard vessel creamed across the bay towards the anchorage. A mass of cruisers stood on their bows, blasting away on their fog horns as if it was New Year's Eve, a World Cup final and the opening of the Olympics all rolled into one. Flash bulbs were going off all around the A-team and Terri felt Shadrach's arm around her waist as he pulled his crew towards the front, the excitement of the moment infecting him as much as the rest of them. Terri felt drunk on happiness and wanted the moment to go on forever.

Jo-Jo left his parents' embrace and walked towards Sam, his hand wrapped tightly around his brother's fingers. Both boys were bare-chested, their eyes wide. Sam beckoned the other girls to her side and waited for Jo-Jo to speak.

'Lady, I say tank you for savin' me and me brudder.'

Sam dropped to her knees and placed her hands on Jo-Jo's shoulders, looking deep into his eyes. 'Jo-Jo, I'm so happy to see you both here alive and well. Everyone on *Rum Punch* knows who saved Samuel and it wasn't me, it was you. Isn't that right crew?'

'Too damn' right,' said Shadrach as they all encircled the boys, gathering them into the protection of their bodies while all around the beach there wasn't a dry eye in evidence.

If the *Caribbean Compass* had a good day's circulation today, thought Terri, then tomorrow's will be a record breaker.

'All look this way,' shouted the cameraman, standing knee-high in water alongside the jetty.

They all turned, fanning out, their hands resting on the boy's shoulders.

'Now, all smile, please.' *Flash*! 'That's a wrap.'

Terri hung back as everyone left the jetty, tapping Sir James's sleeve to get his attention. He took the hint and slowed, waiting for her to speak.

'Sir James, you said yesterday that if there was anything we needed we only had to ask.'

'Ask away, Miss Gillingham.'

'Terri, please.'

He nodded. 'Terri.'

She looked down at *Rum Punch*'s tender crammed amongst others tied to the jetty. 'We seem to have a leak on our dinghy and we don't have a repair kit on board.'

'Leave it to me. Which one is yours?'

'T/T *Rum Punch*,' she said pointing to the dinghy.

'My boys will need to keep it overnight.' His eyebrows arched.

'No problem. We'll get the water taxi back tonight and come pick it up in the morning.'

'It will be here waiting, Terri. It's the least we can do.'

'That's great, Sir James. Thank you.

They were the last to arrive in Belmont and barbecued food was sizzling on two halves of a metal drum above smouldering coals as Terri climbed out of Sir James's car. She caught George's eye and blinked, the message passed and understood.

Maybelline, the boys' mother, was helping the chef cook the steaks, chicken wings, Mahi Mahi and Wahoo, the smells mingling together in a riot of aromas. Shadrach passed by with a tray of rum punches, each glass sprouting a floral display of tropical fruits reminding Terri of the cocktails at the Bay Gardens Hotel in Rodney Bay. She shook her head.

'Come on, missy, dis is not de day to abstain.' Shadrach's grin was infectious.

'OK, but it'll be me carrying you home, not the other way round.'

'In your dreams, lady,' insisted Shadrach, then winked and walked on.

'Why does everyone wink at me?' she muttered as Mount Gay rum hit her taste buds, the national cocktail tasting like nectar.

Evie's teeth were black from barbecued spareribs and Sam was making suggestive signs to a group of youths with a hot plantain. George was behind the bar teaching the barman how to mix her special Stanhope cocktail, which seemed to comprise three parts white rum, two parts Cointreau, pineapple juice, coconut milk and a shot of Sambuca, all over ice. Terri decided that that was a step too far and grabbed a Coke from the cooler before resting on the steps of the boys' shack. Samuel came to sit at her feet as his father eased his arthritic joints down beside her.

'Tank you, missy,' he said, smiling gap-toothed at her. 'Tank you for savin' my boys.'

Terri looked at the care-worn man, realising that he was probably not a lot older than herself, wrapped her arms around his neck and kissed him on the cheek. 'My pleasure.'

His eyes were like doorstops and Samuel was rolling on the floor, holding onto his stomach, giggles coming over him in waves. Maybelline turned up, clipped him around the ear, picked him up off the ground and gave him a massive hug.

'Now yous stop rollin' around in de dirt in dem new clothes, Samuel Mansfield Jackson Brown.'

His giggles started her and his father off too, and before Terri could stop herself they were all guffawing like buffaloes.

Someone handed Shadrach a guitar. He righted a sawn-off log with his foot and sat down, laid the instrument across his knee and began to strum a few cords. The A-team looked at each other, shrugged their shoulders and waited. Seconds later the strains of 'Michael, Row the Boat Ashore' filled the clearing, people swaying to the beat, women singing along and Jo-Jo keeping time with a tambourine. His dad handed Terri a pair of maracas and she joined in, singing along each time the chorus came around.

The music went on and on, the repertoire endless as Shadrach entertained the Bequians with songs from John Denver, Simon and Garfunkel, Roy Orbison and Bob Marley, the A-team getting ever-more hoarse as they sang every lyric. Terri was word perfect.

'Showing your age, Gillingham?' shouted Sam as they went into the third verse of 'Leaving on a Jet Plane.'

The rum punch flowed, the moon crossed the heavens and by midnight they were all loaded into dollar buses and transported to Princess Margaret Beach where a steel band rocked the shore as visitors and locals alike danced the night away.

Terri seemed to have danced with every man over the age of twelve and a few under that age by three in the morning. Her legs ached, her hips seemed to have become detached from her pelvis, and her voice had disappeared into the ether. Time to go, she thought, as she sniffed sweet smoke coming from somewhere to her left.

She went in search of the others. Evie was astride a big Bequian's shoulders jigging to ABBA with her hands in the air, sandals dangling from her fingers. George was trying to walk a straight line along the curved beach, Sam was doing crutch bumps with the barman by the beer stack, and Shadrach was laid out under a palm tree talking nonsense to the tree frogs.

'Time out,' croaked Terri to each in turn.

It took three goes but she finally gathered her crew together and they grabbed a passing dollar bus back to the Frangipani then hailed the water taxi. Shadrach went aboard horizontally, explaining in slurred sentences how to start the outboard motor.

Getting him onto *Rum Punch* wasn't easy with his legs flopping over Terri's shoulders, his backside resting on Sam's and Evie's crossed arms and his upper torso draped against George's chest. They dumped him on the saloon floor, placed a cushion under his head and left him to stew in his own alcoholic juices.

'I don't think we'll be going far in the morning,' muttered Sam as she wandered off to her cabin.

'Christ, my feet ache,' moaned George, sitting on the settee and rubbing her instep.

'That was some jump-up,' croaked Evie, filling a large glass with cold water, only one word in three decipherable.

Terri opened her mouth intent on agreeing. Her lips moved, nothing came out so she shook her head, pointed to her sore throat and retired. The last thing she heard as she flopped onto her bed and doused the lights was Evie spluttering good night to young Geordie below the keel, somewhere out on the foredeck.

Chapter Nineteen

Mayreau

Shadrach opened one eye, felt steel pins skewer his brain and closed it again. Perhaps, he thought, the other eye might fare better. This time the steel pins cauterised his cornea as they went in so he decided to stay blind.

'Morning, Skip.'

The voice was too close, too loud and far too bouncy.

He pulled himself up against the side of the settee and banged his head on the underside of the table. 'FUCK!'

'Not feeling too happy this morning?' The voice was now enemy number one. If he could just get onto his feet he could cut it off at source. There was only one problem, he had no idea where his feet were.

'Here, let me help.'

Two arms straddled his armpits and he levitated onto the seat, his head bouncing off the back cushion. 'Now, isn't that better?'

Just come a bit closer, he thought, and I can throttle you to death.

'I've made some scrambled eggs for breakfast if you're interested. Or would you prefer a hair of the dog?'

Dog, what dog? He was having difficulty functioning. He slumped down against the cushion, dropped onto his right shoulder and groaned. His legs followed all on their own and he lay full length along the settee, trying to remember who he was, where he was and who the hell that voice belonged to.

Time passed, bodies moved around in no fixed order, mumbled chatter entered his subconscious from afar and his mouth felt like a bag of ball-bearings.

'Shadrach, have you surfaced yet?' That voice again. He could have sworn it was his mother having a hissy fit. 'Shadrach, for goodness' sake, it's half-past twelve.'

'I don't care if it's half-past sunset. Now go away.'

'Girls, I think it's time for the water-board treatment.'

Shadrach was on his feet, eyes wide open, head on back to front and stomach trying to get out. He swayed to and fro, his hand flapping in the air trying to find a solid surface as Terri's face emerged from the haze holding a glass of water.

'Here, try this.'

He would have swallowed the glass if she hadn't kept her hand on the base. 'More,' he croaked, leaning against the chart-table for support.

Gallons of the stuff went down before he could get a handle on his life then he remembered who this woman was and little segments of memory started to lock together like a jigsaw puzzle. 'Oh, Christ.' He staggered down to the head, eased himself into the shower and didn't come out until he could remember his name.

'Yous better call Daffodil Marine,' he stuttered as he came up the saloon stairs. 'We need more water.'

'Well, well, well. If it isn't our infamous skipper.'

Shadrach appeared from below the towel and glared at the source of the second voice, wondering if suffocation was in order. Probably not, he decided as he sat at the chart-table, head in hands with the sound of Daffodil Marine answering on VHF. 'Where's de dinghy?' he asked no one in particular.

'Tied to the jetty where you left it yesterday.'

'Den get Daffodil to tow it out here. I's in no fit state to go and get it.'

'Wilco, Skip.'

'And don't sound so damn' chirpy.'

'No, Skip.'

Daffodil Marine delivered the dinghy minutes later along with bags of food and drink, compliments of the locals, and began to fill the catamaran's water tanks. As Shadrach walked back to the helm, his EC dollars unused, he noticed his inflated dinghy tied to the stern. Leaning out, he looked again. 'Now dat's damn' strange,' he muttered, thankful he didn't need to use the foot pump.

The total population of Bequia seemed to be on the beach as 'African' released *Rum Punch*'s mooring line from the buoy and the catamaran moved out of the anchorage, the A-team waving madly at the stern and fellow cruisers giving them a rousing send off with a chorus of foghorn blasts.

'Jesus!' moaned Shadrach, his eardrums rattling his molars. 'I gotta get outta here.'

The four-hour passage to Mayreau was purgatory for *Rum Punch*'s captain. He sat at the helm, hanging on to the wheel for support as the sun frazzled his brain and the sea turned his innards to mush. There was no way he could face raising the sails so he motored down the west coast of Bequia and out into the channel like a novice on his maiden voyage. Finally, George had had enough.

'Shadrach Jonathon William Bligh, if you think we're motoring all the way to Mayreau you're sadly mistaken. Now, what do I do to hoist the mainsail?'

Shadrach gave her an evil stare.

'Fine, I'll make a hash of it without you.' She walked to the mast and undid a yellow and white rope, wrapped it around the winch and pulled for all she was worth. Nothing happened.

'I think you have to open this black handle thing,' offered Evie, her fingers stretching for a halyard jammer.

'STOP!' screamed Shadrach.

They both went rigid, the catamaran slowed and their skipper left the autopilot to turn the catamaran to port while he shuffled to the mast. Elbowing George out of the way, he waited for the bow to come up into wind then pulled on the red mainsail halyard. The sail appeared from its stowage on the boom and headed for the mast head, George winding on the winch handle to take it the last five yards while Shadrach hung onto the line to stay upright.

'Feeling a bit wobbly, are we?' she asked, sarcastically.

Shadrach grunted and rolled his way back to the helm, brought the vessel on track then eased the main sheet, pain from both temples fusing somewhere around his frontal lobe. 'I take it you're now satisfied, missy?'

'No.'

He could have killed her.

'There's the little matter of the front sail.'

'Genoa.'

'Whatever. What's the point of having it if we don't use it?'

She had a point, he thought, but dragging it off the forestay was more than Shadrach could bear. 'Right, if you wants it, you do it.'

He directed proceedings from the calm of the helm, George and Evie working in unison as Terri watched from the foredeck. 'Now, missy, winch it in tight . . . and if you must grunt, do it quietly.'

'Why can't we visit Mustique?' called out Sam, examining the chart in the saloon.

'We ain't got time.'

'But we're going to miss Basil's Bar and it's very famous.' She appeared rubbing suntan lotion into her shoulder.

'Den go rent a villa dere. I'm sure David Bowie's rates are reasonable.'

Sam stuck out the tip of her tongue and went to join the others. 'Obviously, Captain Bligh doesn't do celebrities,' she shouted over her shoulder.

'Mr Christian,' he called back, 'yous gonna walk de plank if yous not careful.'

The island of Canouan passed by on the port side as *Rum Punch* kept up a steady seven knots sailing down her heading towards Saltwhistle Bay. Shadrach was feeling more himself and stowed the sails well in advance of arrival, knowing that without his chart plotter he needed to keep a constant look out for off lying coral reefs and sand cays.

'Ladies, will yous please tell me de minute de water changes colour?'

Terri and Sam took up look-out positions on the forward seats and peered at the sea. It was cobalt blue. 'What are we looking for exactly?' asked Terri.

'Brown coral heads under de water and a sudden sandy bottom.' Shadrach scanned the horizon for the Dry Shingle buoy.

'We've got one of those on board,' quipped George, looking at Sam's gold bikini.

'I can see a stick poking out of the water,' yelled Sam, ignoring George and pointing to starboard.

Rum Punch's bow moved ten degrees to port and Shadrach breathed out. 'Right, Evie, unlash de anchor head and stand by to attach de snatch line once we settle.'

The catamaran motored along Mayreau's north-west coast and turned into Saltwhistle Bay, keeping well into the centre to avoid low-lying rocks. The A-team stood watching, mesmerised by the bay's beauty, a Caribbean picture postcard of white sand, aquamarine water, palm trees on a sandy spit and the Atlantic rollers crashing into the shore beyond.

As pelicans hovered on the east wind, Shadrach manoeuvred *Rum Punch* between the monohulls with their deeper keels and dropped anchor close to the beach, checked the anchor head was well dug in and gave Evie the nod. She hooked the snatch line to the anchor chain and let out a few more feet.

'Done it, Skip,' she boasted, and received a round of applause from her mates.

Shadrach leant his arms on the wheel and stared out across the expanse of beach. 'Well, ladies,' he announced, 'yous now be in one o' de most beautiful anchorages in de Caribbean. De Saltwhistle Bay Club and Beach Bar is hidden in de trees over dere and dey do some mean Happy Hour drinks. Dinner will be on board at eight-tirty.'

'What are we having?'

'Goat curry on saffron rice.'

'Mmmm, sounds tasty.' Terri stepped over the guardrail, balanced on the edge of the coaming then dived into the bay before beginning her fifty laps.

'Does young Geordie like goat?' enquired George, balancing on tiptoe on the port pontoon seat.

'I've no idea,' replied Sam, painting her toenails cerise pink. 'Go ask him.'

'Okey-dokey. Here I go then.' *SPLASH!*

'For Christ's sake, George, you've just ruined my nails!'

The barman carried three Saltwhistle Dreams and a non-alcoholic fruit punch to a secluded alcove and placed them on the circular stone table.

'Cheers,' said Evie. 'Welcome to Saltwhistle Bay and have a nice day.' The glasses clinked and there was a moment's silence.

'Wow, that's potent.'

'I wouldn't know.'

'Well, don't blame us, you were the one who decided to go on the wagon.'

'About time too.'

'Thank you, Sam.'

'No problem, Terri. Maybe now you'll remember to ring me when CJ's not in Pont Street.'

Terri's fingers sort of imitated Winston Churchill's then she picked up her fruit punch and banged it on the table. 'Let's get back to Shadrach.'

No drugs had been found on board but Sam had discovered a note in the chart-table desk with some latitude and longitude positions listed on it, which they thought might be secret rendezvous points. Evie had come across an American flag screwed up in the back of a wardrobe and George had found an orange plastic pistol and cartridges in the pyrotechnics grab bag. Shadrach's guitar, meanwhile, was wrapped in a soft suede cover inside its hard casing underneath their baggage as Terri discovered during her locker check.

'I don't know what to make of it all,' she said, sipping her fruit punch.

'Me neither. All we know so far is that he's blackballed from his family, he's on the breadline, he plays a mean guitar, cooks great food, and is one hell of a sailor.' George sat back, scratching her head.

'To say nothing of his charismatic charm.' Terri blushed, and buried her nose in her glass.

'*Rum Punch* must have a chequered history too,' pointed out Sam. 'I don't know much about yachts but this one seems a bit battered around the edges.'

'I wonder where he found it,' queried Evie.

Terri remembered seeing a number written on the catamaran's stern and decided to make a note of it and see what Google came up with.

'I read somewhere that boats have to fly the flag of the country in which they're registered.' Sam again.

'Well, what flag are we flying? The only thing I've seen is the little flag by the mast in St Vincent colours . . . and that battered American flag stuffed amongst the wet weather gear.' Evie raised her hand and the barman nodded.

'Search me. Perhaps we should ask Shadrach?'

'Well, at least we didn't find any drugs,' said George, stretching forward for a handful of peanuts. 'Did you see his face when Daffodil Marine brought back the dinghy?'

'I did think of asking Sir James for a new hatch cover for my cabin,' added Terri, sucking on a sliver of orange, 'but decided not to push my luck.'

'Thanks,' said Sam, taking her second Saltwhistle Dream from the barman. 'Any chance you could let me have the recipe for this?' She raised her glass. 'I'd love to see CJ's face when I produce it at home.'

'Then you'd better get a grass skirt and a couple of coconut shells to make it authentic,' muttered George, licking froth from her lips.

'Maybe Shadrach could serenade you from the broom cupboard with Bob Marley's "*No Woman, No Cry*",' suggested Evie.

'Or Tammy Wynette's "*Stand by Your Man*",' cut in Terri. 'Although, if CJ had seen Sam making those rude suggestions to the local lads with that banana last night . . .'

'I didn't?'

'Yes, you did.'

'Rubbish.'

'I've got it on film, Sam.'

'Get out of that,' said George, triumphantly.

If young Geordie did like goat curry, he never got the chance to sample it. The pan was wiped clean, the A-team washing the meal down with a bottle of French Chardonnay compliments of the Frangipani.

'Will you play for us, Shadrach?' asked Evie, rising from the table and walking towards the trampoline netting.

'I would, Evie, but I don't have a guitar.'

Terri's head shot up. 'Yes, you . . . Oh, shame.'

'That's funny,' said Sam, refusing to let the matter drop. 'When I went to get my Jimmy Choo sandals yesterday, I could have sworn I saw a guitar case lying in the locker.'

Terri swept up the plates and headed for the galley.

'I'll look, shall I?' shouted Evie, pulling the hatch open and moving baggage about. 'What's this, Shadrach?' She stood up, guitar case in hand.

'Er . . . It needs re-stringing.'

'Balls,' muttered Terri at the sink. She locked eyes with him across the saloon. 'Why don't you want to play?'

Shadrach scratched the nape of his neck and tapped his foot.

'Come on, Skip, Evie told us your history and you can hardly deny you played a mean guitar last night. Who taught you?'

'Self-taught. Me younger brudder and me, we 'ad a band back in de seventies.' He returned Terri's stare, the end of his lips beginning to lift. 'We called ourselves de Moonshine Boys. I played guitar, me school pal, Bronco, played drums and Meshach played de electric keyboard.'

'Meshach?' queried Terri as the rest of the A-team wandered into the saloon.

'Me brudder. You see, me mam, she was a devout Christian, so we was named Shadrach and Meshach. Me tird brudder, he was called Abednego, but he died of pneumonia when he was two.' Evie bit the inside of her lip. 'On de udder hand, me dad, well now, he was a "Mutiny on de Bounty" fan, which explains why I be called William Bligh.'

'And Meshach?'

'Meshach Fletcher Christian Bligh.'

'So, who was Jonathon?' asked Sam.

'Me grandpappy. He worked de sugar plantations in Jamaica but he was long dead before I was born.'

'Were you any good?'

Shadrach looked down in embarrassment. 'We was terrible.'

The saloon exploded with laughter as Evie handed him the guitar case and kissed him on the cheek. 'Sam would like to hear "The Banana Boat Song", on the foredeck, under the stars.'

'Den yous better get me a drink . . . On second toughts, make dat two.'

Chapter Twenty

Harry's Hideaway

Terri was on her forty-third lap when Shadrach leant over the port guardrail, nodded to the stern and wandered off.

Funny, she thought, and continued on her lap, coming to rest clinging to the stainless-steel crossbar of the rear starboard steps and looking up at two hairy shins. Shadrach's body was folded in a heap on the top step, his foot tapping madly.

'I need to tell you sometin'.'

Terri held her breath.

'We 'ave a problem wid de batteries. Dey not be holdin' dere charge.'

She was out of the water, bum on the bottom step, her back to the skipper, trying to work out what this actually meant. 'And?'

'And unless I run de engines for two hours, I ain't able to charge 'em.'

'Fine, then run the engines.'

'Dat ain't so easy.'

'Why not?'

''Cos we needs fuel to run de engines and fuel is what we be short of.'

She turned her head and looked at him over her shoulder. 'What d'you want me to do about it?'

'I just tought tellin' de udders might come better from you, Terri.'

Silence prevailed as young Geordie's tail flicked idly beneath the swim ladder and its body completed a two-point turn.

'Shadrach, what's going on?'

'Nuttin'.'

'Then why are we short of fuel?'

'I was a bit hungover yesterday . . .'

'A bit?'

'. . . Allright, sozzled. Anyways, I forgot to uplift some in Bequia.'

He was lying but Terri decided to keep up the pretence. 'Does anyone on Mayreau have fuel?'

'Harry's Hidewaway, maybe. Dey need it for dere generators but I don't tink they'll sell us any.'

'Well, we won't know unless we ask, will we?' She was on her feet and stepping past him. 'I'll get dressed.'

It was a long, uphill walk along a stony track amongst thick undergrowth. When the pair finally appeared on the ridge they were in a small village dominated by a church, the road, now concrete, winding downhill on the other side to a beach and the Caribbean Sea stretching beyond it clear to the horizon. Terri was hot, sweaty and in need of a drink.

Children appeared from shacks on both sides of the road as they began their descent, circling Shadrach like a long-lost uncle, the smallest one being tossed in the air by his strong arms and duly plonked on his shoulders, the child's tiny brown hands buried in his dreadlocks.

He'd make the perfect father, thought Terri, and wondered why he'd never had a family of his own.

Shadrach suddenly dived into an entrance, the words 'Harry's Hideaway' painted across a piece of driftwood swinging from two hooks.

The white, colonial, two-storey building had fretwork-clad verandas running along both sides and a profusion of flowering plants growing alongside the pathways and up the walls. A drop-dead gorgeous local girl stood at the end of the main path, eyes alight with pleasure to see who was arriving. Terri took stock of her slim body wrapped in a scarlet sarong, looked down at her own stained khaki shorts and wanted to retreat.

'Hi, Shadrach, what brings you here?' the girl asked.

'Is Harry in?'

'No, he's out takin' guests over to Tobago Cays, snorklin'.'

Shadrach seemed to shrink three inches. 'When's he expected back?'

'Maybe tree. Sometimes four. Depends on de visitors. Dey usually have lunch on board.'

'Any chance of a beer?'

She turned and walked back into the bar as Shadrach lowered the infant to the ground, patted his bottom and sent him on his way, then turned to Terri. 'Guess we've had a wasted journey.'

'Glass half-empty, Shadrach?' She followed him inside, noticing copies of the latest *Caribbean Compass* laid out in a pile on the reception desk.

'What can I get you, miss?'

'Just water, thanks.'

She opened a rusted fridge door, pulled out a bottle of Carib and one of mineral water and placed them on the bar top.

'Shadrach Jonathon William Bligh,' came a deep voice from the bowels of the building, and a replica of Jo-Jo's and Samuel's mother suddenly filled the door-frame.

'Now dat's what I calls telepaty!' Her arms encased his neck, her bust billowed either side of his chest and she almost engulfed him whole.

'I was only talkin' about yous to our guests at breakfast. "Dat's our Shadrach," I says. "Always dere when you needs him." Now, what's all dis about rescuing dose kids from Bequia?' She dragged him into the restaurant, pulled out two chairs, plonked her expansive frame down on one and elbowed Shadrach into the other.

Terri held back, not sure what to do. The young girl smiled and handed her a glass of iced water. 'Are yous walking out wid Shadrach?'

Terri's skin took on the colour of the girl's sarong as she fumbled over her denial.

'Here, missy, come and join us.' Big Mamma was beckoning from the restaurant, the flesh on her underarms swaying alarmingly. 'Now, Shadrach, introduce me to your lady friend here.'

'I'm not his lady . . .'

'Delilah, dis be Teresa. Teresa Gillingham. She's outta England.'

'Well, hello, Teresa, and welcome to Saline Bay.' She looked Terri up and down like a goat carcass hanging from a butcher's hook in the market and slapped Shadrach on the back. 'Yous got good taste, mon, I'll say dat for you.'

Shadrach's shoulders quivered as he downed his beer. 'She ain't mine, Delilah,' he managed, eventually.

Delilah's eyes travelled back to Terri. 'Why, is she married? Come here, Missy, I don't bite.'

Terri walked around the table as Shadrach hunched his shoulders.

'Are yous married, missy?'

'No,' she said, convinced she'd walked into a scene from *Alice in Wonderland*.

Delilah leant into Shadrach and pulled his ear. 'Den yous be bloody daft, my boy. Dat or yous gone blind.'

Terri choked on her water and was seized by a coughing fit.

Shadrach sprang to his feet and whacked her several times on the back, her sunburnt skin stinging from the impact.

'Dere's no need to look at me like dat, Shadrach Bligh. I ain't said nuttin' dat ain't true.'

With normality restored, Terri explained the reason for their visit. Delilah seemed to hesitate at the mention of fuel but undeterred Terri soldiered on.

'It's our fault. That is, me and my girlfriends. We . . .'

'How many yous got?'

'Three. There are four of us on *Rum Punch*.'

'Any men?' continued Delilah, not taking her eyes off Shadrach.

'No, only us.'

'Yous running a knocking shop on board dat catamaran, Captain Bligh?'

194

'Lordie, Lordie,' exclaimed Shadrach, his eyes rolling to the back of his head. 'I should be so lucky.'

Delilah winked in Terri's direction. Here we go again, she thought.

'Delilah, de point is, we ain't got much fuel left, de batteries need constantly chargin' and I 'ave to get dese ladies to Tobago Cays, den Union Island and den Carriacou before I's can get more juice. If I don't stick to de schedule I'll be 'ung, drawn and quartered by four man-eatin' women.' He paused and looked across at Terri. 'So, will yous help me or not?'

Terri tried the evil stare on him, but he was immune. 'We'll pay double,' she suggested, and hit the spot. Shadrach turned a sickly grey round the gills.

'It ain't anytin' to do wid money, missy,' said Delilah. 'It's about wantin' to help widout leavin' ourselves short.'

'I see.'

'No you don't, dearie. Dis ain't London wid a fuel station on every corner. Yous be in de Grenadines now.'

Terri thought she should go and stand in the corner. Delilah appeared to think so too and let her wriggle on the line for a minute before placing her hand on Terri's knee and patting it in a motherly fashion. 'Leave it wid me, missy. I'll see what I's can do. Shadrach's no good to you 'ung, drawn and quartered, now is he?' The sexual connotation was clear.

They retraced their steps through the trees and down the steep track, Shadrach in front, Terri bringing up the rear, wondering if Delilah was a reincarnation of her deceased grannie. She chunted to herself as she walked.

'Did you say sometin'?'

'Er . . . no. Well . . . yes, actually.' She decided to go for the jugular. 'Shadrach, how long have you been working for Blue Lagoon Caribbean Cruises?'

'Why d'you ask?'

'Because I looked them up on the web in Bequia and *Rum Punch* isn't listed among the craft on their site.'

His stubbed his toe. 'Oh, about six weeks. One of dere catamarans hit a reef and was holed. It'll be out of action all season.'

'And you just happened to be around?' Man-eating woman indeed, she thought.

'That's right. I was anchored in Prickly Bay at de time, lookin' for work, and one o' der guys asked me if I could help 'em out, seein' as *Rum Punch* was a Lagoon model o' catamaran.'

Terri hadn't a clue where Prickly Bay was, but it all sounded annoyingly plausible.

'Why ain't you married?' he asked, out of the blue.

She tripped over a stone and landed on her hands and knees. Thanks a lot, grannie, she said, telepathically. Now get back to your cloud!

'Yous OK?'

Picking herself up, she brushed goat droppings off her shorts. 'Yeah, I'm fine.'

'Well?' He was obviously waiting for an answer.

'I got fed up kissing frogs.'

'Eh?'

'Joke,' she quipped. *No, it's not, dear,* said a disgruntled grannie in her inner ear. Terri clenched her jaw. Will you sling your hook?

'Have any of yous bin married?'

'George, once,' she said, continuing downhill.

'What happened?'

'Her fella left her for a bloke called Chantelle.'

'Sounds complicated.'

'It was. Chantelle was a lady-boy in Phuket.'

'How long had dey been married?'

'Three weeks. They were on their honeymoon.'

Shadrach came to an abrupt halt. 'She must have been gutted.'

'Incensed would be a better description,' said Terri, colliding with his back. 'Still, she ended up getting the house and the business and has never looked back.'

'What did he get?'

'AIDs. He died two years later.'

'Jesus!'

It was half-past ten when the pair arrived back on the beach. Terri didn't comment as Shadrach pressed his fingers into the fully inflated dinghy, shrugged and pushed it into the water. She was about to clamber in when Evie appeared from the beach bar, arm-in-arm with Dale.

'Terri, look who's here!'

'G'day, bro. How's it going?'

Shadrach stiffened.

'Hi, Dale. Fine. Just fine.' Terri dragged her leg out of the dinghy.

'I reckon you'll be going over to Tobago Cays now.' Shadrach was holding the Rib, his mouth firmly shut.

'Not sure, Dale. We're waiting for a message from base.' Evie's mouth opened then closed as Terri's nose twitched.

'Gee, that's a shame. Why don't you girls join us for the trip? I could have you back before dark.'

'Ooh, that would be fantastic, Dale. Wouldn't it, Terri?'

Shadrach had his back to Dale and dropped his eyelids in agreement. 'Yes,' Terri quickly responded, 'assuming our skipper has no objection.'

'What d'you say, bro? Can I steal your women for the afternoon?

'Sure, why not, mon?'

'See you back on board, Evie' said Terri, and quickly clambered into the dinghy. Dale pushed them off, Shadrach started the outboard and they puttered back to *Rum Punch*'s stern.

'What will you do?' Terri asked as she tied the dinghy's rope to the cleat.

'Wait for word from Delilah and, if I gets de green light, take *Rum Punch* around to Saline Bay, load some fuel and be back here awaitin' your return.'

'What shall I say to the others if we get back before you?'

'Don't.'

'Oh, there you are,' said George, hanging over the stern and sounding like Delilah. 'Wherever have you been?'

Terri ignored her and stepped aboard. 'Anyone for coffee? I'm parched. By the way, Dale is taking us over to Tobago Cays on *Southern Cross* for the afternoon while Shadrach cleans out the bilges.'

'I didn't know they were dirty,' remarked George, filling the kettle.

'Figures. You never were good at housekeeping.'

Southern Cross negotiated the North Channel and crept between two verdant islets, coming to rest in a lagoon protected from the Atlantic by the crescent of Horseshoe Reef, with nothing else between it and the west coast of Africa.

The eighty-three-foot Jongert was everything *Rum Punch* was not. Big, impressive and expensive. Dale handled her like the professional he was, and Evie spent the whole afternoon super-glued to his side.

With masks, snorkels and flippers in place, they all swam along the reef watching Parrot Fish, Bluehead Wrasse, Sergeant Majors, Sharpnose Puffers and Angelfish in every colour and hue imaginable.

Terri followed a Green Sea Turtle as it meandered between the coral heads, nibbling on the rocky garden, and was wondering if young Geordie would have enjoyed the view when she turned a corner and came face to face with an evil-looking fish, its silver body perfectly still in the water, vicious teeth bared to strike. She went into reverse at speed, her flippers beating the retreat like an outboard propeller on full throttle, and came up the side of *Southern Cross* gasping for breath.

'Seen a ghost, Terri?' asked the Irish First Mate.

'No, a bloody big silver torpedo with sharp teeth.'

'Barracuda. Probably attracted to your silver locket,' he said nonchalantly. 'Better take it off if you intend to go in again.'

'Thanks, pal. You could have told me that before I went in the first time.' His accent irritated her, due, in the main, to too many annoying delays at Dublin Airport in the seventies waiting for Air Lingus ground staff to get their act together.

He handed her the deck shower hose, obviously thick-skinned. 'I did, but you were too busy chin-wagging with the others.'

Cheeky bugger, she thought, and let a jet of water accidentally wet his groin.

The sun was setting when Terri came aboard for the final time, her skin all wrinkled. The others were already in the cockpit enjoying a sundowner.

'Harvey Wallbanger, Terri?' asked Dale, pouring the cocktail from an iced jug into Evie's crystal tumbler.

'No, thanks. I'll have one later.' She was trembling from being too long in the water. 'Any chance of a proper shower?'

'Be my guest, doll. Turn left at the bottom of the companionway steps. Second door on the right.'

As the Jongert negotiated Tobago Cays Southern Channel and motored clockwise around Mayreau she crossed her fingers and hoped *Rum Punch* had made it back before them. There was no sign of the catamaran as the yacht passed Saline Bay and Terri relaxed, waving her fingers at Harry's Hideaway, all lit up on the skyline.

It's been an interesting day, she thought as *Southern Cross* anchored in Saltwhistle Bay. Evie announced that she was staying aboard for dinner, so the other three climbed into the Jongert's smart white tender and were whisked across to *Rum Punch* by the Irish mate.

'Where's your owner?' Sam asked him as Shadrach took the rope and made fast on the cleat.

'Still in St Thomas,' came the reply. 'He decided not to meet us in St Lucia after all, so now we're off to Grenada to pick him up there.'

'Nice work if you can get it,' said George, taking Shadrach's hand and stepping aboard.

'Oh, I don't know. Too much hanging around for my liking. I'd rather have your skipper's job.' His hand contacted with Terri's left buttock and he pushed her upwards. She jerked as Shadrach pulled her onto the starboard step.

'Thanks for the lift,' she said, gritting her teeth and adjusting her sarong.

'Don't mention it. See you in Grenada.'

Not if I see you first, Terri thought. When she turned, Shadrach was giving him the evil stare. 'Have we got fuel?' she whispered from the side of her mouth.

'Yeah, but dinner will be a bit late.'

'Can I do anything to help?'

'Nope. Where's Evie?'

'Where d'you think?' Terri nodded to *Southern Cross*.

'Guess we won't be seein' her till mornin', den.'

Chapter Twenty-One

Shark Attack

By day nine the A-team were well used to *Rum Punch*, handling the sails, controlling the helm and working the VHF radio.

Shadrach proved to be a good teacher and his students were quick to learn, not even bothering to look up when a cruise liner went by. Terri spent her free time photographing anything that moved, Evie chatted away on VHF Channel 8 to Dale, Sam was turning a darker shade of mahogany and George tried her hand at whipping rope-ends.

Tall, jagged mountains cut through the haze as they approached Union Island, so different from the undulating terrain of the previous two days. Terri scanned the horizon through the binoculars and paused when a pirogue came into view, following in their wake. She was convinced she'd seen it before.

'Hey, girls, have any of you noticed this pirogue before?' She handed the binoculars to George.

'They all look alike to me,' said George, passing the Zeiss glasses over to Sam. 'If they're not red, yellow and green, then they're green, yellow and red.'

'But this one's got a black and white flash along the side, you can see it as it bounces around in the waves,' insisted Terri.

'Search me,' said Sam. 'But then, I'm not that desperate for a man.'

Evie studied the pirogue as it veered to starboard and dropped away. 'I don't know why you're worrying, Terri. They seem to be heading out to sea. Must be going fishing.'

Terri was less sure. 'Has anyone noticed anything unusual while we've been at anchor?'

'Oh, stop being a drama queen, Terri.' Sam turned over and realigned herself in the sun's rays. 'You'll be telling me next that the Pope is the head of the Italian Mafia.'

'Well, isn't he?' enquired George, dropping into Sam's cabin from the open hatch and landing on her bed.

Sam pulled her sunglasses down lower on her nose. 'Where d'you think you're going, Georgina Stanhope?'

'For a pee,' came the response as her head disappeared.

'Then use the damn' stairs.'

'I saw a chap lying on a surf-board paddling around the anchorage in Bequia,' mumbled Evie. She had everyone's attention, including George whose head reappeared out of the hatch. 'I thought it seemed an odd thing to do, but the bloke smiled and waved at me as he passed so I didn't think anything of it.'

'West Indian?' asked Terri

'Rasta, like Shadrach.'

'Would you recognise him again if you saw him?'

'Doubt it, I didn't take that much notice.'

The A-team stepped out of the dinghy and onto Janti's Happy Island bar, perched on a pile of conch shells above the reef at the seaward end of Clifton Harbour as Shadrach backed away and headed for the shore.

'Do you think that West Indian was casing the anchorage?' asked Evie, pulling out a chair on the raffia-covered terrace and looking around for Janti.

'It's possible, I guess. On the VHF cruiser net this morning the controller reported that a number of yachts had lost their dinghies and was advising cruisers to "lock it or lose it",' replied Terri.

'Well, they're not having ours, we've only just had it repaired.'

'I don't think it's the dinghy they're interested in, Evie, they're after the outboard motors.'

'Well, I'll say it again, they're not having ours. Now, anyone interested in a Saltwhistle Dream?'

'Sorry, lady. We only has rum punch or beer.' Janti stood behind Evie's chair waiting to take their order.

'Rum punch all round then,' said George, whispering as he left, 'it's probably made with moonshine.'

'Can't that send you blind?'

'Who said that?' asked George, pretending to look through them.

'Talking of Saltwhistle Dreams, has anyone seen my drink mat with the recipe scrawled on the back?' asked Sam. The others shook their heads. 'It's really odd, I could have sworn I'd stuck it in the side of my cabin mirror but it's disappeared.'

'Must be senility setting in, Sam. Where's Shadrach gone?'

'Over to the airport to clear us out.'

'But we've only just got here.' Evie could see another catamaran trying to anchor next to *Rum Punch* and it appeared to be dragging alarmingly.

'I know, but tomorrow we're off to Carriacou which is part of Grenada so he has to tell Customs here that we're leaving St Vincent and the Grenadines.' Terri took her drink from Janti. 'Down the hatch, girls. First and last today.'

'Do cruise ships have to do all this clearing in and out thing as well?' The catamaran was having another go at setting its anchor and Evie crossed her fingers.

'I guess so, but collecting and distributing two thousand passports amongst their passengers every time must be a nightmare. Look, there it is again.' Terri was on her feet pointing at the fairway.

'What, the cruise liner? I shouldn't think that could anchor in here.'

'No, you idiot, the pirogue. It came around the reef and is heading towards the town quay. Look, over there.'

'They probably live here, Terri. Now, give it a rest. Better still, stay on the booze. That way, we might get some peace.'

'Don't say I didn't warn you, Sam, when our dinghy's missing in the morning.'

Shadrach made the long walk from Clifton to the airport in the height of the midday sun, wishing he could just sit under a palm tree and drink beer. He was still worrying about his batteries and thanked his lucky stars that Delilah had persuaded Harry to off-load some of their diesel. He had given them an IOU and intended to pay them back once he got the balance of his charter fee.

A light aircraft slid onto the runway as he walked through the perimeter gate, taxied to a stop outside the terminal building and cut its engines. The Cessna's door opened and two men got out, swarthy skinned and well-dressed. Shadrach stood and waited for them to enter the arrivals hall then followed them inside. He took up residence on one of the metal chairs against the back wall, knowing it was going to be a long wait.

The heat of the terminal and the drone of the ceiling fan lulled him into a stupor. Slowly his eyes closed, his head dropped back and he dozed.

He dreamt of the first time he had seen *Rum Punch*. She was being escorted into English Harbour, Antigua by the local Coastguard. At the time she was called *Rum Runner* and glided past Shadrach as he stood on some wooden scaffolding, polishing the hull of a Grand Banks motorboat. He was curious to know why she had been impounded.

That evening as he worked in the Lagoon Bar on Dockyard Drive, an off-duty customs officer walked in, sat on a bar stool and ordered a beer. By his fourth Carib, Shadrach had learnt that *Rum Runner* was an American-flagged catamaran running drugs between Port of Spain, Trinidad and the US Virgin Islands. The crew had been arrested and their drug haul confiscated following a tip-off from the Drug Enforcement Agency (DEA) in the States.

The catamaran had remained at anchor in English Harbour for weeks with Shadrach eyeing her from afar, convinced no one would ever come to claim her. Then, one November night in 1999, Hurricane Lenny hit Antigua, wrecking homes, uprooting trees, decimating the coral reefs and causing havoc in the anchorages and marinas.

By morning, Antigua looked like a bomb site. Shadrach rushed down to English Harbour and witnessed the devastation all around for himself. At first he couldn't see *Rum Runner* due to wreckage piled up in the lagoon and assumed the yacht was in pieces. Then, using his binoculars, he caught sight of her coach roof. She had sunk in three metres of water in the centre of the lagoon, only her upper structure and mast visible above the waterline.

'De customs officer is free now,' shouted a female from behind a screen.

Shadrach came to with a start and took a minute to remember where he was. 'OK, lady.' He shook his head, trying to clear his mind, walked over to the door and knocked.

'Yeah, mon, what can I's do for you?'

Chatham Bay, on the leeward side of Union, was deserted at midday, just a huge, curved beach bounded by densely wooded hills and swaying palm trees. Before *Rum Punch*'s hook had even bitten into the sand, Shadrach had his arm raised and a brightly painted pirogue left the shore, the words, 'Shark Attack' brightly painted across the bow.

It arrived at their gunwhale, the owner, all solid muscle and wiry curls, holding it stationary against the catamaran's side with his massive hands.

'Yo, mon. Yous lookin' for a beach barbecue?'

'Dat's right, Shark Attack. De ladies here, dey just love lobster.'

'Den I'll see yous at sunset for de Happy Hour drinks.' He revved the seventy-five-horsepower engine and arced his way back to the shore.

'I bet that engine's stolen,' mumbled Terri as she captured his pirogue in her viewfinder.

'Don't let Shark Attack hear you say dat,' whispered Shadrach into her ear. 'He don't take kindly to bad publicity and he's as honest as de day's long.'

'Ignore her, Skip. She's convinced that all Grenadians are related to the Kray Brothers.' Sam lowered herself majestically into the bay and floated off to port.

'No I'm not, but that's a pretty nifty engine for a bloke who appears to be making his living on a deserted beach.'

At that moment a French-flagged monohull cut short any further discussion on the subject as it appeared around the headland, cruised around the mile-long bay for ten minutes then dropped its anchor so close to *Rum Punch* it came to rest five metres away from her bow.

'Feelin' lonely?' shouted Shadrach, glaring at the French skipper. 'Why didn't you hook onto our anchor chain instead?' The Frenchman gave him a one-finger salute, stripped off to his birthday suit and dived into the sea.

'Bloody Frogs,' chuntered George. 'They've never got over Waterloo.'

'Georgina,' whispered Terri from behind, 'he's no idea we're English.'

'Then it's high time he did.' She grabbed her St George's Cross beach towel and waved it in the air like a demented football supporter. 'Up yours, *Crapaud!*'

Shadrach stepped ashore with his guitar strapped to his back. Sam, with the A-team's version of a Saltwhistle Dream filling an empty one-litre water bottle came next followed by Evie and George manhandling a cool-box of beers and water, with Terri bringing up the rear balancing a stack of clear plastic glasses and her camera. They all headed for Shark Attack's smoking oil drum where a large plastic box full of lobsters lay alongside.

Much to Georgina's chagrin, the *Crapaud* arrived on the beach with a box full of French cheeses, some foie gras, a bottle of Aquavit and a half-full bottle of Remy Martin cognac. She sat on a wooden crate and glared at him, muttering under her breath, until, an hour later, much mellowed by a surfeit of French brandy and barbecued crustacean, she could be seen chatting away to England's favourite enemy in fluent French.

'I tought George didn't like Frenchies?' queried Shadrach, picking up his guitar as Georgina waxed lyrical about the beauty of the Haute-Savoie and her experiences as a chalet maid.

'She doesn't,' replied Terri, wiggling her toes in the sand. 'Especially Frogs with connections to Napoleon. Her dad was in the Rifles, you see.'

He didn't, but chose not to labour the point.

'The Rifles,' she repeated. 'Back in 1815. They fought at Waterloo.'

Sam wandered down the beach and stood watching the moonlight shimmer off the bay as the lilting refrain of 'Cavatina' began to drift towards her on the air. She sat on a bowed palm trunk and let her long legs dangle below, trying not to feel guilty for enjoying life so much. A turtle popped its head out of the shallows yards from her perch then slowly receded back into the depths. However am I going to put the genie back in the bottle? she thought, and ran her hands through her long hair, trying to imagine life in London after the vivid sights and exotic sounds of the Caribbean.

Evie sat by the driftwood fire watching the sparks rising on the breeze and thought of Dale. They were having one of those mind-blowing holiday romances that usually only eighteen-year-olds experienced, not women in their late forties, yet her body refused to grow old gracefully, tingling whenever she contemplated their next tryst.

She knew she had to be realistic. Once her holiday was ended, Dale would disappear over the horizon on *Southern Cross* and never be seen again. 'Cavatina' seemed to mirror her mood and no amount of sensible argument inside her head could pacify her body's craving for such long-overdue attention.

Until the holiday, Evie had assumed that the rest of her working life would be spent inside some English spa massage room with a succession of pale, wrinkled oldies laid out like fish on a slab, waiting to be pummelled to death as New Age music played in the background. As for her private life, that would remain shallow and ever more lonely. If only I could find a way out of the rut, she thought, picking up some driftwood and playing with the coals. There's got to be more to life than the Belgrove Park Health Spa and massaging mens' egos.

Terri watched Shadrach playing his guitar and mulled over her own problems. If someone had told her back in Ealing that she would fancy a destitute Rastafarian with a chequered past she would have suggested sectioning them. And it wasn't only Shadrach who was getting under her skin. She hated the idea of leaving *Rum Punch* for the sanitised environment of Paternoster Square and the grey men and women who worked in the British Electricity Board's head office there.

A shooting star flashed across the heavens and dropped into the ocean. Terri scooped soft sand into her right palm and let it fall through her fingers like lost time, wondering what it would be like to live aboard *Rum Punch* permanently with Shadrach. The idea made her feel warm inside. Why didn't I do something like this when I was younger? she mused. Where would I be now? Her questions had no answers. At forty-eight, all she had to show for her life were old memories of her flying days, a crumbling Victorian semi in Ealing, a settee that was past its sell-by date, and the on-set of middle-aged spread. She thumped the sand with her fist and studied Shadrach's features in the firelight. The glow from the embers danced across his rippling arm muscles as long nimble fingers plucked the strings, his head bowed, eyes hidden below thick, black lashes; a man lost in a world of his own. Terri liked what she saw and would have given anything to have turned back the clock and become part of his world. Face the facts, Teresa Gillingham, life has passed you by and no amount of wishing on a star is going to change that. She lay back, hands clasped behind her head, and looked up into the heavens. 'All in all,' she mumbled to the universe, 'life's a bitch and there isn't a damn' thing I can do about it.'

The coals were losing their glow and dawn was creeping into the skyline. George and her *Crapaud* were swaying together, ankle-deep in the warm shallows, while the rest sat around the campfire putting the world to rights. No one wanted to break the spell. After days of excitement the A-team were chilling out, letting time and tide wash over them, safe in their Caribbean bubble.

As the sun's first rays touched Terri's forehead, she called everyone together for a group photograph. They all shuffled into line, arms around each other's waists, the Frenchman bringing them into focus through the camera's viewfinder, ready to capture for posterity four ex-air stewardesses, a musical Rastafarian skipper and a Grenadian beach entrepreneur, linked in friendship, all looking out into the morning.

'Now, you say ze cheese ven I say tree.'

'Un . . . deux . . .trois . . . FROMAGE.' *Click*!

Chapter Twenty-Two

PSV

The Frenchman was long gone when Shadrach and his crew eventually surfaced the next morning. Time was running out and a meeting around the chart-table was underway.

'Now den, ladies. We has a choice. Eider we head straight for Carriacou so yous can do an island tour or we can stop off at Petit St Vincent for de day and make for Carriacou tonight.' He looked to his crew for a decision.

'Is that what PSV stands for on the chart?' asked Evie, leaning over Shadrach's shoulder and pointing at a small spit of land south-east of Union Island.

He nodded.

'It doesn't look much. What's there?'

'De whole place is a five-star tropical island retreat where de rich and famous hang out. I tought Samanta might welcome a bit o' class.'

'Are we allowed ashore?' asked Terri, wondering if Johnny Depp was having a couple of days R&R away from filming.

'Sure ting. De rooms are individual cottages scattered across de hillside, which, o' course, are private, but de two bars and two restaurants are open to visitors. If you flash dose eyelashes, Evie, you might even get a massage at de health spa.'

Evie's eyes lit up like Sydney's fireworks.

'You seem to know a lot about this place, Shadrach Bligh,' George observed.

'Well, I should, I used to walk out wid de spa's head honcho.'

'Is she still there?' Evie swivelled him round on his stool to face her.

'It might be a man,' suggested George.

'Would one of yous clap dat girl in irons?' demanded Shadrach, pointing behind him.

'Seriously,' insisted Evie. 'Could you introduce me?'

'What's it worth, Evie?'

'Oh, I don't know . . . the price of a tank of fuel.'

The saloon went deathly quiet. Shadrach looked at Terri who pouted and shrugged, George clipped Evie's ear and Sam scratched her chin.

Evie's eyes darted from one to the other. 'I just thought . . . I mean . . .' She looked to the others for help. They were all tight-lipped. 'Oh, hell, Shadrach, George noticed that the fuel gauge was very low and Dale's first officer told me that you and Terri had been trying to scrounge some fuel in Mayreau.' She bit her lip and looked at their skipper from under her long black eyelashes.

Terri immediately went on the attack. 'We didn't scrounge any, Evie. Shadrach paid for some because he was so drunk in Bequia he forgot to take fuel onboard before we left. As for that Irish leprechaun, he should go back under his toadstool where he belongs.'

'It's OK, Terri.' Shadrach pulled Evie onto his knee like a small child. 'Evie, George is quite right, de fuel tank is nearly empty and I was goin' to fill it up in Carriacou. We'll be sailin' dere anyway but, if you wants to see PSV and dat luxury spa den I can drop you alls off and hop across to Petit Martinique.' He pointed to a second spit of land close to PSV. 'De diesel is real cheap dere, and, as it happens, so is de booze.'

'I'm sorry, Shadrach, I didn't mean to insult you and I really do want to see this health spa.'

'So do I,' agreed Sam, 'and as for the fuel, why don't we use the money from *True Life Movies* to pay for it? It's all one and the same and we've hardly used any so far. Let's be frank, our bar bill onboard must be more than that.'

'Certainly far higher than it would have been for an English couple with two kids,' added George.

'What d'you say, Shadrach?' Terri waved their money-belt in the air from across the saloon, beaming from ear to ear.

'Lordie, Lordie.' Shadrach eased Evie off his knee and leant back against the chart-table. 'Wid yous lot gangin' up on me, I don't stand a chance o' refusin'. Evie girl, I'm gonna get you over to dat Clementine pretty damn' sharpish before de udder man-eatin' women decide to mutiny and take me ship.'

'YES!' shouted Evie, punching the air as Terri 'high-fived' George.

Sam was back in her element, sashaying up the PSV dock in a full-length flowing emerald sarong above a matching cutaway swimsuit. Her hair was hidden beneath a large-brimmed black straw hat, Moroccan earrings dangling beneath, Ray Ban sunglasses hiding her eyes and Jimmy Choo diamante sandals glittering in the sunlight, as were the gold and emerald bangles adorning her right arm. A black and emerald striped linen beach bag completed the ensemble, nonchalantly slung over her shoulder. Guests at the beach bar all turned to watch this six-foot-two-inch apparition, oozing elegance, negotiate the wooden jetty like a world-class model at the Milan Fashion Show.

Evie added to the scene with her white, figure-hugging, all-in-one silk jump suit, setting off her jet-black hair and tanned complexion to perfection, her multi-coloured metal belt and beaded mules enhancing an otherwise blank canvas; while George glided onto the terrace in cream linen trousers and taupe knotted blouse over a matching lace bikini, her hair brushed off her face under a cream Panama hat.

Terri was not to be outdone. She had decided to go all nautical in white cotton cut-offs, a navy and white matelot crop top showing off her bronzed midriff and *Rum Punch*'s communal NYPD baseball hat shading her Polaroid glasses. She had clubbed her hair with a big blue scrunch and borrowed a pair of Sam's Swarovski stud earrings to give the outfit class. Tripping along behind the others she felt superior, her bare feet and hands edged with bright orange nail-vanish.

The A-team were quite a sight.

'I'll have an espresso,' announced Evie as she pointed to the reception area, waved a piece of paper in her hand and headed in that direction.

'Two espressos, a cappuccino and a latte, please,' said Terri to the waiter hovering by their table. 'Well, girls, I don't think cruise liner passengers get to see this.'

Sam did a Sharon Stone 'crossed legs' impression, causing two men at the opposite table to gawp and their female partners to bring them to heel with sharp words. She lifted her Ray Bans and glanced at her friends with serious-looking eyes. 'Terri, I think it's time the A-team thanked you for giving us all one hell of a holiday.'

'Hear, hear,' added George, watching a well-toned, Scandinavian-looking man walk up to the bar and speak to the barman. 'Umm, tasty.'

Terri followed her gaze and agreed, the man in question being the right age, the right height and definitely the right income bracket. His Rolex watch and impeccably white espadrilles oozed quality. 'You know, this holiday might have started badly but it has made me realise that there is more to life than the British Electricity Board and take-away curries,' she said.

'I couldn't agree more,' said George, eyes still locked on the Rolex watch. 'Where have we been all our lives?'

'Don't beat yourselves up, girls. Beagle Air was certainly not BOAC, where the passengers were all out of the top drawer,' said Sam. 'If it hadn't been for my accidental meeting with CJ, right now I would probably be working in some NHS hospital wiping geriatric patients' bums.'

'Do you miss it?' asked Terri, taking her coffee from the waiter.

'Not working in the NHS, but they do say staff in the Wellington opposite Regent's Park get very good tips.'

'Well, they would, wouldn't they? It's full of Russians.'
George smiled discreetly as Rolex Man passed by her right
elbow.

'Are you really that shallow, Sam?' asked Terri, frowning.

'No, of course not, but you have to agree,' she scanned the
bar and the beach beyond, 'this beats the hell out of Clacton.'

Terri watched Evie approach them, smiling.

'Shadrach's note worked,' she announced as she lowered
herself into the spare chair and picked up her coffee.
'Clementine is going to let me give Sam a massage on the spa
terrace overlooking the sea in fifteen minutes, so she can see
how good I am.'

'Then don't yell out, Sam,' ordered George, 'this could be
Evie's last chance at a better life.'

'Don't we get one too?' asked Terri, watching *Rum Punch*
disappearing across the channel to Petite Martinique.

'Only if you pay.'

'How much is it?'

'If you have to ask, you can't afford it,' said Evie. 'Anyway I
thought you hated massages.'

'I do. Half the time they tickle and the other half hurt like
hell.'

'You're such a wimp, Gillingham. Count me in, Evie, but
don't expect a tip.' George's eyes followed Rolex Man until he
disappeared from view then she sighed.

'Allright, you lot, have it your own way. I'm going to
wander about taking some photographs,' Terri said.

'You run the risk of getting arrested, pal, and we won't be bailing you out, so think about that before you go snapping some Colombian drug baron and his floozy.'

'Very funny, Georgina.' Terri extended her hand across the table. 'Sam, can I have the kitty?'

Sam stretched to the floor to retrieve her linen bag and the men at the opposite table immediately peered down her cleavage. The first received a slap on the arm and the second was dragged bodily away from the terrace.

'Whoops,' whispered Evie, finishing her espresso.

Clementine handed Sam a white towelling robe and a locker key then walked Evie over to the terrace, pulled a soft white muslin curtain to one side and exposed a massage table, draped in white linen, resting on an open wooden deck with a view that would put a Kuoni holiday brochure to shame. A trolley full of oils and body lotions stood to one side and a wicker, high-backed chair occupied one corner.

Evie, now dressed in the resort's standard-issue uniform, a white overall with the PSV logo embroidered on the breast pocket and a pair of white Scholl sandals, walked over to the deck balustrade and looked out. 'My, oh, my, this certainly beats the view at Belgrove Park.'

A matching muslin curtain to her right wafted in the breeze, separating her from the massage area next door. As she turned she saw Sam appearing from the powder room, swathed in soft towelling, her feet in PSV Resort slippers, her blonde hair gathered into a bunch on the top of her head and all her jewellery discarded. 'Good morning. Madam, my name is Evangelina and I am your masseuse today.'

Sam's lips cracked as she discarded her robe and walked into the monogrammed linen towel held out by her fellow cruiser, who was deliberately looking the other way. She settled onto the massage bed, face down, crossed her arms under her chin and looked out on the Caribbean.

Evie checked Clementine's reaction. She was sitting in the wicker chair, her black hair falling around her face in cornrow braids embellished with coloured beads and shells, her rich chocolate-coloured eyes shadowed in soft beige and gold, plump lips coated in neutral lip gloss. The woman had an hourglass figure under the white PSV overall and her long, delicate fingers looked well-manicured and enriched from constant contact with the very best hand and body lotions.

I can see why Shadrach fancied her, Evie thought as Clementine nodded back at her. I wonder what went wrong. She turned her attention to her client.

'What type of massage would Madam like today?'

'What would you suggest?' answered Sam, giving Evie free rein.

'Well, if you would like to be invigorated, I can use peppermint oil and give you a Hot Stone or Thai massage. If, however, you wish to feel relaxed and stress-free I would suggest a sweet almond and lavender oil Swedish massage.'

Sam wiggled her toes. 'Swedish, please. After the past few days I could do with some de-stressing.'

Evie pinched her on the thigh, turned, smiled at Clementine and approached the trolley. Rubbing her hands together, she inspected the row of bottles and selected the one she wanted, allowing her mind to empty of everything but the next hour's work. If Clementine liked what she saw, Evie knew she might be on her way to working with the rich and famous in this tropical setting. She gently pulled back the linen towel, exposing Sam's long spine, moved to the head of the table and dribbled sweet almond and lavender oil onto her friend's shoulders.

Forty-five minutes later Sam was floating on a fusion of exotic aromas and lapping waves, faint sounds of Caribbean music drifting by on the breeze as Evie laid cotton-pads soaked in chilled rosewater on each eyelid, placed a glass of lemon-infused cold water by her side and departed with Clementine for the reception area.

George met them at the desk. Her left eyebrow lifted. Evie blinked and continued the charade. 'Good morning, Madam, are you here for your pedicure?'

'Dat's OK, Evangelina. I'll deal wid dis client. You go and change. We should talk over lunch.' Clementine made no further comment, taking George gently by the arm and leading her to a display of nail varnishes. 'Now, Madam, which Dior colour can I tempt you with?'

Terri was having the time of her life, sitting in the passenger seat of a golf-cart being given the grand tour of PSV by the under-manager.

She had completely bamboozled him with a fictitious story about being a travel journalist for the *Sunday Times* and wishing to do a piece on the resort for a future article about exclusive, exotic holiday destinations. Taking one look at her Sony DSLR zoom camera, he had immediately agreed to give her everything she needed and whisked her off around the island, pointing out all the benefits on offer.

'We have a policy of complete privacy for our guests, Miss . . .?'

'Gillingham.'

'Miss Gillingham. There are no telephones, Wi-Fi or televisions in our twenty cottages. We use a charming driftwood flagpole system, unique to this resort, for communication.'

Terri recalled her days in the Girl Guides flapping her arms about doing semaphore, and was intrigued. 'How does it work?'

'Oh, it's quite simple,' he said, negotiating a one-hundred-and-forty-degree bend in the road. 'If our clients do not wish to be disturbed they raise a red flag. If they require service they use a yellow flag.'

Terri pointed to a yellow flag alongside cottage number six. 'Like that.'

'Exactly.' At that moment a staff member arrived in another golf-cart, drew to a halt, nodded to the under-manager and walked up to number six's entrance.

'May I take a photograph?' asked Terri politely.

'Be my guest, but be quick before the clients hear the ship's bell telling them their order has arrived. We don't want them thinking we are spying on them.' The under-manager chuckled and did an emergency stop.

Photograph taken they continued on their way, a running commentary accompanying Terri's pauses to get yet another shot. Red flags appeared above a number of the cottages and

Terri wondered if Johnny Depp and his wife were among those signalling. She touched the orange bead on a piece of whipping string around her neck and recalled another Caribbean beach.

By the time they arrived back at the reception area Terri's camera was filled with blue skies, aquamarine seas, stone and wooden cottages, elegant dining areas, spa facilities and water-sport equipment. She thanked the under-manager profusely, requested a brochure and business card, and went to find the others.

Sam had drifted in and out of sleep after her massage, a muted conversation going on next door, the muslin curtain allowing her to glimpse the hazy outlines of a client and her beauty therapist.

'Is this your first visit to PSV, Madam?' Sam couldn't help earwigging on the reply.

'Yes, but we will definitely be back. CJ and I are really loving the peace and tranquillity here after our hectic schedule in New York, and I just love your red and yellow flag system.'

Sam's cotton-wool pads hit the floor and she was off the bed in seconds, robe pulled around her body, nose peeking round the edge of the muslin curtain. All she could see was the masseuse's white overall bending over the massage table and the client's jet black ponytail held aloft with what looked like a pair of dark wooden chopsticks.

Evie nearly fell over her as she entered Sam's area to wake her client. 'What the . . .?'

Sam rammed her hand across Evie's mouth and dragged her outside into the ladies' powder room.

'What the hell's going on?' demanded Evie, readjusting her jump suit.

'Evie, I want you to do something for me. I need to change, but I also need to know who the client is in the next bay to ours and which cottage she's staying in.' With that, Sam plucked her locker key out of her robe pocket, accessed her clothes, shoes, hat and linen bag, and disappeared into a changing room.

'Why?' asked Evie as the door closed.

Sam's head reappeared, her next words whispered through gritted teeth. 'Because unless there are two CJs in the world, she's shacking up with mine!'

'You're joking?'

'Just get me the information, Evie. I need to know who she is.'

'Right.' Evie was out of the door and moving towards the reception desk when Terri walked through the door to the spa.

'Hi, Evie. How'd it go?'

Evie ignored her, the appointment book under close inspection, finger running down the entries as she looked at her watch. 'What time do you make it?'

'Half-past one. Why?'

'Right. Jasmin Wong, cottage eighteen. Follow me.'

Evie retraced her steps to the powder room with Terri in hot pursuit, convinced something was afoot but not having a clue what it was.

'Evie!' came Sam's voice through the changing-room door.

'Here with Terri.'

'Did you get it?'

'Yes. Jasmin Wong.'

'And the cottage number?'

'Eighteen.'

'Right, I'll meet you in the beach bar in ten minutes. Terri, have you got your camera?'

A lot of rustling was coming from behind the door. 'You know I have. What the devil is going on?'

'I'll tell you at the bar. Now make yourselves scarce so we don't attract attention.'

Evie filled Terri in on the way to the bar.

'She can't be serious? He's in Alaska with his wife,' argued Terri, trying to remember where cottage eighteen was. She plonked herself into the same chair she had vacated earlier and pulled out the resort brochure. 'Now, let's see. Oh, here we are.' Her finger pointed to a small arrow above the number eighteen on the resort map. 'It's a beachside cottage at the end of Cross Pointe.'

'Good,' said Sam, joining them, her straw hat and Ray Bans hiding her features. 'All we have to do now is check that CJ is in residence and the shit is going to hit the fan.'

'Can I get you anyting, ladies?'

'No . . . thank you.' Sam tried a smile but it came out more like a grimace.

'Actually, yes,' countered Terri. 'We will have four Planter's Punches please.'

'Terri?' groaned Sam, eager to sort out her life.

'Now, listen to me, Samantha. You are to sit there, calm down and think this through rationally. Firstly, you may have misunderstood what was said. Secondly, this resort prides itself on giving its clients total privacy, so you can't go barging in on people without notice, especially if their red flag is up.'

'Red flag? What red flag?'

Terri explained as the waiter handed them their drinks. 'And thirdly, if, God forbid, it is CJ, then exposing him during post-coital bliss may not be the best policy.'

Sam bit her knuckle. 'I don't need to hear this.'

'Terri's right, Sam. Well not necessarily about the post-coital thing,' Sam drew blood ... 'but about making rash decisions that you may regret later. We're here to support you all the way but there's no need to panic. The occupants of cottage eighteen aren't going anywhere in a hurry, now are they?'

'Exactly,' agreed Terri, handing Sam her iced punch. 'Now drink this, and let's wait for George to join us before you make a plan of action. With luck this will all be a storm in a teacup and we can get back to enjoying PSV over a nice lunch.'

Sam sank into her chair, trying to disguise her six-foot frame, her brain whirling. George, by contrast, floated over to the bar, her big toes sporting white palm trees on blue backgrounds, a small diamante bead positioned in the fronds, glittering as she moved. She lowered herself into the vacant seat, placed her feet on the arm of Terri's chair so her toenails could be admired, and frowned. 'What's up?'

'Here, drink this,' said Terri, 'you're gonna need it.'

'Now, are we all agreed?' They were sitting on sunbeds on the beach as far away from other people as possible. 'Evie and I are going to wander down to Cross Pointe for me to do a photo-shoot off the rocks. With my telephoto lens, I should be able to pick up anyone on the terrace of the cottage so Sam can confirm it is not CJ after all.' She looked at the others who all nodded, except for Sam. 'George, keep her occupied here and don't let her out of your sight.'

'Wilco,' said George, daring Sam to argue. 'What happens if you can't get a good enough shot?'

'I'll raise the yellow flag on their pole and wait for a staff member to turn up. This CJ's bound to answer the door so I can photograph him then.'

'But, what happens if the red flag is up?' Sam knew if it was CJ that was exactly what would be flying.

'I'll think of something. Right, are you ready, Evie?'

'Yeah. You never know, I might make the centrefold of *Playboy* magazine.'

'Now that's a good way to get this bloke's attention,' remarked George, waving them off down the beach.

Evie was the ideal model, imitating fashion-shoot poses like a professional, pulling the zip of her jump-suit lower and lower as she swung from side to side, her boobs expanding to fill the space provided.

'That's great, Evie. Keep going while I walk around you. I need to face the terrace in case he's sunbathing.'

Terri's impression of David Bailey was equally as impressive, her camera lens going in and out like a racing car's piston, finally settling on cottage eighteen where Miss Jasmin Wong, fresh from the spa, could be seen leaning against the stone balustrade watching their every move. She's quite a stunner, thought Terri, as she knelt on a rock below Evie and pretended to get a sky shot, instructing her model to shake out her curly locks.

Evie let the zip slide further and did a twirl, stretching out her arms as her nipples peeked beyond the fastener, making sure the full effect could be appreciated from the cottage before turning her head back to Terri, hands clasped behind. She winked as Jasmin's partner came out onto the terrace naked, placed his hands inside her robe, caressed her breasts, buried his nose in her neck and let the robe fall.

'Come on, you pillock, bring your head up,' whispered Terri to herself.

'Problem?' muttered Evie.

'His head's buried in her hair.'

'Not for long,' announced Evie, and dropped her all-in-one to her ankles, exposing her well-tanned, well-toned body to anyone who happened to be around. The man's head snapped up, he focused on the naked model on the rocks and Terri got just the shot she was hoping for. 'Jesus Christ,' she uttered under her breath as she stared at the Peeping Tom in all his naked glory. 'That's only the bloody Chairman of the British Electricity Board!'

The beach restaurant was filling up as the A-team stood at the entrance waiting for a table. Sam's colour had returned and her usual proud posture was back when the head waiter led them to a table and handed out large wooden clipboards with the menu clipped to them.

'What are we drinking?' asked George, another waiter hovering by her shoulder.

'A brandy and Benedictine for me,' announced Terri, all thoughts of abstinence gone.

'A bottle of still water,' ordered George, 'and a bottle of your house white with three glasses.'

'Thanks, pal. With friends like you, who needs willpower?'

'Forgive me for mentioning it, Teresa, but didn't you say I was to stop you drinking alcohol?'

'That was last week. Right now I need a sedative to get over the fact that my Chairman is screwing some oriental beauty in an exclusive resort in the Grenadines, compliments of the profits from my hard, boring work. Not only that, if it hadn't been for some quick thinking on the part of my grannie, his bloody objection to the BIE logo could also have landed me without a job!'

'I thought your grannie was dead?'

'She is.'

'Pass the Panadol, I can feel a headache coming on.' George leaned her elbow on the table and pressed her fingers to her head.

'How are you feeling, Sam?' asked Evie in counselling mode.

'A lot better than an hour ago.' She placed a hand on Terri's arm and patted it comfortingly. 'Don't fret, love. Just take a deep breath, count to ten and let the A-team take the strain.'

'Listen to Miss Agony Aunt here. If you'd used CJ's real name over the years instead of all this cloak and dagger nonsense, I would have stayed oblivious to my Chairman's extra-marital affairs and able to enjoy my lunch in peace.'

Sam quickly sat back and looked the other way.

'Too right, Hutchins. You've been running rings around us all morning because of your precious CJ. I think it's high time you gave with the info. What the hell *is* his name?' George's well-placed rebuke shot straight across Sam's bows.

Her eyes narrowed, her full-lipped mouth squeezed tight and her hands clenched into fists. 'If I tell you, you'll have to promise to keep it to yourselves.'

'For Christ's sake, Sam, what d'you think I'm going to do? Write it in large letters on Prestige Travel's shopfront window: Mr So-and-so has been shagging Miss Samantha Hutchins for twenty-five years over in Knightsbridge?'

'Keep your voice down.'

'Well, for goodness' sake.'

'OK, OK. Chill out. His name's Charles Julian Cranbourne-Smyth, owner and CEO of Betelgeuse Ultra-dynamic Securities. Satisfied?'

'Never heard of him,' remarked Evie.

'He sounds very Old Etonian to me.'

'Winchester, actually.'

'Not likely to know Cyril then?' Terri's retort silenced the others as she clicked back through her photographs.

'Cyril?'

'Yes. Cyril Trowbridge. Ex-eighties Labour MP for some constituency in the Black Country, now Lord Trowbridge of Leek.'

'Great,' said Evie. 'Two bastards with over-active libidos.'

'Charles isn't a bastard,' huffed Sam.

'Funny,' said Evie, leaning over Terri's shoulder. 'I could have sworn you were calling him that an hour ago.'

'Well that was when I thought he was two-timing me,' she argued, trying to justify herself.

'Three-timing, Sam. He's been two-timing his wife for over twenty-five years with you.' George peered over her sunglasses and gave Sam a withering look. 'What would you have done if it had been your CJ fondling our nubile Miss Jasmin Wong?'

'How the hell do I know? Probably pinned his balls to the bedhead and demanded compensation.'

'Now there's an idea,' muttered Terri, expanding Cyril Trowbridge's testicles in her viewfinder.

'What's the "J" for?' asked Evie.

'What?'

'Cyril J. Trowbridge. CJ for short.'

Terri looked at the nearest palm tree for inspiration. 'D'you know, I've no idea. In fact, I thought his name was Cyril Kenneth Trowbridge.'

'CJ. CK. Not much difference, is there?' muttered Evie.

'None in Sam's hearing,' said George, raising her clipboard in the air.

'You do realise, Evie, you've just exposed yourself to a peer of the realm, because Madam here needs her ears syringing.' The waiter arrived at the table just as Sam kicked George under the table.

Shadrach dropped *Rum Punch*'s anchor in PSV's harbour and checked his watch. It was two-thirty and he thought his crew would need another hour at least for lunch, giving him just enough time to get up to the hillside spa and find Clementine without being seen. He checked the still-inflated dinghy attached at the stern and decided to swim underneath before leaving, to find out what had had happened to the leak.

With young Geordie for company, he paddled around the underside of the Rib checking the seal, and came across a large patch stuck to the rear starboard pontoon. Well, I never did, he thought, running his fingers across the repair.

Coming up for air, he sat on the lower step and chuckled to himself. 'How de hell did dey organise dat?' A picture of the Bequia jump-up filled his mind. 'Lordie, Lordie, dose women sure be sometin' else.'

He took the shower hose from its stowage, washed sea water from his hair and skin, climbed into his shorts and t-shirt, jumped into the dinghy and headed for the shore.

Giving the beach restaurant a wide berth, he made his way to the health spa, coming to a halt at the back door and tapping lightly. One of the beauty therapists answered, smiled at Shadrach and let him pass. When Clementine walked into the staff room, he was reclining on a wicker settee, fruit juice in hand, reading *Elite Traveller* magazine.

'Well, look what de cat dragged in,' she said, a muscle in her right cheek twitching.

'Afternoon, Clemmie, how'd it go wid me lady passenger?'

'Fancy her, do you?' asked Clementine, leaning against the wall, arms crossed.

'No, but I tell you, Clem, all four o' dem are like nuttin' you've ever seen. I wouldn' say it to dere faces, hon, but dey be angels, absolute angels.'

'Well,' said Clementine, coming to sit by his side, 'Evangelina certainly knows her stuff when it comes to de massage. Dat Georgina told me she'd trained at Champneys.'

Shadrach raised his eyebrow.

'It's one of de best health spas in de world. I'd just love to have her work here. She'd bring real class to dis place, and dat's no lie.'

'Did you tell her dat?'

'No. I was going to over lunch but she shot off like a rat up a broomstick. I don't know what happened but de tall one . . .'

'Samanta?'

'. . . Yeah, Samanta. Well, she looked as if she'd seen a ghost and de next minute . . . poof!' Clementine's hands shot into the air. 'Poof!'

Shadrach scratched his dreadlocks. 'What d'you tink happened, Clem?'

'Search me. Must have been sometin' I said, but for de life o' me I can't tink what.'

Shadrach looked at his watch. 'Got time for a quickie?'

'If you're payin', Shadrach Bligh.'

'I's payin', Clem.'

'Well, miracles will never cease.'

They both left the health spa and headed for the staff quarters.

Evie put down her spoon, wiped her mouth and sat back. 'This has to be the best beachside restaurant I've ever been to.'

'Me too,' said Terri. 'Coffees all round?'

'Not for me. I want to talk to Clementine and find out what she thinks about my chances of working here.'

'Would you really give up Belgrove Park for this?'

Evie glanced sideways at Terri as she rose from the table.

'Daft question,' admitted Terri. 'If you are offered a position, can I be your first client?'

'Only if you pay the going rate.'

'I always suspected you were mean, Evangelina Shapiro.'

'Must be my parsimonious side coming out,' replied Evie as she lifted her bag from the back of her chair and made her way to the exit.

'No wonder Dale has stars in his eyes,' commented Sam, watching their friend depart. 'She can find muscles I didn't know I had.'

'Perhaps she could give us all lessons on the way down to Grenada. You never know when it might come in useful.'

'I second that,' said Terri. 'And I'll tell you something else. I'm gonna be green with envy if she ends up working here while I'm stuck in Paternoster Square.'

'No problem,' said George. 'Threaten Cyril with exposure in the *News of the World* and spend your golden handshake running the Ladies Best Detective Agency in the Grenadines. You won't be short of clients.'

'Can we change the subject?' said Sam, calling for the bill. 'I think I've had enough detective work for one day.'

'Say no more, Samantha. Next stop Carriacou for the night. Let's hope it's a quiet one. Has anyone seen Shadrach?'

Evie walked along the path toward the spa wondering if this could be her lucky break. A guest stopped his golf-cart and asked her if she wanted a lift, eyes homing in on her breasts. She declined and sent him on his way, wondering, not for the first time, why men assumed every female was up for sex.

Entering the spa, she walked up to the reception desk and heard Shadrach talking to Clementine in the office beyond. Evie shot round the corner out of sight and saw their reflections in the glass as they left by the back door, arm in arm. Following at a safe distance, she watched them approach the staff quarters. Evie dodged behind a tree as Shadrach checked from left to right to see if anyone was looking then disappeared inside a wooden hut and closed the door. The words: 'Used to walk out with the head honcho' filled her mind as she quickly backtracked and headed for the dinghy dock.

You're a bloody liar, Shadrach Jonathon William Bligh. Just like CJ and CK, you can't keep your prick in your trousers, Evie decided, and kicked a stone along the path in disgust. It was irrational of her to be angry but she knew Terri would be gutted if she'd witnessed the scene and felt protective towards her friend. Suddenly PSV had lost its charm. Evie just wanted to get back onboard *Rum Punch* and sail away.

Chapter Twenty-Three

Carriacou

There was a definite change in the atmosphere on the boat that afternoon but Shadrach couldn't put his finger on what had caused it. Terri seemed distracted and Evie was down-right rude.

At the top end of Petite Martinique he turned the yacht's bow south and made passage for Tyrell Bay, intent on overnighting there while he checked them all into Grenada. There would be a barbecue in the local Yacht Club grounds, which he thought his passengers might enjoy.

Sitting at his position by the helm, the sails powering them along at a steady six knots, the fuel tank full and the booze cupboard replenished, he felt content, his world back in balance, and relived the hour spent with Clemmie, the memory making him smile. Then Evie walked by, book and towel in hand, without glancing in his direction once.

'What de hell is wrong wid her?' he chuntered as his euphoria tarnished around the edges. PSV had started out as a really great idea, he'd thought, his crew full of mischief and determination, but somewhere along the way, the mood had turned sour, the women metamorphosing into grown-up, serious, charter passengers, their morning laughter and *joie de vivre* replaced by monosyllabic answers and quiet reflection. Shadrach was feeling confused, out of his depth and insecure. He adjusted the sails as the wind came onto the port bow and decided to concentrate on hand steering *Rum Punch* to take his mind off the atmosphere. 'Bleedin' women,' he muttered. 'Dere's no pleasin' 'em.'

Sam needed some thinking time. She'd had the fright of her life on PSV and now had to face the truth head on. If CJ had been in cottage eighteen her whole life would have been turned upside down. Even now she questioned whether her lover actually was in Alaska with his family.

What proof did she have after all? He could be anywhere he pleased, enjoying the delights of a replacement mistress . . . someone just like Jasmin Wong. As young as Jasmin Wong. Sam's stomach churned. It was time for damage limitation, she decided, and knew that the first thing she needed to do was to hire a lawyer. If it came to a fight, she must know her rights. Her reflection in the cabin mirror looked newly determined.

Opening the top drawer of her dresser, she pulled out her Ray Bans and suntan lotion and made for the door, pushing the drawer closed with her hip as she went. It stuck halfway. Huffing, she dropped her stuff on the bed and put two hands to the problem but no amount of pressure would sort it out.

'This yacht is definitely past its sell-by date,' she grumbled as she opened her hatch, stuck her head out into the breeze and shouted to Shadrach.

'There's something wrong with my drawer.'

He stood up. 'What's wrong wid it?'

'I can't close it.'

'Can't it wait till Tyrell Bay?'

'No.'

With eyes closed he countered to ten, then he punched the auto-helm button, asked George to keep watch and went below.

'Here, let me try.' He eased Sam out of the way and tried pushing and pulling the drawer, with no success. Returning to the chart-table, he picked up a Maglite torch and checked the drawer's inside runners. All seemed to be in order. 'Maybe it's expanded wid de humidity.'

'Either that or I've got something jammed behind it.'

Shadrach pulled out the drawer and balanced it on Sam's knee, then shone the torch on the interior bulkhead and tutted. 'Dere's a piece o' batten hangin' down at de back.' He stretched in and wiggled it, looked up and saw the mirror move. 'Hold on, I'll get a screwdriver. We'll need to take de mirror off to screw de batten back in place.' He poked his head out of the hatch. 'George,is everytin' all right up dere?'

'Yes, Skip.'

'Keep your eye on dat freighter, he be headin' for Hillsborough so shout if he don't change course in de next three minutes.'

'Wilco.'

By now Terri was hovering in the corridor. Sam placed the drawer on her bed and held up the mirror as Shadrach undid the four screws holding it to the wall. He then took the weight at one side and together they lifted it onto the floor, propping it up against the drawer unit. As they looked up at the bulkhead Sam's hand shot to her mouth.

'What de devil!?' Shadrach shook his head, blinked and looked again.

Evie dropped down the cabin hatch onto the bed to see what all the fuss was about as Terri stood on tiptoe trying to peer over Shadrach's shoulder.

He'd expected to find a solid bulkhead behind the mirror but instead was met by the sight of a two foot by three-foot cavity packed full of black polythene packages. Sam's Saltwhistle Bay drinks mat was pressed to the surface of the right-hand package.

'Dear me,' said Evie.

Shadrach pulled the drink mat off the polythene and handed it to Sam.

'So that's where it went.'

'Would somebody mind telling me what's going on?' Terri was jumping up and down in the cabin doorway.

'Samanta has just discovered a secret hideaway inside her bulkhead,' announced Shadrach, eyes still fixed on the cavity.

'What's inside it?' demanded Terri.

'I've no idea,' replied Sam. 'Drugs, by the look of it.'

'Don't touch a thing until I've photographed it,' yelled Terri as she disappeared up the stairs.

'Does this lot belong to you, Captain?' demanded Evie, in a hostile tone.

Shadrach leant against the opposite bulkhead, allowing Terri to squeeze past and aim her camera lens at the recess. 'Does I look like a drug dealer, Evie?'

'How would I know? But you are the owner.'

His eyes dropped to his feet and he clenched his fists. 'Dis lot don't belong to me, Miss Evie, but I've a pretty good idea who de owner is.'

'Skip,' shouted George, 'the freighter still hasn't change course.'

Shadrach elbowed Terri out of his way and stormed off, leaving Evie wilting under the scowls of her friends.

'Don't make me feel bad. A few days ago you were all convinced that's exactly what he was.'

George poked her head into the hatch. 'Was what?'

'A drug dealer.'

'Christ, what have I missed?'

'This,' said Sam, pointing to the stash of contraband.

'Bloody hell. Is that Shadrach's?'

'Hardly,' said Sam. 'If this lot were his, the last thing he'd do is expose it.'

'She's got a point, Evie.' Terri dropped her camera strap over her head. 'I know it doesn't make sense but he's got to be telling the truth.'

'Not necessarily,' said Evie, her words dripping with acid.

'Well, we'd better find out what the truth is before we're all arrested.' George jumped onto the bed and headed for the saloon.

'Would you stop doing that!' demanded Sam, pushing the batten back into place.

'Pass me the screwdriver, Evie.'

'What for?'

'I'm going to check what's behind my mirror,' said Terri, and left.

Sam appeared at the helm with an open black package in her hand.

'They're not drugs, Shadrach. They're US dollars. Thousands of US dollars. And Terri has found a similar stash behind her mirror.'

Shadrach lifted his sunglasses and took the package out of her hand, dragging his thumb across the edge of the wad. 'Well now, ain't dat a surprise? Perhaps I should do a runner and go live in South America.' He pointed to the gap between Point Cistern and the Sister Rocks and aimed *Rum Punch*'s bow at the middle of it. 'Let's get settled in Carriacou then we can discuss what I should do.'

Forty minutes later they were anchored in Tyrell Bay, all sitting in the saloon, packs of high-denomination US dollars piled on the table, Terri's camera battery on charge and no one wanting to be the first to open the conversation. Finally Terri took the lead.

'Shadrach, you said earlier that you thought you knew who owned this lot.'

He sat at the chart-table, tapping the chart-plotter with his dividers, trying to find the right words and ending in a cul-de-sac of indecision. Whatever he said, it was not going to go down well. He scratched his head with the point of the dividers, walked across to the galley, and seemed to come to a decision.

'*Rum Punch* ain't de yacht's original name.' Having started, it became easier to carry on. 'Her original name was *Rum Runner* and until last year she was bein' used by a drug cartel based outta Trinidad, shippin' drugs up to de US Virgin Islands. De first time I sees her was in English Harbour . . .'

Minutes ticked by, the A-team hanging on their skipper's every word.

'. . . When Hurricane Lenny hit Antigua, *Rum Runner* sank in tree metres of water, blockin' de fairway in de lagoon. Dey all said she was a write-off but I knew different.' He rubbed his hand along the galley surface in a caress. 'After a lotta arguin' de boatyard pumped her out and moved her outta de way, dumping her amongst de mangroves where she was abandoned.' Shadrach wandered back to the chart-table and sat down, twisting a pencil between his fingers, while the A-team sat on the edge of their seats.

'I offered one hundred US dollars to take her off everyone's hands on de understandin' dat de boatyard lifted her out onto de hard for free. It was a no-brainer. De boatyard tought I was nuts but de Customs, dey had de drugs, de crew were banged up in jail, and as no one had a clue who de owners were, dey decided to take me money and signed her off as scrap.'

'What did you do then?' Terri slid onto the floor, legs crossed.

'De first ting I did was change her name to *Rum Punch*. Den I spent me spare time and all me life savin's makin' her seaworthy before launchin' her in June dis year. I handed in me notice at de boatyard, did a two-week shake-down cruise to Grenada, and arrived in Prickly Bay needin' to find work. Dat's when de manager of Blue Lagoon Caribbean Cruises approached me.' His eyes found Terri's. 'De rest is history.'

'Why you?' asked Sam, the tension in the cabin mounting.

'One o' dere catamarans had hit a reef off Canouan and was holed. She will be out otta action for de rest of de season and dey had charter commitments to fulfil.'

'Like us.'

Shadrach looked suitably embarrassed.

'I'm gonna kill that Adrian Falks when we get back to England,' announced George, pacing the saloon floor. 'And as for you, Shadrach Bligh, there's the little matter of misrepresentation.'

'What?'

'You should have told us the truth.'

'But I just have.'

'A bit late in the day wouldn't you say? We could have drowned out there if this tub had sunk.'

Shadrach was also on his feet. 'She ain't a tub!'

'That's your opinion. Personally I think she's falling apart. However, right now we could end up in jail for carting black money around the Caribbean.' George picked up a packet of dollars and aimed it at Shadrach's chest. 'And I'm bloody sure the British Consulate wouldn't bend over backwards to get us out in these circumstances.'

He plucked it from the air and dropped it back on the pile. 'You tink *you* got problems? Wid my past I could be banged up for years wid no parole.'

'So you did go to jail?' Evie accused him. 'Another one of your little lies.'

'What did you go down for?' asked Sam.

'I ain't told any lies and I didn't go down for nuttin',' he shouted, hackles rising. D'you tink the Po'lice here are gonna take my word as gospel?'

They were ganging up on him like a pack of wolves. He was cornered and came out fighting. 'What about you lot? Yous ain't so bleedin' honest? Dis holiday was wangled on a pack o' lies and as for you, missy,' he turned on Evie, 'all you wanted dis mornin' was de free use of dat health spa to impress your friends. Pulled de wool right over me friend Clemmie's eyes, didn't you?'

'She's more than a friend,' said Evie, her lip curled. 'That's another of your lies.'

'No, she ain't.'

'Yes, she is. I saw you both disappearing into her room for . . . what did you call it? . . . a quickie.'

'What?' said Terri, looking from one to the other of them sharply.

Shadrach burst out laughing, the sound raucous. 'Is dat why you been so miffed, missy. Jealousy, is it? Tought I was screwin' our Clemmie, did ya? Well, you be wrong, girl. She was givin' me a shoulder massage for me spondylosis. I've suffered wid it for years and sleepin' on dat bleedin' roof ain't helped.'

'Leave Evie out of this!' shouted George. 'If you'd been honest with us in the beginning you wouldn't have had to give up your cabin because we'd have told you what to do with your damned heap of salvage.' She was now eyeball-to-eyeball with Shadrach, resembling Medusa on steroids. 'You, matey, are nothing but a chancer, out to get whatever you can for yourself, and I'm not sure I believe a word you've just told us.'

'For Christ's sake, shut it!' yelled Terri, jumping to her feet. 'Screaming at each other isn't going to sort out this mess.' She glared at them all, daring them to utter another word. 'Right, let's get back to the matter in hand.' She picked up a pack of dollars. 'I assume, Shadrach, you think this lot belongs to that drug cartel.'

He nodded.

'Then why didn't Customs find it in Antigua when they had possession of the yacht?'

His sighed. 'I don't know, Terri. De same reason I never discovered it, I presume. Customs found drugs in de bilge and must 'ave assumed dey'd got everytin'.'

'And assuming you're telling the truth, what do we do now?'

'Throw the bloody lot overboard,' demanded George.

'What, here in the anchorage? Don't be stupid, Georgina,' snapped Sam.'

'Jesus, will you all stop having a go at each other?' Terri went to the chart-table and examined the chart. 'If we could find something heavy to weigh it down, we could drop it all overboard off this place "Kicking Jenny", and no one would be any the wiser.' Her finger rested on a spot off the north-west corner of Grenada.

'Planning to destroy de evidence, Miss Teresa?' Shadrach's voice was full of reproach. 'Dat's a great way to look guilty.'

She turned her head, stung by the reproof. 'Well, it's better than being caught red-handed, isn't it?'

'Maybe, but if I contacted Customs in Antigua I could tell dem what happened. Dey know *Rum Runners*'s history and, as sure as me mudder is a Baptist, dey won't want egg on dere faces.'

'But how do we do that on VHF without everyone hearing us?'

Shadrach walked over to Terri and placed his hands on her shoulders. 'We don't, missy. The signal wouldn't reach Antigua from here anyway. I need to check us into Grenada here in Carriacou, so I could telephone English Harbour while I'm in town. Wid luck, dey will notify de local Coastguard who will take de bleedin' money off our hands, leavin' us free to reach our intended destination. I assume dat's what yous all be wantin', now?'

'Too right,' said George.

'I agree,' added Sam.

'The sooner the better so far as I'm concerned,' announced Evie.

Each statement twisted the knife further into Shadrach's guts. He searched Terri's face, hoping for a glimmer of friendship.

'Well, I guess I'm out-voted,' was all she said. 'Let's hope Antigua carries some clout down here.' She turned and began gathering the packages of dollar bills together. 'If not, we'll be spending the night in Carriacou's police cell.'

Chapter Twenty-Four

Double Trouble!

The whole evening had been a disaster. Shadrach hadn't been able to contact Antigua because the Customs Office there was closed. He'd spoken to his old boss at the boatyard who had promised to relay his message when they opened the next morning and he'd returned to the Yacht Club to face another diatribe from George, who was convinced he was bluffing and had other plans for the money.

Sam spent her time on the club's computer, searching for a family lawyer in London whom she could meet the moment she got back to Knightsbridge. Evie only spoke when spoken to and hitched a ride back to the yacht with some other cruisers immediately after dinner while Terri spent the time having a one-way conversation with the dining table or trying to keep the peace. Added to this, she was convinced her barbecued jerk chicken was attacking her stomach lining, horrible rumbling noises coming from it ever more frequently.

She climbed into the dinghy still unsure what to believe. Having spent her private life mixing with male waifs and strays who ate her out of house and home then buggered off, Terri had to admit, she was no judge of character.

Nor did she know what to do about Cyril Trowbridge. Blackmail was not an option, she decided, but if she was to face disciplinary action when she returned to the office, then the

Chairman was going to feel the full force of her wrath, somehow.

It was all one big mess, and like Humpty Dumpty, Terri had no idea how to put it all back together again. 'God, I wish I'd never won this damned holiday,' she mumbled under her breath as she picked out *Rum Punch*'s little twelve-volt anchor light at the outer reaches of the anchorage, guiding them home.

The moon was casting a ghostly glow over the bay, the outlines of the other vessels barely visible, only their masthead lights and the odd garden solar light indicating their location. *Rum Punch*'s dinghy passed them in silence, the two-point-five horsepower engine chugging along at walking pace. As they rounded the stern of a powerboat the breeze came in and *Rum Punch*'s bow swung towards them.

'Christ, what's that?' said Terri, pointing ahead. No one spoke. She stood up to get a better view.

'Sit down, you nutter, or we'll all be in the drink.'

'But, George, look. There's a pirogue attached to our bow.'

Shadrach immediately cut the engine, grabbed the two oars from under his feet and turned the dinghy one hundred and eighty degrees so he could get a better view.

They were all now alert and Terri's stomach chose that moment to rumble alarmingly. She clenched her buttocks, crossed her fingers and hung onto the dinghy grabrail, trying to ignore her innards. Shadrach slowly rowed towards the catamaran keeping well in shadow and heading for the bow. There it was, the white flash on both sides of the bow illuminated in the moonlight.

'See, I told you,' Terri whispered to the others. 'I *said* they were up to no good.'

'Shush,' muttered Shadrach. 'Whoever dey are, dey could be armed.'

'Dear God,' whispered Sam, her hand shaking against her mouth.

'I want you all to stay put. I'm going to climb onto de foredeck to see what's happenin'.' With that Shadrach hauled himself up. They watched him swing his legs over the trampoline netting and land flat on his stomach, crawling crablike towards the saloon window, while the A-team walked the dinghy between the twin hulls, ducking almost to the floor as they made their way under the yacht and came out at the stern. Terri's heart was playing catch-up with her stomach as she slipped the dinghy rope around the starboard cleat and went to step out.

'Stay here,' demanded George, hanging onto her trousers.

'Sod off.' Terri pulled her hand away, crept up the steps and peered carefully over the stern coaming. What she saw made her blood run cold.

Evie was crumpled on the saloon settee, knees bent, ankles tied together. Her arms were secured behind her back and what looked like a tea towel had been rammed between her teeth and tied behind her head.

Terri's body took off across the stern deck like Boudicca saving the Iceni, her Gillingham temper in full flood. The cabin door slid open. Evie's head snapped up, the whites of her eyes protruding from their sockets glaring at the port staircase.

Terri didn't need telling twice. Grabbing the BCF
extinguisher from the galley bulkhead and breaking the seal, she
took the stairs in one jump, turned into Sam's cabin doorway
and aimed the contents at a stranger, bent double, who was
dragging all Sam's beautiful lingerie from a drawer and tossing
it on the floor. He sprang up and the nozzle got him straight
between the eyes, his head and upper body rapidly enveloped in
a mist of expanding chemical spray.

He screamed, then choked, the foam reaching his tonsils as
his aggressor swung the fire extinguisher with maximum force
and smacked him under the chin with the metal casing. He
went backwards onto Sam's mirror, lying discarded on the bed.
It shattered on impact, shards of glass burying themselves in
every soft surface they touched and the would-be thief lay
pinned to the bed looking like a bloated marshmallow.

'Christ, I've killed him!' Terri yelled, and promptly dropped
the extinguisher on her big toe.

Shadrach had watched in horror as Terri rose above the stern
coaming then raced across the deck and dragged back the
sliding door.

'Nooo!' he'd choked, crabbing along the gunwhale and leaping
round the helm in an effort to stop her, landing seconds too
late.

Evie watched him crawl into the saloon and nodded her head
violently to starboard as Terri disappeared down the port steps,
leaving Shadrach in a quandary as to what to do first. Evie
looked desperate, eyes out on stalks, shoulders heaving as she

tried grunting through the gag while jerking her chin towards the other stairs.

A fire extinguisher went off, then Terri screamed at the top of her voice: 'Take that, you bastard!' followed by a crunching whack. Shadrach grabbed his heavy-duty spotlight from under the chart-table to use as a weapon, jumped into the starboard stairwell and hit his nose on Terri's cabin door as it slammed shut in his face.

'Gottcha, mon,' he shouted as he braced himself with his arms against the bulkheads, flexed his right leg and concertinaed the door off its hinges. A stranger balanced on the bed, the blue duct-taped hatch above him partially open, his head and shoulders rammed between the plexiglass and broken bin bag, straining to gain momentum. Shadrach dropped the lamp, grabbed the intruder's legs and dragged him bodily back down. He turned the man over, leapt on top, pinned him to the mattress and laid him out cold with a boxer's upper cut. Shaking his hand, Shadrach gingerly stretched his fingers as the joints cracked and blood seeped from his knuckles.

The room was a mess, clothes, shoes and toiletries scattered everywhere, the mirror propped up against the wardrobe, an empty cavity gaping in the wooden bulkhead like a toothless mouth. Shadrach heaved the still figure into a fireman's lift and carried him into the saloon as George and Sam came through the door. He dropped his load on the floor like a sack of coal and rushed to the port side, shouting, 'Tie him up.'

Coming to a sudden stop, he took in the chaos in Sam's cabin and felt his adrenalin level go into reverse. Gently, he turned Terri away from the prostrate body splayed out on the bed and wrapped her in his arms.

'It's OK, hon, it's over. You did good.'

She lost the use of her legs and slid between his arms, coming to rest in a heap on the floor, coughing toxic fumes from her lungs. Sam's words came back to him.

'The area must be ventilated as soon as possible after use.'

He placed his arms under Terri's armpits and knees and carried her bodily onto the stern deck, lowered her to the bench seat and went to open the starboard forward hatch as she took deep gasps of fresh air, coughing and spluttering between breaths.

'Sam,' he shouted from the bow, 'I'm gonna need your help.'

Sam looked up, having just freed Evie from her restraints. 'Can't it wait?' she called back.

'No,' came the reply. She turned to Evie. 'I'll get you a brandy in a minute. Are you alright?'

Evie nodded, rubbing her neck, the welts on her wrists beginning to swell.

'Dunk those in cold water while I go and see what Shadrach wants.'

Sam passed George finishing some Girl Guide knots on one prisoner. He lay on his stomach with his wrists and ankles tied securely together with webbing tape. Sam could see that Terri was suffering from the effects of chemical poisoning. 'George, get Terri some water and a cold flannel.' Shadrach, meanwhile, was bending over the starboard hatch and Sam went forward to join him. 'What's up?'

'That,' he said and pointed into Terri's cabin.

The lining of Terri's bronchial tubes felt like burning polystyrene and her eyes were raw. George pushed a wet flannel at her, the cool surface soothing the mess that was her face.

'Jesus . . .' cough '. . . this reminds me of Manston Airport . . .' cough '. . . during Beagle Air's fire drill.' Gasp.

'Take slow deep breaths and drink this.' George handed her a glass of water.

'Have I killed him?'

'No idea. Sam and Shadrach are dealing with him now.'

'It was that damn' mirror . . . He annihilated it as he fell backwards . . . His back must be peppered with glass . . . to say nothing of a broken jaw.'

'Stop trying to talk and drink.'

'But . . .'

'No buts. Drink. Evie can I get you anything?'

'How is she?' Terri came out from under the flannel. 'I nearly died on the spot when I saw her trussed up like some kidnap . . .' wheeze '. . . victim.'

'What you did was go ballistic,' croaked Evie, standing by the sink, her hands and wrists plunged into a bowl of water. 'I've never seen you move so fast.'

'How long had you been like that?'

'Will you stop asking questions and drink?' George took charge.

'We're gonna leave Tyrell Bay, now,' announced Shadrach as he preceded Sam onto the stern deck.

'Eh?' croaked Evie.

'There may be more of them out there.' He jerked his thumb at the anchorage. 'I needs some sea room to sort dis lot out and question dose thugs. Evie, how is you doin'?'

A tear ran down her cheek.

'Go and lie down on de settee while George and I haul de anchor up and get us on our way. Sam, you need to tie up the Abominable Snowman down there before he comes round, though I don't tink he'll be goin' anywhere wid his injuries.'

'You mean, he's not dead?' Terri asked.

'His chest was movin' when I left a minute ago, but he'll need dental treatment if he ever makes it to shore.'

A shiver ran down her spine. 'Is there much blood?'

'A bit like an abattoir,' said Shadrach as Terri grabbed her stomach and rushed to the starboard head.

Rum Punch motored along in the moonlight heading south, the dinghy and pirogue bouncing around in her wake.

Sam picked glass out of her patient's bloodied polo shirt with a pair of tweezers while he lay alongside his accomplice in the saloon, arms hugging the table pedestal, his wrists and ankles separately secured with electrical ties.

Both thugs were now awake and both groaning from their injuries with Evie keeping watch over them, sitting curled up on the settee, a large brandy goblet in her hand and murder in her eyes.

Terri went to inspect the crime scene which was Sam's cabin and found George wiping down the bulkheads with a sponge.

'There's no way Sam can sleep on that mattress, George,' she said, gobbets of blood and glass shards still glittering from the cabin wall light.

'True, but I need to do something. My nerve-endings are jangling.'

'I know what you mean. Who the hell are these two?'

'Search me, but from the look on Shadrach's face when he carried you through the saloon, I don't think it'll be long before we find out.'

'GEORGE!' called Shadrach from the helm. They both came on deck as he throttled back. 'Right, I'm goin to take dere pirogue and tie it to dem rocks over dere.'

They looked at the outline of the jagged islet, not a building in sight.

'Terri, are you up to helpin' me?'

She nodded, not sure what he expected her to do. 'Good. Now, George, keep *Rum Punch* slowly goin' round in circles and watch your depth. We be in ten metres here so don't wander too close in, dere's a reef off to port.'

George threw the sponge on the stern deck table and plonked her derrière onto the helm seat as Shadrach beckoned Terri to the stern steps. 'I plan to tow de pirogue into dat islet using our dinghy.' She could hardly see it. 'When we get dere I wants you to stay with de dinghy and keep her off de rocks. Once the pirogue is secure, I'll swim back to yous. Here, take dis head torch, and, Terri . . .'

She watched him untie the pirogue and jump into the dinghy, tying the wooden boat to the grabrail. 'What?'

'. . . you was amazin' back dere.'

Terri was still suffering from shock and just shrugged.
'I mean it, hon. You was sometin' else.'

So there she sat, alone in the dinghy in the shadow of some
rocks called Frigate Island, looking like a Yorkshire coalminer
with a head torch plastered to her forehead. It was pitch black
and eerie all around, Shadrach having disappeared in the
pirogue minutes earlier and the hull of *Rum Punch* lying way off,
hidden in the darkness. 'What the hell am I doing here?' she
asked the night and got no response.

Time dragged and the silence began to get to her so she
started to hum 'Amazing Grace'. It seemed to steady her nerves
until grannie decided to put in her half-penny's worth.

*'Well, Teresa Gillingham, so much for your Caribbean cruise. Next
time you think of texting True Life Movies, go put your head in a bucket .
. . assuming you ever get out of this alive!'*

Terri clamped her jaws shut and mentally told her grannie
what she could do with her bucket then went back to
humming, hoping that she wasn't drifting too far out to sea.
'Come on, Shadrach,' she begged, rubbing her hands against
her upper arms to try and keep the circulation going, 'get a
move on before I end up in Nicaragua.'

The minutes ticked by and she began mentally to write her
last will and testament when the sea to her right suddenly
erupted and two wrinkled hands clawed themselves round the
rope handle. Terri nearly jumped out of her skin.

'It's only me,' gasped Shadrach, pulling himself into the Rib
and wetting her through in the process.

Relief turned to anger as cold water sloshed down Terri's neck. 'If you soak me one more time on this trip, Shadrach Johnathan William Bligh, I'm going to sue you for . . .'

Her words were smothered in the longest kiss since Burt Lancaster smooched Deborah Kerr on a beach in *From Here to Eternity*. Strong hands were holding both sides of her head as warm, soft lips pressed lovingly against her own, the electrical impulse between their mouths making the earth move. Terri closed her eyes, leant into the most protective embrace she'd ever experienced and put her life on hold. Grannie, meanwhile, was leaping about her cloud doing a highland jig as her granddaughter refused to come up for air.

Eventually the pair parted. 'Oooh!' Terri spluttered, grabbing lungful's of ozone. 'What was that for?'

'Nuttin',' replied Shadrach, then started the outboard, sat on the coaming and carried her out to sea.

Back on deck, they secured the engine back onto its mounting and towed the dinghy as before. With George acting as First Mate, *Rum Punch* sailed west into the night under a heavily reefed mainsail and genoa, going nowhere in particular, as Terri mentally tossed the world's frogs into the Caribbean Sea.

'Did you bring back dem leftovers from tonight's barbecue for young Geordie?'

Shadrach's 'business as usual' voice brought her down to earth with a bang. How do men do this? she thought, trying to remember about the scraps. 'They must still be in the dinghy.'

Shadrach hauled on the rope, stretched down into the Rib and extracted a plastic bag from the bow. 'Yeah, they's here.'

'Why?' she asked, still not firing on all cylinders.

'You'll see.' He said, and winked.

Now, *he's* definitely not a frog, she thought, and placed the plastic bag in the sink.

'You seem to have a better colour, Terri.' Sam was examining her face in a professional way.

'Must be the sea air,' Terri replied, and went to hide her blushes in the starboard head.

Rum Punch was ten miles offshore as dawn lightened the horizon and Shadrach turned into wind to stow the sails.

Sam had finished her Florence Nightingale ministrations and was sitting on the foredeck staring out to sea. George and Terri had made some progress on Sam's cabin and Evie was still sitting guard on the settee, a large sheath knife in her hand taken from the big thug's pocket earlier.

He had a swollen jaw from Shadrach's upper cut while the other man had minor lacerations all over his back, his jaw was broken and he had lost four front teeth. He looked like a Caribbean version of Quasimodo and spent the journey spitting blood onto a towel laid below his chin.

They had stopped sailing and were bobbing on the morning waves, drifting very slightly westward. Shadrach came into the saloon, took an electrical tie from the pack lying on the table, told George to untie the webbing securing the thugs wrists and ankles together and re-secured his hands behind his back, pulling the plastic unnecessarily tight. The thug banged his head on the underside of the table.

'I know how dat feels, mon,' said Shadrach, dragging his charge out to the rail. 'Terri, get the bait.'

She hadn't got a clue what Shadrach had in mind and didn't like the sound of his voice.

'Now, you bleedin' terrorist, what I wants to know is who you be workin' for?' The thug spat in Shadrach's face and got belted across the cheek in return. He spun with the blow and toppled headfirst over the rail, his centre of gravity only checked by Shadrach's powerful grip on his trousers. 'Well den, I guess yous be goin for a swim wid dem sharks. 'Terri, de bait.'

She threw some scraps over the side and waited. Come on, Geordie, she prayed, don't abandon us now.

Shadrach pushed the West Indian further out over the water, his knees catching on the rail, blood dripping into the sea from where he'd bitten his tongue and strong hands around his ankles, checking his fall. Suddenly the water below bubbled, a fin cut the surface and a tail flicked backwards and forwards as the underwater creature spun and dived for the food.

'Are yous gonna tell me who you be workin' for or do yous want to be fish food like dem scraps?'

Terri lobbed more of them into the sea and young Geordie did a great impression of shark-infested water.

'Bloody hell!' shouted George, pointing towards the stern.

Shadrach and Terri looked up and saw a large black fin cutting through the sea a hundred yards off, leaving a water trail similar to that of a jet engine in flight.

The thug saw it too and arched his back, desperate to get as far away from the waterline as possible.

'I'm waitin',' said Shadrach, his tone icy.

Terri's fingers were crossed behind her back as she imagined young Geordie being eaten by a real shark. 'Scoot, Geordie,' she whispered under her breath. 'Scoot!'

'El . . . Dia . . .'

'What?'

The fin was getting closer. 'Diablo! El Diablo!'

Terri scanned the water trying to see if Geordie was still there but the shadow from *Rum Punch* was hampering her view.

'His name. Give me his name.' Shadrach loosened his fingers and the thug dropped another few inches.

Terri gasped.

'For Christ's sake, mon, give him de name,' screamed George in his ear, 'before de bleedin' skipper kills you, eh?'

'Paco . . . Paco Segui,' he shouted. 'For de love o' God, mon. FRANCISCO SEGUI!'

'And where's dis Segui bloke based, den?'

'PUERTO RICO.'

Shadrach hauled the thug back on deck just as the black fin cruised by, a dark torpedo-shaped shadow moving west, close enough to touch. Terri shot into the saloon and retched into the sink. As she turned round she saw the other thug with his trousers around his ankles, Evie sliding the knife back into its sheath. 'It's OK, Evie,' she said, wiping her mouth on the back of her hand, 'Shadrach got it.'

'So did I,' croaked Evie, and climbed back onto the settee.

A dull thud echoed through the saloon as a limp body hit the window and slid down the plexiglass. Shadrach walked inside, rubbing his bloodied knuckles. 'That bastard won't be botherin' us again for a while.'

Chapter Twenty-Five

Prickly Bay

Rum Punch rounded the headland at Prickly Bay, Grenada in the late afternoon and anchored in six metres of water between a Moorings charter yacht and a gentleman's cruiser. It had been a long day and an even longer night.

The A-team looked as if they had participated in the twenty-four-hour endurance race at Le Mans, Shadrach had eyeballs the colour of Sandeman's Port and the prisoners resembled two of Muhammed Ali's more unfortunate opponents.

Sam looked worried, convinced that Terri and Evie were still in shock, her training in post-traumatic stress confirming her suspicions. They both need counselling, she thought, but had no idea how that could be arranged in Grenada. George appeared to be holding up well, but once they'd reached their destination she too had gone quiet and uncommunicative.

Sam pulled Shadrach to one side. 'I think I should get the others to a hotel where they can chill out, away from all of this.'

They both scanned *Rum Punch*'s interior which still looked a bit like a war zone.

'Dere's one in Mount Hartmann Bay just across de hill.'

'Will it be full at this time of year?'

'No idea. I don't do 'otels, but I'm sure de staff here will find out. Failin' dat, dere's always de Calabash. It has a good reputation but could be a bit on de expensive side.'

'Do they have internet?'

'What, de Calabash?'

'No, this marina.'

'Dey 'ave tree computers in an office behind de Tiki bar.'

'Great. Can you take me ashore? I need to check my emails.'

'Sure ting, but can we wait until de Coastguard get 'ere?'

Sam could understand Shadrach's dilemma. 'Of course. When do you expect them?'

'In de next half hour. Dey knows where we are 'cos I spoke to dem on VHF. I don't tink dey'll leave us stewin' for long wid so much cash on board.'

Sam wandered onto the deck to find the rest of the A-team sitting around the stern table, each with a Mojito to hand.

'Should you lot be drinking under the circumstances?' she chided.

'What else would we do?' argued Evie, and downed a large gulp of minted cocktail.

'Cut the Mother Hen impression, Sam, and grab yourself a glass,' said George, holding up a jug of alcohol. 'We're at journey's end. We should be celebrating.'

Terri looked completely washed out. 'I think I'll go for a swim.'

'Is that wise?' Sam couldn't help herself from saying.

'I want to see if young Geordie's alright.'

'Fine. I'm coming with you then.'

They lowered themselves into Prickly Bay and swam under the hull. Young Geordie was nowhere to be seen. Terri hung off the port step and pressed her forehead against the cold steel. 'I bloody knew that shark had got him! Why did he have to die?'

'You don't know that,' Sam argued, trying to comfort her friend, but she'd also grown fond of the Remora and the thought that it had been eaten pricked her conscience too. 'I think we all need a break from this yacht,' she suggested, and waited for a response.

Terri just sank between the wavelets, surfaced and started her fifty laps of the yacht.

'Terri, are you listening to me?'

The reply was lost in a splash of kicking feet as Terri headed for the bow.

'Jesus!' said Sam, and climbed out.

The A-team watched the Coastguard vessel scream into the bay, a replica of the one in St Vincent. It slowed, the bow wave instantly dropping as it motored slowly past the other boats and hovered at *Rum Punch*'s side.

Shadrach waited to take their lines, fully dressed for the first time in two weeks. He nodded to the captain then frowned as two heavily built guys in casual attire and baseball hats appeared from the cabin and stood alongside a Grenadian police officer, obviously waiting to board. Moving to the stern, Shadrach tied their rear line to the catamaran's cleat and whispered to the others out of the corner of his mouth, 'I's seen dese two landin' at de airport in Union when I was clearin' out.'

The local police officer was the first to board. He shook hands with Shadrach and moved on deck. The other two waited for an invitation so Shadrach nodded to them, gestured with his hand and they both came over the guardrail in tandem.

Rum Punch's crew stood by the helm waiting for the visitors to join them.

'Good evening, ladies. It seems you've 'ad an exciting trip,' commented the police officer.

'You could say that,' said George, stepping forward and shaking hands. 'Georgina Stanhope.'

Terri, Sam and Evie did likewise, leaving Shadrach till last.

'Shadrach Jonathon William Bligh at your service, gentlemen.

'Officer Colin Burroughs,' said one of the casual duo in a Texan drawl that sounded doubly out of place after two weeks of island patois. 'Officer Jose Rodriguez and I are from the DEA and are here to take possession of the haul.

'DEA?' queried Evie.

'Drug Enforcement Agency, ma'am. We help the Eastern Caribbean police departments investigate drug smuggling between South America and the States.' He turned to Shadrach. 'Captain Bligh, we have the full report on this vessel from Customs in Antigua.'

Shadrach visibly relaxed. 'Well, officer, we got a bit more to dat haul since yesterday.' He slid the saloon door open.

The police officer went first, stopping in his tracks as he saw the thugs tied together in the starboard stairwell. 'Well now, what do we 'ave 'ere?'

Officer Burroughs pulled a pair of handcuffs from his back pocket and descended the stairs. 'Captain, perhaps you'd tell us where these two came from.'

'Dey boarded *Rum Punch* in Tyrell Bay last night, but we was able to overpower dem.'

'We?'

'Yes, sir, Miss Gillingham and me.'

'Good Lord,' said Officer Rodriquez, taking the sheath knife from Evie. 'You should be working for the DEA.'

'Dere pirogue,' continued Shadrach, 'is safely tied to rocks on an islet close to de south of Carriacou. I 'ave de co-ordinates for you.' He stretched across to the chart-table and handed Officer Rodriquez a piece of paper.

Burroughs took another set of handcuffs from his partner, looked at the co-ordinates and shook his head. 'Amazing.'

'What will happen to these two once you have them in custody?' asked Sam.

'They'll be interrogated, ma'am. We need to know who they're working for and we'll do our best to get it out of them.'

'As it happens, Officer, that won't be necessary.' Terri nodded to Shadrach to do the honours.

'And why's dat, missy?' enquired the policeman as Officer Burroughs pushed the two West Indians up the stairs.

'Because,' said Shadrach, 'I used a bit of me own interrogation in de middle o' de night and found out dat dere boss is some bloke called El Diablo.'

'You definitely should be working for the DEA,' laughed Rodriquez, taking hold of the smaller thug.

'We understand El Diablo's real name is Francisco Segui,' added Terri, 'from Puerto Rico.'

'We know who he is, ma'am, he's been on our Most Wanted list for years.'

'Then you'd better hurry up or you'll miss him,' announced
Evie from the saloon door. She had everyone's immediate
attention. 'Because he's just leaving.'

'He's what?' demanded Officer Burroughs, barging past
everyone to see what she was pointing at.

'You heard me. He's on that big ketch moving out of
Prickly Bay right now. The one called *Southern Cross*.'

The four officials and their prisoners were on the deck, across
the guardrail and calling for their ropes before the rest of the A-
team had registered what Evie had said. Shadrach threw the
stern rope to a member of the crew as their powerful engines
churned the water. The bow moved ahead, its rope released
from *Rum Punch*'s cleat by another uniformed crew member,
who vaulted the catamaran's rail dragging the trailing line
behind him.

'We'll be back for the cash just as soon as we've
apprehended El Diablo,' shouted Officer Rodriquez. 'I assume
it's still safe?'

Four heads nodded, their eyes rising to a point at the top of
the mast.

'What in God's name is dat?' called out the Grenadian.

'Shadrach's guitar case stuffed full of dollars,' shouted back
George. 'Evie lashed it up there for safe-keeping.'

'Den I suggest Evie brings it down again while we're away.'
The Coastguard vessel veered to port, described a semi-circle in
the anchorage and charged, full bore, for open water.

'EVIE!' shouted the rest of the A-team in unison.

'What?' she replied, coming out onto the deck.

Three hands lifted into the air, index fingers pointing to the mast head.

'Oh, no, not me again.'

They all shrugged, including Shadrach.

'Fine, but let's get this straight. This is the last time I'm shinning up that damn' mainsail rope, circus or no circus.' She stormed to the base of the mast and grabbed the red halyard. 'As for you, Shadrach Bligh, you owe me, BIG TIME!'

With El Diablo, Dale and the Irish leprechaun clapped in irons and *Southern Cross* impounded, the officials returned.

'If you've got nuttin' better to do wid dat Jongert,' suggested Shadrach, 'I'd be happy to take 'er off your 'ands.'

'Nothing would give me greater pleasure,' said Burroughs as he opened the lid of the guitar case sitting on the saloon table and exposed a stack of black plastic packets, the top one open to expose a wad of large-denomination dollar bills.' He whistled. 'Unfortunately, it's not my decision but I'll be sure to keep you posted when she comes up for auction.'

'So that's what you do with all the confiscated booty,' said Sam, handing out glasses of iced Coca-cola to their visitors. 'How much did you get for the cocaine?' The air instantly chilled. 'Joke,' she said hurriedly. 'Obviously you Americans don't share our British sense of humour.'

Shadrach struggled to keep a straight face. 'We expect yous to count all dis on board and den give us a receipt,' he said, pointing to the stash, his implied distrust not lost on the officers.

'Oh, we know how much is here,' replied Rodriquez.

'Really. How's that then?' George stood by the stairs, arms crossed.

'Because we were the ones who planted it in the first place.'

'You's gotta be jokin'?' Shadrach's eyes narrowed to slits.

'Well, we didn't actually plant it here but we knew it was still on board when Customs in Antigua sent us their inventory, which only listed the cocaine.'

'Den where did you plant it?'

'With the cartel in Trinidad.'

'That's friendly.' Shadrach shoved the guitar case against Burroughs's knees. 'So, why didn't you tell Antigua about this?'

The officer shoved it back and rubbed his kneecaps. 'It seemed a good way of luring the drug cartel out into the open when we let slip in certain quarters that no money had been found on *Rum Runner*.'

'Lordie, Lordie. So me and *Rum Punch*, we was used as your bait?'

'You bastards,' spat George. 'What would have happened if we'd been murdered in our sleep?'

Burroughs reclined back in his seat, oozing confidence. 'Unlikely, ma'am. We had you under constant surveillance.'

'Oh, really? Where from . . . a bloody submarine.'

'No, ma'am, our eye in the sky.' He looked smug.

'Then why didn't you see those jokers coming aboard last night?' Terri's temper too was beginning to flair.

'That's something we're investigating right now, ma'am. My boss will want answers to that.'

'*I* want bloody answers,' screamed George. 'Who the hell d'you think we are, *NCIS Miami*?'

'Please, ma'am, we fully recognise the danger you were in and the US Government is truly grateful for everything you've done.'

'Put your money where your mouth is, sonny. If you don't want an international incident then this is definitely gonna cost you.'

'How much is in this stash anyway?' asked Sam.

'Ten thousand bucks short of four million,' said Rodriquez nonchalantly.

'What happened to the other ten thousand?'

'Expenses, ma'am.'

'Fine, then you keep another ten thousand for your time today and we'll take the rest as blood money.' George stormed out of the saloon leaving a yawning silence.

Evie coughed to gain attention. 'What will happen to the crew of *Southern Cross*?' Sam looked at Terri who looked at Shadrach.

'We'll be shipping them back to the States to stand trial. From what you've told us, we assume they were keeping tabs on *Rum Punch* and informing their boss of your movements.'

Evie grabbed the edge of the sink for support. 'Why are you so sure they're involved?'

'They have form, ma'am. That Dale fella is actually a South African gun runner and we know that the Irish . . .'

'Leprechaun,' cut in Terri.

'. . . First Mate has links to the IRA.'

'I bloody knew it,' declared Terri.

Burroughs decided to change the subject. 'Perhaps you'd tell us how you got the burglars to talk.'

'Yes, Evie.' Shadrach turned to face her rubbing his chin. 'How did you get that loser to tell you El Diablo was on *Southern Cross*?'

'Simple, Skip. I used a well-known Mafia technique.' She paused. 'I gave him two choices. He could either keep his balls or become one of the Castrati.'

Burroughs crossed his legs.

'She's half Italian, you see,' explained Terri, putting a loving arm around her friend, 'and lethal with a knife.'

'Bleedin' man-eaters,' muttered Shadrach, and took the receipt Officer Rodriquez had written out.

'If dere's nuttin' else, gentlemen, we 'ave some clearin' up to do around 'ere. After dat, I's gonna take my crew out to dinner at dat fancy Calabash place in de bay and yous will be getting' de bill!' He stood by the saloon door as Burroughs picked up the guitar case and walked out. 'Oh, no, you don't, mon. Dat be my guitar case. You go find your own.'

Chapter Twenty-Six

Spice Island Blues

George was pacing around on the foredeck muttering to herself as the others waved away the stash of cash. She was beside herself with anger and wanted someone to feel the full force of her displeasure. Adrian Falks of Global Adventure Holidays neatly fitted the bill. She had been convinced for some time that he had ripped off *True Life Movies* by using Blue Lagoon Caribbean Cruises instead of a more professional and reputable charter company. The TV station probably believed that the lucky family of four were cruising the Caribbean on a flashy charter yacht with all the trimming and would certainly have been invoiced accordingly, a situation that was not uncommon in her industry.

After Shadrach's revelations and the events of the past night, George had had enough. Adrian Falks didn't know it yet, but Global Adventure Holidays were about to lose their lucrative TV contract to Prestige Travel.

'Skipper,' she shouted from the bow, 'I need to go ashore.'

While Sam and George sat in the marina office checking their emails, Terri and Evie were pulling their cases out of the deck locker ready to pack for the homeward journey. Terri stood in her cabin looking vacantly at her empty suitcase, clothes scattered across her bed like confetti. She could still feel the warmth of Shadrach's lips whenever her mind dwelt on the events of the previous night. She couldn't make up her mind if it had been an act of impetuosity on his part or whether he really did have designs on her. The latter thought made her skin tingle.

She picked up her creased and soiled Primark cheesecloth dress and laid it in the bottom of her case, recalling the night at Bang between the Pitons . . . remembering Shadrach's expression as the rain exposed her curves. She gave up on the packing, her whole being refusing to leave *Rum Punch*.

What she needed was a drink. Heading for the galley, all resolve gone, she passed the chart-table, hesitated, lifted the lid and rummaged around the navigation charts with her index finger. The wine-red cover of Shadrach's passport peeked out from under some Notices to Mariners. Before she could change her mind, she pocketed it, shot back into her cabin and closed the door. Seconds later she was examining the back page where, under the heading 'Emergencies', two names and addresses were written in Shadrach's spidery hand.

Mr and Mrs A L Bligh
Flat B, Bath House,
Bath Terrace,
Elephant and Castle,
Southwark,
London SE1
and
M F C Bligh LLB (Hons)
Flat 12, Grosvenor House,
Lisson Grove,
Marylebone

London NW8

If there's one thing I can do for Shadrach, she thought, Mount Gay rum now erased from her mind, it's to give him back his family's respect. She quickly noted down the details and picked up her copy of the *Caribbean Compass*, placing them both in the front compartment of her case. Poking her head around the cabin door, she tiptoed up the stairs and slipped the passport back under the charts, her action dislodging something stuck to the underside of the lid at the back. A photograph fell onto her hand. She turned it over, her eyes taking in the scene, and all her loving intentions of the past few minutes flew straight out of the saloon window.

From: cjSW1@hotmail.com
Subject: Hi from Alaska!
Hi lover,
Now back on dry land and able to get an email off to you. Nothing in my Inbox from you so assume you're sulking? Flying into Heathrow on 6th at 07.50 and will come straight to Pont Street for you know what! Trust you're missing me. Need to talk.
Much love CJ x

Sam re-read the bit about needing to talk and didn't like the sound of it at all. She deleted the email and moved on to the next.

To: Ms S Hutchins
From: Broadfield, Sampson & Tye Solicitors
Subject: Meeting

Dear Ms Hutchins,

Thank you for contacting BS&T Solicitors. One of our Senior Partners –
Mr Reginald Sampson - specialises in family law and will be delighted to
offer his expert advice regarding your query. Would 3 August at 11.30am
be convenient?
We look forward to receiving your confirmation in due course and to
meeting you here at our offices in High Holborn.
Kind regards
Pauline Fitzgerald
Partnership Administrator

Sam pressed 'Reply' and hit the keyboard without
hesitation.

To: Ms Pauline Fitzgerald
From: Ms S Hutchins
Subject: Appointment on 3 August
Dear Ms Fitzgerald,
3 August at 11.30am will be fine. I look forward to meeting Mr
Sampson. Should circumstances prevent me from attending this meeting I
will, of course, contact you further to rearrange.
Regards
Samantha Hutchins

George plonked herself down at the vacant computer
alongside and Sam quickly moved her solicitor's email and the
response into a sub-folder away from prying eyes.

'Any problems?' George nonchalantly asked as she logged
on.

'No, just the usual junk mail and confirmation of my next
dental appointment.'

'What, nothing from Charles?'

'No, I told you, he's on a ship and can't communicate. I'll probably get a text message when he lands at Heathrow.'

But George wasn't listening, Ralph's latest update from Prestige Travel now occupying her attention.

Hi Boss,

Not sure if you'll get this before flying back but your dad has cocked up our Sage accounts programme and I can't access any of our invoices. Rang the techno bloke who normally deals with this stuff but he's on holiday until the 5th. Made back-ups of all my stuff but not sure if Fran bothered. Too much on her mind . . .

By the way, she's produced a 9lb baby boy who they're calling Herbert!!!!! Minimum cost for flowers was £25. Went ahead anyway, hope that's alright.

P.S.: your dad insists he didn't do anything wrong and is convinced your Excel software programme is faulty. I'll leave you to deal with it when you get back.

P.P.S.: Janet at Holidays Are Us couldn't help out due to staff shortages. She wants to talk to you ASAP. Wouldn't say what it was about. Said it was personal.

Hope your holiday is going well. Don't forget, I leave for Cumbria, fell-walking for two weeks, immediately you get back.

Have a good one!

Ralph

'I'll bloody kill him,' muttered George under her breath.'

'Who?' asked Sam, signing out of Hotmail.

'My dad. He's apparently buggered up my accounting software. I tell you, Sam, I'll swing for him one of these days.'

Sam stood and patted her on the shoulder. 'You'll sort it, George, you always do. See you at the Tiki Bar.'

George grunted and typed Ralph a non-committal reply then did an internet search for the name and contact details of *True Life Movie's* Chief Executive Officer. Once found, she cupped her hands to her mouth, breathed hot air into her palms, rubbed her hands together and belted out a letter to a Mr Brendan O'Donnell, her fingers flashing across the keys.

In Evie's cabin all was not well. Clothes were being rammed into her silver Samsonite with total disregard for either care or order. Dirty shoes rubbed against delicate bras and salty bikinis mingled with freshly laundered knickers, each item pummelled mercilessly to make more room as she imagined doing the same thing to Dale's head.

She had done what she'd sworn she would never do. She had let her guard down and been kicked in the guts in exchange. What was worse, she now realised she had been used. Used and abused by a South African gun runner with a penchant for cocaine.

'You bloody idiot, Evangelina Shapiro. You bloody stupid idiot.' The bristles of her hairbrush made indentations in her white leather trousers as she sat on the suitcase lid and tried to fasten the clasps. Her beads got caught between the hinges as the full force of her bodyweight compressed the two sides together, snapping the nylon thread and jettisoning coloured balls all over the cabin floor. Evie dropped to her knees, head in hands, and let the floodgates open.

'Evie? Evie, open the door.' Terri could hear her friend wailing, her body acting as a mortice lock against Terri's attempts to gain access. Running up on deck, she flicked open the handles on Evie's hatch and landed, feet first, on the bed beneath, pain shooting through her left calf as a wooden bead buried itself in her instep.

'OW!'

Evie looked up, her face a crumpled mess.

'Oh, Evangelina.' Terri was quickly on her knees rocking Evie backwards and forwards like a mother cradling an injured child. 'Come on, love. He's not worth it. He's a con artist. He knew exactly what he was doing. You didn't stand a chance. He eyeballed you across the dance floor at Bang between the Pitons and homed in like a bloody mosquito.'

Her words only seemed to exacerbate the situation and Terri could have kicked herself for being so insensitive. 'Don't cry, lovey. In years to come you'll look back on this and be glad it was you who put him inside. He deserves all he gets.'

'Yes . . .but . . .' Evie's sobs were too intense for her to speak.

'Let it go, Evie. Ships in the night and all that. As my grannie always said, "beware Greeks bearing gifts". You weren't to know. We all had the wool pulled over our eyes . . .' Terri paused. '. . .well, except me with that bloody leprechaun, I *knew* he was no good.'

Evie buried her face in Terri's shoulder and shook with pain.

'Why do men have to be such bastards?' Terri was picturing that photograph she'd found, the one of Shadrach standing alongside a beautiful West Indian girl, both of them dressed in wedding attire and surrounded by palm trees, a small boy standing between them, his little face a mirror image of his father's. 'I tell you, Evie, if I had my way, I'd drown every one of them at birth.' Terri's words dripped pure venom. 'I don't know if this helps, lovey, but I hope I never see another Rastafarian for as long as I live!'

Shadrach quietly backed away from the hatch and went to sit on the coach roof, Terri's words ringing in his ears and cutting him to the quick. Within thirty-six hours, he thought, his passengers would be back home under the grey gloom of a British sky, while he headed to St Lucia with the next Blue Lagoon charter - and he was still no nearer to understanding Terri than he had been when he'd first clapped eyes on her in Rodney Bay.

'Well good riddance,' he whispered, anger rising in him like bile. 'Bleedin' hell!' he cursed, sliding down the saloon window, 'I's not cut out for dis charter business.' He stripped to his birthday suit and tossed his clothes on deck. 'Dat damned ex-air stewardess, dat ball-bustin', man-eatin' jezebel. She sure fucked up my plans for de future and no mistake.' He climbed over the guardrail and dived below the hull, taking out his frustration on the moonlit waters of the bay.

Young Geordie met him when he levelled out, gliding alongside as they both swam towards the underside of *Rum Punch*'s hull.

'Well, hello dere, mon,' Shadrach mouthed. 'Has you bin gettin de cold shoulder as well?'

Chapter Twenty-Seven

Homeward Bound

Caribbean Island Airway's Boeing 747 lifted off from Maurice Bishop International Airport as dusk settled over Grenada, the aircraft banking steeply as it arced out into the Atlantic Ocean heading for London Gatwick, some four thousand miles to the north-east.

The A-team were each lost in their own thoughts, all trying to make sense of what had happened to them in the past two short weeks. Evie still had red rings around her eyes even though she had spent most of the morning lying by the pool at the Spanish hacienda-style hotel overlooking Mount Hartmann Bay with slices of cucumber over her eyelids, while Terri attempted to circumnavigate the pool fifty times and gave up after twenty-three, having stubbed her toe several times.

George, by contrast, had been annoyingly chirpy, whistling away to herself all through breakfast and lunch until Sam lost her temper and told her to take a running jump. She duly complied, wetting the others through as they reclined on sun loungers envying the yachts rounding the reef at the entrance to the bay, heading out on the next sector of their sea-borne holiday.

Dinner at the Calabash Hotel the previous evening had been cancelled, none of them feeling in the mood for candlelight or fine dining, so they had left Shadrach to dine alone while they retired to their king-sized beds and room service. Sam's peppered steak looked delicious as it came through the door on a trolley but it was still congealing on her plate two hours later as she drifted in and out of a disturbed sleep, mind still racing after too much black coffee on an empty stomach.

By the time they arrived at departures, blurry eyes hidden behind sunglasses, feet cramped inside high-heeled shoes, the atmosphere was more *Brief Encounter* than *Summer Holiday*. Terri still had the note Shadrach had left at reception wishing them a safe flight home, a standard farewell scribbled across a Prickly Bay Marina compliments slip. She had screwed it up and pushed it inside her skirt pocket.

Even George's effervescence had gone flat. She knew her email to Brendan O'Donnell would, by now, be playing havoc with Global Adventure Holidays, but any satisfaction at Adrian Falks's discomfort seemed insignificant besides the prospect of a wet Fulham Broadway and running Prestige Travel single-handed for two weeks. Finally, as the aircraft reached its cruising altitude, she zapped all thoughts of home from her brain and demanded champagne.

'Right, girls, this holiday is not over until the fat lady sings and I think a bottle of Moet will be a good way to finish.'

'You'll be lucky,' said Sam. 'The nearest thing to champers on this festering metal tube will be soda water with a splash of Blue Nun.'

'Is she the fat lady?' enquired Evie.

'No, Evie. That's the stewardess with the Zimmer frame.'

George was up out of her chair and heading for the galley, the words 'Have faith, Hutchins' hanging in her wake. Five minutes later she was back, a bottle of iced champagne and four plastic glasses under her arm.

'How the hell did you manage that?' demanded Sam.

'Simple. I told the CEO of *True Life Movies* that if he didn't give us some first-class service on the flight home, his company would be front-page news in the Travel Section of the *Mail on Sunday*.' The champagne cork hit the underside of the hat rack as liquid fizz filled each glass and the A-team smiled for the first time in twenty-four hours.

'How many bottles did you order?'

'How many can you drink?'

Terri checked her watch. 'In eight hours?' She looked at the others. 'Any advance on a dozen?'

They were all unsteady on their feet as they dragged their cases through Customs and out into the arrivals hall at Gatwick.

'Look,' shouted Evie, 'some bloke is holding up a clipboard with your name on it, Terri.'

She searched the mass of humanity waiting by the barrier and saw a middle-aged man in pale grey uniform and peaked cap holding her name aloft on a sign. Well now, she thought, things are looking up.

Within minutes they were all settled in a large limousine and gliding north along the M23, more bubbly frothing in crystal glasses.

'Where to, Miss Gillingham?' asked the chauffeur.

'Pont Street, Knightsbridge,' cut in Sam.

Shock rippled around the interior.

'Knightsbridge it is then, miss.'

'Why Pont Street?' asked Terri, sinking back into the cream leather upholstery.

'I've decided, as we missed out on the Calabash, we're gonna make up for it by eating in style tonight at L'Escargot. CJ can foot the bill.'

'Now that's what I call finishing the holiday in style,' said George.

'You can all kip down at my place and taxi home tomorrow.' Sam was in decisive mood.

'What happens if CJ cuts his holiday short and turns up while we're still there?' asked Evie.

'He won't. He isn't due back until the sixth. But if he does, he can damn' well make the toast while we're getting dressed.'

Three pairs of eyes peered at her over crystal rims.

'There's no need to look at me like that. It's high time Charles realised that I also have a life.'

'I say nuttin',' muttered George, her hands in the air. 'I comes from de Caribbean, and in de Caribbean, missy, de mon, he no do de toast!'

Chapter Twenty-Eight

Terri

Terri walked into 45 Deloitte Villas and dropped her case on the floor. The hall smelt musty, her Victorian pile a far cry from the sun-blushed decks of *Rum Punch*, the bubbling and stained wood-chip wallpaper a metaphor for her life.

She felt depression descending and headed straight for the wine rack, gathering up two weeks' worth of post on her way through to the kitchen. Pulling out a bottle of Cabernet Sauvignon she paused and looked at her watch. It was eleven-thirty in the morning and old habits were returning to haunt her.

'Put that back, Teresa Gillingham, and get a life.'

She shoved the bottle back in place, filled the kettle and dropped onto a kitchen chair, head in hands. She thought she'd prepared herself for those post-holiday blues on the way back from Knightsbridge to Ealing in a taxi, but Terri's world was in free fall and she was hanging on by a thread.

Shuffling through the bills, junk mail and flyers, trying to make sense of life, she spotted an envelope with a British Electric logo in the bottom right-hand corner.

'Do I want to open you?' she asked as the kettle shook violently and clicked off. She ripped the white flap open and extracted the contents, smoothed the letter out on the work surface and made a cup of tea.

The words were short and to the point. Teresa Gillingham was to report to Human Resources on Monday morning at nine o'clock following a report by the BIE Marketing Manager that she was not fit for purpose and would now be offered a suitable position elsewhere in the organisation. It was the death knell to Terri's day and it wasn't even lunchtime.

Looking back, she couldn't say what made her do it. Maybe she was still suffering from the pain of unrequited love or worried about paying her mortgage or simply needing to lash out. Whatever the reason, her tea went cold as she grabbed her camera from her hand luggage, shoved the memory card in her Epson printer, slotted some A4 photographic paper in the paper-tray and took evil delight in printing out all the images she could find of Cyril Trowbridge in flagrante delicto. A short note accompanied them to Anne Blakemore:

Dear Ms Blakemore,

Having returned from a Caribbean vacation this morning, I find that, in my absence, my position as the British International Engineering Division's Marketing Co-ordinator has been terminated, due to our Chairman's objection to the BIE logo. After fifteen years of loyal service to the company I find this action astonishing and totally without justification. Perhaps Lord Trowbridge will look into this matter and bring some pressure to bear on Human Resources to reverse this decision if the organisation is to avoid a legal challenge for constructive dismissal.

Yours

Teresa Gillingham.

enc: A few holiday snaps for your delectation.

The local courier office assured Terri that her letter would be delivered to Paternoster Square within the hour and she returned home, feeling smug, and began to unpack. A copy of the *Caribbean Compass* lay on the bed alongside the addresses noted down from Shadrach's passport. Terri tried to ignore them but each time she returned to her case they seemed to attract her like a magnet.

'OK, OK. Life's too short to hold a grudge.'

She stuck a copy of the article in an envelope addressed to Meshach Bligh and put the original in one addressed to his parents in the Elephant and Castle. She thought of enclosing a short note but then decided against it. She couldn't think why any of them would want to contact a stranger, but if they did, they could always track her down through the editor of *Caribbean Compass* who had her business card. She smiled as she licked the envelope. Knowing my luck, she thought, he probably binned it before I'd even closed the office door. She shrugged and went back to her unpacking.

Monday morning was a revelation. Terri was met at the revolving entrance door by Anne Blakemore who looked like Golda Meir with toothache and whisked up to the top floor before she could even wave to the receptionist. Once there, Terri was ushered into the PA's private office and the door firmly closed. They sat either side of the desk.

'Now, Teresa. May I call you Teresa?'

'Certainly, Anne.'

'Excellent. I have discussed the unfortunate situation regarding your position within British Electric with Lord Trowbridge and he assures me that the fault was entirely his. Not only did he not object to the BIE logo, but he has gone on record to state that he considers the design to be a perfect depiction of the BIE Division's worldwide activities.'

She took off her designer spectacles and cleaned them with a hankie. 'It was all a misunderstanding between himself and the Board, you see.'

Terri bit the inside of her cheek.

Anne hurried on. 'Any suggestion that your position has been compromised is categorically not true and the Human Resources Director has not only rectified the matter forthwith but, as the BIE Marketing Manager's post is now available, he considers you to be the ideal candidate to fill this position after so many years in that department. You will see that the associated salary level and pension rights are very generous.'

She pushed a contract across the desk pointing deliberately to the remuneration section.

'Really?' said Terri, her intonation not lost on Anne. 'What has happened to Happy Hands . . . Harold Crompton's successor?'

'Oh.' Anne flicked her hand as if swatting a fly, 'He was merely a caretaker manager until a suitable successor could be found.'

'I see.' Terri pushed the contract back across the desk. 'And what about Lord Trowbridge? Will he be remaining in his post?' She knew she was on firm ground here. Anne Blakemore's clandestine affair with the Chairman had been the talk of the ladies' toilets for years.

Anne coughed, cleared her throat and gritted her teeth, her blue eyes glacial. 'Lord Trowbridge is making a statement to the Board this afternoon informing them that, due to his other extensive commitments, he feels he cannot continue in his role as Chairman and will be resigning his post forthwith.'

'Oh, shame,' said Terri, sounding like Margaret Thatcher accepting Michael Heseltine's resignation. The contract slid back towards her.

'Naturally, I'll need time to consider the company's offer.'

'Naturally.' Anne dropped the contract into an envelope and handed it over.

'If there's nothing else, then, I'll be on my way.'

'Teresa?' Anne screwed the top back on her fountain pen very slowly. 'I trust we can now close the file on this matter.' Terri raised her right eyebrow. 'That's assuming, of course, you accept the promotion.'

'No doubt, Anne. IF I accept the promotion.' Terri tucked the contract under her arm and headed for the lift, the prospect of her blue Dralon -covered Chesterfield going to meet its maker putting a jaunty spring in her step.

The department secretary was hovering by the coffee machine when Terri walked into the Marketing Department five minutes later.

'Hi, Terri. Great to have you back.'

'Really?' She was deliberately obtuse and started clearing the contents of her desk into a Tesco plastic bag. The secretary backed away, obviously assuming Terri had been fired, and shrugged to the others in the open-plan office as she returned to her station.

Remaining suitably blank-faced, Terri placed Anne Blakemore's envelope on top of fifteen years' worth of detritus, gathered the whole lot up in both arms and vacated the area, shouting over her shoulder to one and all; 'I'm not sure when

I'll see you next but if anyone wants my job I suggest you get your application into Human Resources PDQ.'

The sound of computer keyboards leaping into life accompanied her exit and she couldn't help chuckling as she descended the stairs, imagining her associates' faces when they found out who would be making that decision. 'Of course, I may not accept the post of Marketing Manager,' she declared, breezing past reception.

'*Over my dead body*,' said grannie.

'I'll head over to the cemetery then, shall I?' remarked Terri as she walked out through the revolving doors and straight into Costa Coffee.

Placing a hot croissant and espresso on the ledge by the window, she lowered herself onto a stool as a 7 series BMW pulled up across the square. The chauffeur got out and opened the passenger door with a flourish. Terri paused, mid-bite, and watched Cyril Trowbridge alight, stump over to the revolving doors and disappear inside. It triggered an image of a certain elliptical, red birthmark prominently positioned on his left buttock, as captured through her camera's viewfinder back in PSV.

'Gotcha, Cyril,' she whispered, sipping her espresso. 'Next time, keep your libido where it belongs. You never know who might be watching!'

Chapter Twenty-Nine

George

You could have cut the atmosphere with a knife in Prestige Travel on Saturday morning. George sat at her desk, thumping away at her computer, while her father sat opposite, chest puffed out, an expression of righteous indignation stamped across his features.

'In my day, young lady, we had secretaries to do all this computer stuff.'

'In your day, Dad, they didn't have bloody computers.'

'There's no need to swear, Georgina, and I'll have you know our IBM main-frame at British Steel was so big it filled a whole warehouse unit.'

George looked at her father over her bifocals. 'Neanderthal,' was her only comment.

'Rot,' countered the old man.

'It's not rot. All that fanfold paper stripped the Amazon of a third of its trees.'

Mr Stanhope shuffled in his seat. 'The trouble with you young ones today is that you think you invented everything.'

'Young ones!' shouted Georgina as she searched in vain for any semblance of her accounts programme. 'For Christ's sake, Father, I'm forty-eight years old. I stopped being young thirty years ago, and if *you* hadn't interfered with my computer software I wouldn't now be in danger of suffering a mid-life coronary!'

'If you'd had a normal marriage and a house full of kids there wouldn't have been any need for all this technical twaddle. Your mother and I have been denied the pleasure of grandchildren because you chose a husband who preferred men, so don't blame *me* for the present crisis!'

'That's right, drag up the past.' George's computer screen froze. 'You never did give me credit for making the best of a bad situation. Any other daughter would have come back home crying her eyes out and looking for moral and financial support. I, meanwhile, licked my wounds and got on with life, and have given you and Mum more free holidays than you can shake a stick at ever since. Anyway, if you'd wanted grandchildren so badly, why didn't you have more kids?'

'I'm not going to sit here and be insulted,' said Mr Stanhope, shoving his arms into the sleeves of his North Face anorak. 'If you want my help again, I suggest you climb down off your high horse and show some respect to your father.' With that he was out the door, bumping into Mrs Featherbridge from down the road, who had come to pay the balance on her two-week holiday in Jersey.

'Christ, I hope she has her invoice with her,' muttered George under her breath as she rose and smiled sweetly. 'Hello, Clarisse, and how are you today?'

The afternoon flashed by with customers coming and going and George fielding phone-calls, holiday bookings and package holiday complaints with her legs crossed, any chance of a visit to the ladies' on hold until closing time. She was just explaining the delights of a Nile cruise to a couple looking for a honeymoon destination when the door opened and another customer walked in, nodded to her and took a seat by the rack of holiday brochures. George thought he looked different to her usual clientele and turned her attention back to Luxor and romantic nights in a Bedouin tent. She saw the couple out of the door armed with a plethora of brochures and an assurance that they could ring her if they had any further queries. She suspected they hadn't got a clue where Egypt was, and that brought to mind her years at Beagle Air and the in-house joke going around at the time.

'Where did you go for your holidays this year, Mick?'

'Benidorm, Paddy.'

'Where's that then, Mick?'

'I don't know, Paddy. We flew.'

'Excuse me.'

George spun round and found herself toe to toe with the customer who, she decided, was extremely eye-catching. He had a head of chaotic dark brown curls which set off his vivid green eyes, and was dressed in a pair of Levis and an Irish rugby shirt.

'Would you be Georgina Stanhope, by any chance?'

The Irish accent turned her cheeks pink. 'Yes, that's me.'

'Miss Stanhope, my name's Brendan O'Donnell from *True Life Movies.*'

'Good God! . . . I mean . . . good afternoon, Mr O'Donnell, nice to put a face to a name.' George retreated behind her desk, straightened her skirt and sat down demurely, torn between gazing at his drop-dead gorgeous features and trying to appear totally disinterested in this matinee idol from the Emerald Isle.

He smiled, revealing a set of perfectly aligned white teeth. George's mind was already forming suggestive images of hot bodies in steamy locations when he spoke again.

'How was the flight home?'

For Christ's sake, Georgina, get a grip. 'Fine. Well, if you call steerage fine. I had been expecting Business Class.'

He had the grace to look embarrassed. 'You might be interested to know that we are investigating Global Adventure Holidays following your email. I'd like to talk to you about it some more over dinner tonight.'

Before George could get a handle on this invitation her mouth opened and she heard herself accept.

'Great, that settles it then. If you let me have your address, I'll have a taxi pick you up around eight-thirty. Do you like fish?'

She felt as if she was being flattened by a steamroller. All she could do was nod.

'So do I. I'll book a table at Sheekey's in St Martin's Court.'

George finally caught up and decided to stamp her authority on the conversation. 'Mr O'Donnell . . .'

'Oh, please, the name's Brendan.'

'. . . Well, Brendan, let's just slow this right down, shall we? I've had a very busy first day back at work after a very trying two weeks cruising the Grenadines in a bathtub, which happened to include saving the lives of two drowning West Indian fishermen, running the risk of spending the rest of my life in a Caribbean jail and capturing a bloody drug baron from Puerto Rico on behalf of America's Drug Enforcement Agency, all while I was supposed to be having the holiday of a lifetime! Right now, I just want to go home, pour myself a stiff drink and have an early night.' She sat back in her chair and studied her visitor, whose mouth was now hanging open. 'So, if you want the full SP on Adrian Falks and his little scam, I suggest you start by getting your secretary to phone for an appointment and leave *me* to decide on a convenient date.'

He raked his fingers through his hair and George went weak at the knees. 'My apologies. I didn't mean to . . .'

'Accepted. Now, if you're still interested in that dinner, I'm free next Wednesday evening. And as I never give out my address to strangers, I suggest we meet at my club for pre-dinner drinks and take it from there.'

'I won't be in London next Wednesday,' he countered, walking towards the door. 'I'm only in town for a couple of days.'

George could have kicked herself.

'But if we can compromise on tomorrow evening, I would be delighted to meet you at your club and, as you say, take it from there.'

She burst out laughing. 'Brendan O'Donnell, you drive a hard bargain! Let's say seven-thirty in the cocktail bar at the RAC Club on Pall Mall.'

'Do I have to wear a tie?'

'Too right. Unless you want to conduct our conversation through the lounge window.'

'Damn' Brits,' he groaned, and went on his way with a backward wave.

Well, Terri, thought George as she locked the office door minutes later, you certainly couldn't call *him* a leprechaun!

Pall Mall looked grey and dismal as George climbed the steps to the RAC Club and entered. She was met by the doorman who recognised her immediately, the Stanhopes having been associated with the club since her grandfather's day. George used it regularly when she was in town, both socially and for business.

'I'm expecting a guest, Harry. A Mr Brendan O'Donnell.' She scribbled his name in the visitor's book and signed him in. 'I'll be in the cocktail bar when he arrives.'

'Right, miss,' said Harry taking her coat.

She was sitting reading the *Sunday Times*, G&T in her hand, when Brendan appeared in the bar entrance and scanned the interior. He caught sight of her over by the window and walked across, his easy gait and lopsided smile giving him an air of authority and quiet charm. George rose to meet him, enjoying the envious looks she received from other female members as he stretched out a well-manicured hand, grasped hers in a firm grip then sat, arms casually hanging over the sides of the chair, looking for all the world as if he owned the place.

'Do I pass muster?' he asked as he adjusted his Windsor knot and straightened his tie.

Her eyes slowly progressed from his well-polished brogues to his crisp white shirt and that riot of thick dark hair. 'You'll do. Now, what would you like to drink?'

'Whisky on the rocks.'

'Bushmills or Jameson's, sir?' asked the waiter, standing by Brendan's right shoulder.

He bit his lower lip. 'Bushmills, please.' He uncrossed his legs and leant towards Georgina. 'Is my accent that obvious?'

George pressed her fingers against her smiling mouth. 'Possibly, but personally I think it's that gold harp you left parked outside that gives you away.'

Brendan's infectious laughter could be heard out on Pall Mall. 'Georgina Stanhope, I think we're going to get along just famously. Now, why don't you start at the beginning of your tale and I'll just sit back and enjoy the view.'

Brendan O'Donnell was a consummate flirt, and flirt he did, all through pre-dinner drinks, in the taxi to the restaurant, and throughout the whole of the candlelit meal. George tried every trick in the book to counter his outrageous behaviour with her usual ball-busting techniques, but after imbibing two gin and tonics, a bottle of Pouilly-Fuissé and a brandy she could have bathed in, she was having difficulty stringing her words together, let alone fielding volleys.

It didn't help that she fancied him like crazy and kept having to remind herself that under his suave Irish exterior and delightful soft Gaelic accent, this Prince Charming probably had a wife and a horde of kids back in Ireland.

'Let me get this straight,' he said as the waitress brought the bill. 'The DEA had actually planted four million dollars on *Rum Punch*?'

'No. Stay with it, Brendan. The cash was paid to the drug cartel by an under-cover agent down in Trinidad and was on its way to El Diablo in Puerto Rico with the cocaine when the catamaran was impounded in Antigua. I can only assume that there was a cock-up in communications between the DEA and the Coastguard and *Rum Runner* was boarded prematurely. Although the cocaine was seized, no one around Antigua knew anything about the money, which left us holding the baby, so to speak.'

'Good Lord! No wonder you were spitting bullets when you emailed me. You could have been banged up inside a Grenadian jail for years if the DEA hadn't been there to put the record straight.'

'Exactly. Here, let me.' She reached across to take the bill but he snatched it from under her fingers and shook his head. 'You may be a feminist, Miss Stanhope, but where I come from, men do the paying.'

'Really? Then I'll be a good little woman and let your wallet take the strain.'

Brendan glanced at her over his half-rimmed spectacles, chuckled under his breath, laid a platinum credit card on top of the bill and turned to summon a waiter. George took in his chiselled profile and wondered what he would look like in a pair of Speedos. She quickly rose from the table, headed to the ladies' and stayed there until she had control of her emotions. When she returned, Brendan was standing with her Burberry at the ready. He wrapped her into it, opened the restaurant door and walked her to the waiting taxi.

'I'll be in touch again in the coming weeks. In the meantime you can take it from me, any association we had with Adrian Falks will be ended immediately I get back to the office.'

'If you need a substitute, Brendan, Prestige Travel is at your service.'

'That's good to know, Georgina. Pity it doesn't apply to its owner.'

'What?'

Brendan handed the taxi driver a wad of notes. 'I've no idea where you're taking Miss Stanhope because she won't tell me, but I'm sure this will cover it.'

'Thanks, mate. I'll give the young lady the change.'

'Chiswick,' announced George through the internal partition as the engine sprang to life. 'What were you saying, Brendan?'

'Only that it's a damn' waste.'

'What is?' she asked, craning her neck backwards as the taxi pulled away from the curb.

'That you bat for the other side.'

'But I don't . . .' she shouted, her words swallowed up in a swirl of traffic noise as the cab shot off up the road.

'Did you say something, miss?' asked the driver, peering at her through his rear-view mirror.

She shook her head, sat back in her seat and muttered expletives all the way home. 'I'll kill that Teresa Gillingham.'

Chapter Thirty

Sam

The meeting at the solicitors in High Holborn had proved to be anything but positive. Mr Sampson had been quite clear. There was no such thing as a 'common-law' mistress, therefore she could not make any legal claim for maintenance or pension rights against her provider as the courts would not give her any form of legal recognition unless she could prove either that she had played more than just a sexual role in the relationship or that she had produced children fathered by the said provider.

Mr Sampson bluntly pointed out that Sam would be better off waiting for her partner to die rather than trying to claim against him during his lifetime, as, assuming she was being maintained by him right up to his death, she could then claim off his estate for maintenance and capital, irrespective of the terms of his will, and he felt her chances of winning would be excellent based on the length of time the relationship had lasted.

Sam couldn't see herself greasing the stairs at Pont Street, and giving birth to Charles's children had never been an option. Mr Sampson sympathised but, as he said, the law was the law.

'May I suggest, Miss Hutchins, that you consider starting a business of your own while your relationship with your provider is still amicable? This way you would have something to fall back on if the relationship failed and it would give you the opportunity to fund a private pension for your old age.'

Sam thanked him for his advice and departed, arriving back at Beauchamp Villas dragging a black cloud in her wake. She entered the apartment knowing she had only one option with which to safeguard her position. CJ had to be convinced to open an investment account in her name and place a lump sum in it, commensurate with her years of devotion to him. How she was to make him do this, however, was quite another matter.

She was still mulling over the problem three days later when he walked through the door.

'Hi lover, have you missed me?' He dropped his bag on the hall floor and moved towards her, beaming with expectant pleasure.

Sam looked at the man who had been the centre of her life for twenty-five years, buried her fears in a compartment of her brain marked 'pending' and went into his embrace, knowing her world had already tilted on its axis.

Give it time, she thought, fingers crossed behind his neck as his lips caressed hers, the familiar scent of his cologne invaded her senses and his hands roamed over the body he believed was his for the taking. She closed her eyes, wanting desperately to feel something, anything, of the old flame that had burnt so brightly for so long. But all she could think about was how many girls like Jasmin Wong there were, just waiting to take her place. CJ's fingers dug into the bruise on her buttock and Sam winced.

'Sorry, was I hurting you?'

'No, Charles, I just banged into the glass table the other day. It must still be sensitive.'

'Then let me kiss it better.'

'Not here in the hall! Why don't you open a bottle of champagne and we'll celebrate your return in style in the bedroom.'

'Your wish is my command, kitten.' He disappeared into the kitchen while Sam entered the bedroom, letting her silk wrap slip to the floor. When she turned CJ was standing in the doorway, ice bucket, champagne bottle and two glasses in his hands, his eyes taking in every curve of her naked body.

'Christ, you're beautiful, Sam. You've no idea how much I've missed you.'

With his libido sated, CJ sat in the lounge in his Liberty dressing gown catching up on the BBC news as Sam made them a coffee. She paused mid-way through filling the cafetière and stared out of the window, all colour drained out of the day by the thick grey clouds racing overhead. She longed for the vibrant shades of the Caribbean.

It's no good, she thought, I'm going to have to tell him and face the consequences. She walked into the lounge, bent over the back of the settee and wound her arms around CJ's shoulders. He snuggled into her embrace, one ear cocked to Moira Stuart as she read out the headlines from her auto-cue.

'CJ, we need to talk.'

He patted Sam's hand, more interested in getting the golf results than in listening to his mistress, her presence for the time being a distraction. Something inside Sam snapped. She grabbed the remote, zapped the television and stood in front of him, hands on hips, champagne on an empty stomach strengthening her resolve.

'You're not in Surrey now, CJ. When I say we need to talk, we need to talk. If all you want to do is watch sport, then go back home.'

'This *is* home.' CJ scratched his head, confused.

'Correction. This is *my* home. It has been my home for twenty-five years. For you it's just a place to get your end away.'

'I beg your pardon?'

'You heard me. Your home is in Surrey. If you want to breeze in and out of here whenever the mood takes you, then at least have the courtesy to show me some respect.'

'What's got into you, Sam?

'Your bloody behaviour, CJ. Does it ever occur to you that I might have a life of my own? Would it ever cross your mind to think that I might be cruising in the Caribbean while you're off in Alaska being the perfect husband, or do you assume that by maintaining me in this style,' she extended her arms indicating the whole flat, 'you have the God-given right to keep me locked away like some exotic painting, to take out and admire whenever the mood takes you?'

CJ tried to stand but was pushed back down by Sam's firm hands. 'For twenty-five years I have allowed you to dictate the way I live my life because I thought you loved me. Well, you don't, do you?

Whatever CJ was about to say was cut off at source.

'What you love is having your own personal prostitute . . . after all, you have the money to pay for your own private brothel. Well thanks a bunch, CJ. You're now looking at a forty-nine-year-old whore with neither a pension, family, loving husband nor children. Would you please tell me what the hell is missing from *your* life?'

'Christ, Sam, what has happened around here while I've been away?'

'Life, CJ. Life has happened. I've learnt that there is more to it than being a slave to your libido . . . which, I may add, has become rather boring of late.'

'Well, whose fault is that? Don't think I haven't noticed your lack of passion over the past few years. If I didn't know better, I'd think we were married.'

'But we aren't, CJ, are we?'

'Is that what this is all about?'

'Yes, I guess it is, legally speaking.' Sam walked over to the window and turned to face him. 'Just what do you think would happen to me if you dropped dead tomorrow?'

CJ opened his mouth, closed it and stared at the wall. Sam could see him facing reality and went for the jugular.

'What would I do if you suffered a heart attack here during sex? What am I supposed to say to the paramedics and your wife when they cart you out in a body bag?'

'Jesus, Sam. You're scaring me.'

'Well, it's about time somebody did. You're not twenty-eight anymore. You eat too much, you drink too much, you're overweight, and the only exercise you get is strolling around a golf course and humping me.'

'But . . .'

'Stop kidding yourself. You're getting on and you do nothing to make yourself attractive, either to me or to your family. Have *I* gone to seed?'

'No, of course not. You look as good today as you did when I first saw you jogging in Regent's Park.'

'Then why don't you? Maybe I should trade you in for a nineteen seventies model.'

'Now you're being ridiculous.'

'No, CJ. I'm being realistic. At my age, time is not on my side. If I'm to provide for myself in my later years, I need to start now.'

'Well, I need a drink.' CJ went to the bar and poured himself a large Scotch. 'Do you want one?'

Sam shook her head.

'You're completely wrong, you know. I do love you, I've always loved you, and if I could get out of my marriage without losing my family and suffering a guilt trip for the rest of my life, I would have done it years ago.'

His words hit Sam straight in the solar plexus. She sank to her knees and buried her head in her arms. CJ came over and joined her on the floor. 'What do you want me to do, Sam? Just tell me and I will move heaven and earth to put this right. I don't want to lose you. You're my sanity, my refuge, my reason for living.'

'Then stop thinking about yourself and find a way of making me secure. I need financial security, I need to build bridges with my parents before they die, I need to have a social circle of my own, a life beyond Pont Street . . . and most of all I want your wife to know I exist.' Sam shivered as her words rang around the room.

'She already knows, Sam. She's known for years.'

'What?' Sam glared at CJ.

'I never told you because I didn't think you'd understand.'

'Understand? Understand what, exactly? That your wife prefers you to screw your mistress like a fucking Royal, instead of doing the rounds of grotty London brothels and bringing home some nasty venereal disease.'

'No, Sam, that's not what I meant at all.'

'Then, for God's sake, what *is* the reason?' shouted Sam.

CJ's head dropped to his chest, his words barely a whisper. 'I nearly killed her in a car accident back in the sixties. She's paralysed, Sam. Thanks to me, she spends her life in a wheelchair.'

Dusk was clipping the windowsill as CJ and Sam sat on the settee, Sam's head resting on CJ's lap, a cathartic sense of peace filling the room. After all the years of Sam believing CJ's wife to be her nemesis, she learnt how Felicity had been imprisoned in her own body, loving her man from afar and being unable to express that love physically. It must have been purgatory for her to acknowledge her husband's affair, thought Sam, welling over with guilt as she tried to imagine what it must have felt like, watching him leave the house, knowing he would spend the night in another woman's arms. She rubbed her temples, unable to swallow down the grief and guilt she felt. How could she go on with CJ knowing all this?

'What I don't understand is why you have kept this to yourself all these years?'

'Because I knew you would leave me if you learnt the truth and I was too selfish to let that happen.' CJ kissed her gently behind the ear. 'As the years went by it got harder and harder for me to set the record straight.'

'But how were you able to have children?'

'They're adopted, Sam. Watching them grow up has been Felicity's only real enjoyment in life.' His voice cracked. 'And the grandchildren, of course.'

'Do your children know about me?'

'No, but I'm sure they suspect. They have too much respect for their mother ever to tackle me on the subject, but, as sure as night follows day, they would have raised Caine if I'd tried to get a divorce.'

'Too bloody right,' said Sam, amazed to hear her own reaction. 'And the car accident, was it all your fault?'

CJ nodded. 'We had an Austin-Healey 3000 at the time and used to love screaming through the back roads of the South Downs with the top down. I took a corner on two wheels, lost control and crashed into a tree. In those days no one wore a seatbelt. Felicity flew out of the car and landed on rocky ground, breaking her back. I was in a coma for three days. When I came to, I learnt the devastating news of her injuries.'

'Jesus Christ. No wonder you've spent all these years feeling guilty. Would your marriage have survived if the crash hadn't happened?' Sam's words seemed callous but she needed reassurance.

'Who knows? I loved her at the time but I can't say now if I would have sustained it. Meeting you changed me, Sam, and the fact that I could never make you my wife is the price we've both had to pay.'

'You were right, you know. I would have left you if you'd come clean.'

'Why do you think I've been so possessive?'

'Well, it's time you stopped. We have to come to terms with our lot and plan for the future.' She lay across his lap, head resting on his rotund stomach. She raised her hand ticking off points on her fingers. 'First, you'll lose some weight. Second, you'll set up a trust fund for me for my old age. And third . . .' She stopped talking, dragged his head down to her own and kissed him passionately on the lips. 'You won't get cross when I tell you that I'm just back from sixteen days in the Caribbean where I had a ball!'

Chapter Thirty-One

Evie

Lilting music and lapping waves from the sound system at Belgrove Park Health Spa enveloped Evie and her client in a cocoon of superficial tranquillity. As her hands mechanically travelled across a seventy-year-old body her mind wandered off into the ether. No amount of rational thought had been able to persuade her to accept her old life while Petite St Vincent dragged her back to a wooden deck overlooking Petite Martinique and that lost chance of a new life.

She had thrown herself into her work, taking on extra shifts when asked, standing in for other beauty therapists when they needed to leave early and taking over the water aerobics classes after the regular teacher left to have a baby, but none of it was done with enthusiasm. She was losing weight, had dark rings around her eyes and had refused all attempts to be winkled out for evenings at the pub or an Italian meal with her workmates, her constant excuse being that she had other things to do.

She was depressed and knew it, still licking her wounds over Dale and wallowing in her own self-pity. Sylvia, the reflexologist, was getting worried about her, having no idea what the problem was but suspecting that it had something to do with the Caribbean cruise. Belgrove Park clients were also beginning to notice Evie's lack of interest in her job, often requesting the other masseuse when booking a treatment at reception.

If she goes on like this, thought Sylvia, she will be asked to find another job. And with that thought in mind, she decided to act.

Evie was sitting in the staff room drinking a carrot juice when Sylvia popped her head around the door.

'Oh, there you are, Evie. What's the name of that travel agency your friend runs? My mum's knitting group has decided to spend some of their savings on a trip to the Black Forest.'

'Prestige Travel,' said Evie, unsure if Sylvia's mum would get on with bratwurst and sauerkraut when her idea of a culinary treat was some potted shrimps on Margate prom. 'Georgina is the person she should speak to, Georgina Stanhope. Here, I'll give you her work number.'

Sylvia went back to reception tapping the buttons on her mobile phone and disappeared into the ladies room to get some privacy.

'Hello, is that Georgina Stanhope? . . . Good morning Miss Stanhope. You don't know me but I work with Evangelina Shapiro at Belgrove Park Health Spa. I'm the reflexologist. I'm rather worried about her and wondered if we could meet for a chat.'

George put down the phone and stared at the passers-by through the plate-glass window, her fingers drumming on the desktop. Whatever it was this Sylvia wanted to discuss, it was obviously urgent. George thought the others should also be present at the White Cross pub overlooking the Thames in Richmond later that day. Flicking the Closed sign round on the door, she dialled Terri at work and got some female on the line asking for her name and telling her that the Marketing Manager was currently busy and would ring her back. Sam was equally elusive, probably having colonic irrigation or some other demeaning treatment in Harley Street, George decided, and left a message. Ten minutes later Terri rang back.

'How's life in the upper echelons of the British Electricity Board?' asked George.'

'Interesting,' said Terri. 'For a start, I don't have to get my own coffee and the Chairman's PA is being so sweet she ought to work for Tate and Lyle.'

'What about Cyril?'

'Exiled to the wilderness where all sexually over-active bastards belong.'

George thought Terri's comment had the ring of personal grievance about it. 'I've just had a phone call from one of Evie's work mates . . .'

The pub was heaving when Sam walked through the door and headed for the bar. She seemed to be the first one to arrive so ordered her usual Campari and Soda and beat another couple to the last window seat where she sat watching some rowers sculling down the Thames in the evening sunlight.

A woman of about her own age seemed to be hovering uneasily by the dart board so Sam raised her hand and attracted her attention.

'Are you Georgina Stanhope?' asked the female.

'No, I'm Sam, Samantha Hutchins, another of Evie's friends. George and Terri will be along shortly. Here.' She shuffled over. 'Take the weight off your feet.'

By the time the others arrived Sam already had the full story on Evie. She introduced Sylvia then related the problem. 'Have either of you spoken to Evie of late?'

'No,' said George, 'I've been too wrapped up in my own business.'

'Me too,' said Terri. 'Some friends, eh?'

'Don't beat yourself up, Terri, I haven't spoken to her either. If it weren't for Sylvia we wouldn't have known anything about this until Evie was hospitalised or worse.'

'Jesus, Sam, d'you think it's that serious?'

'I hope not, but she's apparently lost a stone and a half in weight.'

'What?'

Sylvia nodded. 'Now that Sam has told me what happened to her in the Caribbean, I can understand what she must be going through. Apart from this Dale fella, it can't be easy working at Belgrove Park after seeing that exclusive spa in the Grenadines. Most of our clients are in their dotage and have never been further than Benidorm.'

'Well, what the hell are we going to do about it? She won't take kindly to Sylvia spilling the beans. We're going to have to find another way to bring Evie out of her depression.'

'Perhaps one of you could check in for a massage and take it from there.'

'Good idea,' said George. 'I'm up for a full Swedish, what about you, Sam?'

'Count me in. Evie's talents far outweigh those of the masseuses at my local spa.'

'OK, why don't we set aside next Saturday for an A-team pamper day?' Terri turned to Sylvia. 'Is she working on Saturday?'

'Right now she's working seven days a week if she can.'

'That's settled then. George, what about Prestige?'

'No problem, Ralph can take the strain. I'll ring you tomorrow, Sylvia, and book us in. I suggest we don't say anything to Evie. Probably better to make it a surprise.'

'Ring me after ten, Georgina, I can make sure I'm on the reception desk then. I'll book you in under fictitious names.'

'Right. The Three Musketeers are coming to the rescue. Thank you, Sylvia for contacting George, we all really appreciate it.'

'Hear, hear,' said Sam, rising from her seat. 'Anyone for another drink?'

Evie couldn't believe her eyes when she walked into the pedicure room and found the rest of the A-team sitting with their feet up, cotton-wool pads between their toes. The A-team couldn't believe what they were seeing either. Terri leapt to her feet and grabbed Evie in a bear hug. She stared at the others over Evie's shoulder, eyebrows in her hairline.

'Well, Miss Elusive. Where the hell have you been? I've been trying to get hold of you for days to tell you we were coming here today.' George put down her coffee and craned upwards as Evie bent to kiss her on both cheeks.

'I've been so busy,' she said, leaning over Sam.

'Ever heard of an answerphone?' George was not the most diplomatic member of the group.

'Well, we're here now and expect you to give us the best Swedish massage this side of PS . . .' Terri could have kicked herself.

'Actually,' jumped in Sam, 'I fancy the hot stones treatment, Evie. I assume it does what it says on the packet.'

'Oh, yes, Sam. You'll float out of here and be jumping off the wardrobe in no time at all.'

'Then lead me to it while these two find out what's amiss in their decrepit bodies through reflexology.'

Evie led Sam out of the pedicure room and down the corridor while Terri and George sat back in their recliners stumped for words.

Finally Terri made a decision. 'I'm going to have to contact Clementine. I can't believe she wasn't impressed by Evie. Something went wrong that day and I have a sneaky suspicion it was all to do with bloody CJ.'

'CK,' said George, scratching her chin, 'but I agree. Evie looks like something out of Belsen.'

'A slight exaggeration, George, but if we leave her here for very much longer she'll be diagnosed with anorexia.'

'D'you think Sylvia would let us use the spa's computer to get PSV's telephone number?'

'No need,' said Terri, rummaging through her bag. 'I've still got the under-manager's business card in my wallet.'

'Thinking of taking a holiday there?' asked George as Sylvia appeared in the room.

'Right, girls, who's first?'

'Me,' said Terri, trotting to the door. 'You might be interested to know, Georgina, that on my new salary, that's not such a bad idea.'

'Show-off,' said George, and picked up a copy of *Country Life*.

The *Movies4Men* channel was playing on the TV at eleven-thirty that evening as Terri dialled the Grenadines and waited for the number to connect. She clicked the mute button on the remote as she heard a female voice answer and felt a warm glow at the sound of steel drums in the background.

'The health spa please.'

'Sorry, madam, we don't have a telephone link to the spa. Can I help you?'

'Of course you don't.' Terri began to wonder if she was becoming senile. 'I was hoping to speak with Miss Clementine. I'm ringing from the UK. Could she possibly ring me back, or could I ring her again at an arranged time? It's rather important.'

'Just one moment, madam, I'll see when she's free.'

Terri drummed her fingers against her thigh hoping it wouldn't take too long. Transatlantic calls had never been cheap.

'This is Clementine, who's calling?'

Terri couldn't believe her luck. 'Oh, Miss Clementine, sorry . . . I wasn't expecting to speak to you so quickly. My name's Teresa Gillingham. I'm a friend of Evangelina Shapiro's.' A pregnant pause ensued. 'We were all sailing with Shadrach Bligh on *Rum Punch* some weeks ago. Evangelina came to talk to you about . . .'

'Oh, yes, I remember. A very talented masseuse. What can I do for you, Miss Gillingham?'

'Well, it's like this, Clementine . . .'

Chapter Thirty-Two

Shadrach

Shadrach was sitting on the deck of *Rum Punch*, stern-to the quay in English Harbour, watching the tourists admiring the views around Nelson's eighteenth-century dockyard, when Earl Harrison, the Chief Customs Officer, sauntered across the grass and stopped by his port steps.

'Shadrach, are you dere?'

'Yes, mon.'

'Good. I's comin' aboard.'

Shadrach met him at the saloon door with two bottles of Carib in his hand. 'Drink?'

'Let's go inside.'

Shadrach was intrigued. They both sat at the saloon table, Earl with his feet up on a stool, the door firmly closed.

'I hears you gone and quit that Blue Lagoon Cruisin' crowd down in Grenada.'

'How'd you hear dat?'

Earl tapped the side of his nose. 'So, what's de plan now den?'

Shadrach stood up and leant against the sink, swigging his beer. 'I don't know, Earl. Maybe get me old job back in de boatyard if dey'll 'ave me or sail on up to St Martin and see what's cookin' in Simpson's Bay Lagoon. A cruiser told me dey be lookin' for good cabinet makers up dere.'

The chief picked a piece of spinach from between his teeth with his thumb. 'You be finished wid de charters den?'

'Got it in one. I's not cut out for dis passenger lark. Too bleedin' complicated. Give me a piece o' wood and a chisel any day.'

'What will you do wid *Rum Punch*?'

'Keep 'er. Apart from anyting else, dis little beauty is me 'ome.' Shadrach practically had stars in his eyes as he scanned the saloon.

'Den, you don't fancy sometin' bigger?'

'How de hell could I afford sometin' bigger?' Shadrach inclined his head. 'What yous getting at, Earl?'

'Well, it's like dis, Shadrach.' He twiddled the beer bottle between his fingers. 'Yous better sit down.'

Shadrach dropped onto the chart-table stool and rested his elbows on his knees. 'OK, I'm sittin'.'

Earl licked his lips. 'I've had a communique from de DEA.' He pulled an official-looking document out of his inside pocket. 'Dat Francisco Segui dat dey caught in Grenada . . .'

'We caught,' corrected Shadrach.

'Whatever. Anyways, dere was a price on his head.'

'Pull de udder one!' said Shadrach, draining his beer.

'I's not kiddin' you, Shadrach Bligh. Dere's . . . let me see.' Earl ran his finger down the wording on the page. 'Yes, here it is. Five 'undred tousand dollars to de person who shopped him to de po'lice.'

Shadrach dropped his beer.

'I tought you'd be interested. Now, do yous want de good news or de bad news?'

Shadrach snatched the paper out of Earl's hands and was reading the contents for himself. 'Good news,' he muttered, eyes locked on the figure $500,000.

'You seem to qualify.'

Shadrach resembled a giant wrasse with lockjaw. 'And the bad news?' He didn't want to hear it.

'You need to go to Miami to collect it.'

'Lordie, Lordie!' shouted Shadrach, doing a jig around the galley. 'Pinch me, Earl. Dis ain't happenin'.'

'It sure is, mon, and I can't tink of a better bloke to benefit from dis windfall.'

Shadrach couldn't stand still. 'What about *Southern Cross*?'

'She goes up for auction on de fifteenth.'

Shadrach looked at his watch. 'Christ, mon, dat's only a week away.'

'Den I suggest you gets your butt up to Florida PDQ.'

'When's de next flight outta here for Miami?'

'Today at two forty-five.' Earl pulled an airline ticket out of his back pocket, a wry grin on his face. 'Make sure you're on it, boy.' He threw the ticket on the table. 'And, Shadrach,' he slowly rose to his feet, 'mine's a trip to Disneyworld wid de kids!'

Chapter Thirty-Three

Late December

Terri was sitting in the conference room listening to the CEO rabbiting on about the annual budget, doodling palm trees on her note pad, when her mobile vibrated. Having learnt her lesson from a previous occasion, she chose to ignore it. The mobile doggedly persisted, massaging Terri's right thigh and buzzing like a swarm of bees. The CEO looked up from his report as she zapped the sound from under the table and stared severely at her number two. Leaning down to pick up a deliberately dropped pen, she quickly read the text.

Man in reception asking for you.
Says it's personal. Name of Bligh.
Sandra.

Terri came up fast, ramming her mobile back in her pocket, hands shaking. She sat trying to appear interested in estimated costs, department overheads and projected income while her head spun and her heart stampeded around her ribcage. Stay calm, Terri, she told herself. It didn't work. It took all of her self-control not to levitate off the seat. The CEO finally brought the meeting to a close and Terri excused herself, pointing to the toilets, and legged it into a cubicle where she sat fully clothed on the lid, a hand across her mouth. She was still there ten minutes later when her mobile vibrated again.

Are you coming down or do I tell this bloke to sling his hook?
Sandra

Terri tapped a quick response and checked her appearance in the washroom mirror. 'You look a bit different from the way you looked in Rodney Bay,' she told her reflection and examined herself critically. 'Actually, Terri, you don't look bad. You've lost weight, your eyes are clear, your hair looks rather fetching in that new bobbed style, your Jaeger suit looks expensive and those gold earrings from John Lewis give you a very executive appearance. All in all, you look years younger than forty-eight. Pity about the drooping eyelids.'

She came out of the lift with her fingers rammed in her jacket pockets to keep them still and looked about. There he sat, reading a newspaper, minus the dreadlocks.

'Afternoon, Shadrach. What brings you to London?'

His eyes left the page. He looked Terri up and down and smiled. Instantly she was back in the dinghy off Carriacou and had no idea what to do or say next.

'Miss Gillingham?'

Miss Gillingham, she thought. What is this? Shrugging, she continued the charade. 'That's right, Mr Bligh, I understand you wanted to see me.'

'I do. Allow me to introduce myself. Meshach Bligh. I believe you know my brother.'

The afternoon whizzed by as Meshach and Terri sat in a bar café on Fleet Street comparing notes. She was able to fill in enormous gaps in her knowledge of Shadrach.

'He never told us he had a twin.'

'To be fair, Terri, I'm not surprised. As he came out first he always referred to me as his younger brother. I guess that's why I tried so damned hard to get one over on him.'

'Well, you certainly did that. I understand you're a well-respected race relations lawyer who plays the electric keyboard. The Moonshine Boys, wasn't it?'

He ran his tongue over his upper lip as Terri tried to stop thinking of him as Shadrach in a city suit. They were identical. 'It was a good job Shadrach played a mean guitar and Bronco was a demon on the drums as I missed more notes than I played. Cheers.'

They were now halfway through a bottle of wine. 'What did your parents think to the article in *Caribbean Compass*?'

'They were so chuffed, Terri. I can't tell you. For years they have longed to see Shadrach, but he's refused to come home. Some arguments obviously run deep and our father can be pretty cutting when he's had a few.'

'How long is it since you've seen him?'

'Six years.'

'You have children, don't you?'

'Yes, two. My son is now twelve and my little girl is five.' He pulled out his wallet and handed over a family photograph. 'They're the apple of my mother's eye.'

Terri took it. 'What's your son called?'

'Abednego. We call him Abe for short. He was six last time Shadrach saw him at our wedding. As for Jessie,' he pointed to his little girl, 'she's yet to meet her uncle.'

Terri's wasn't listening, her eyes locked onto his wife's beautiful face, one she had seen before. 'Meshach, exactly where did you get married?'

'Jamaica. In my grandfather's village. Harriet and I lived together for some years before we tied the knot.'

'Fuck!' she muttered, pouring Viognier down her throat to drown the expletive.

Next time check before you jump to conclusions, you idiot,' said grannie, bending her left ear as wine ran down Terri's chin.

Evie came out of the swimming pool dripping water across the tiles, heading for the changing rooms as her aerobics ladies gathered together at the other end of the pool helping themselves to cups of mint tea.

Sylvia met her by the lockers. 'This was sitting on the reception desk when I came in.' She laid a white envelope face down on the slatted wooden bench and walked out. Evie assumed it was a note from the management and ignored it.

Walking into reception some time later, her hair a riot of curls with wet ends, she met Sylvia hovering by the mineral water stand.

'Anything important?' Sylvia asked, nodding to the envelope sticking out of Evie's sports bag.

'Sorry?'

'The letter. Was it anything important?'

'I doubt it. Probably some complaint from a customer.'

'Oh. Still, it might not be.'

Evie looked at her workmate, hesitated, took the envelope out of her bag and ripped it open.

Everyone in Belgrove Park could hear her shrieks of delight at Clemmie's offer of employment.

CJ walked into the bedroom, a legal document hanging from his fingers.

'Here, you should keep this somewhere safe. It's a copy, the original is with my solicitor for safekeeping.'

Sam stretched across the bed to take it, read the contents then looked at her lover, noting the slight reduction in his waistline. 'That's very generous, CJ. Do I need a financial advisor?'

'No, the hedge fund will manage it while I'm alive, but if you're not satisfied at any time, you can find an alternative advisor to handle your affairs.'

She pulled him onto the bed and buried her head in his neck. 'I love you, you know. I always have.'

'And I love you, you rich bitch.'

She lay back on the silk pillows and ran her toes along his arm. 'While I was in Prickly Bay you sent me an email.'

'Umm,' he groaned, running his tongue around her left nipple.

'In it you said we needed to talk.'

'Umm.'

'What did you mean?'

His head came up and he kissed the end of her nose as she wound her long legs around his waist. 'I said I was going to make it up to you after the holiday. Well, I have. I've bought us a holiday villa in Bequia. You can go there whenever you want, and if you wish to take your friends, go ahead. Just keep a few weeks free for us.'

The cocktail bar in the RAC Club felt very empty as George sat sipping a Daiquiri and reading the latest ABTA report. It was nearing Christmas, the twinkling baubles on a huge Norwegian pine sparkling in the light from the candles dotted about the room. She was waiting for her parents to join her for dinner, an olive branch after months of strained relations. A lot had happened since she'd returned from the Caribbean, the main change being her decision to sell Prestige Travel to Janet at Holidays Are Us, who was looking to expand, and then starting a new company specialising in executive vacations for the rich and famous. Georgina now ran 5 Star World from her home in Chiswick, keeping the clientele to a manageable level and the profits in the stratosphere. She was enjoying herself for the first time in years, and had earned more in commission in a few months than she had in two years in Fulham. PSV featured prominently in her website and she had already booked herself in for a Swedish massage with Evie on her next inspection visit.

'Would you like another cocktail, Miss Stanhope?' asked the waiter, hovering close by.

'No, thanks, Philip, I'll wait until my parents arrive. They seem to be running late.'

He moved away as her mobile rang. 'I know, you're going to be late because of the traffic,' said George, assuming it was her father calling, but a familiar Irish accent greeted her instead. 'Brendan, what a surprise and quite a coincidence. Right now

I'm sitting in the cocktail bar at the RAC Club, waiting for my parents.'

'I know, they're standing alongside me in reception. Your dad is kindly signing me in.'

George was on her feet and striding to the door, her mobile pressed against her ear.

'If Mohammed won't come to the mountain, Georgina, then the mountain will have to come to Mohammed.'

'For God's sake, Brendan, what the hell are you talking about?'

'There's no need to swear, Georgina,' said her father as she stormed into the entrance hall. 'Mr O'Donnell has kindly offered to take us all to Sheekys in St Martin's Court and hopes we can persuade you to go and speak to his . . .' He looked to Brendan for help.

'Script-writers,' said Brendan, taking George's arm and marching her back into the bar.

'How did he find you?' she asked over her shoulder.

'Through the club, dear. They forwarded a message to us from *True Life Movies*.'

'Your parents have been very helpful in filling me in on your past, Georgina. I understand you have an intense dislike of Thailand.'

George staggered to a stop, poked a finger in Brendan's chest and leant in to whisper in his left ear. 'What the fuck are you doing here, Brendan O'Donnell, and what's your game?'

'Your daughter certainly has a way with words, Mr Stanhope,' said Brendan, plonking her in her seat. 'I'm afraid we'll have to edit out her foul language when we make that TV movie of her holiday in the Grenadines, early next year.'

'I'm sorry, son, we did try, but something got lost in translation,' said George's father as he ordered Bushmills on the rocks all round.

'Georgina,' said her mother, settling into a seat by the window, 'Mr O'Donnell tells me he's taking you to St Lucia for Christmas. I have to say, I'm very jealous.'

'Mother,' announced George, her voice frosty as she glared at Brendan, deep in conversation with her dad. 'That man has two chances of taking me anywhere. A dog's chance and no chance at all.'

'That's what I like, Mr Stanhope,' said Brendan, 'a girl with spirit,' He looked at George and winked, then downed his Bushmills in one. 'Would you be at all agreeable to me taking her off your hands?'

'Anytime, my boy. Any time at all.'

Terri dropped onto her Chesterfield and sipped a glass of Prosecco. I really must buy a new settee, she thought, as her hips promptly sank between the webbing. She shuffled her derrière until equilibrium set in then stretched over to the coffee table and picked up the photograph album labelled 'Millennium Caribbean Cruise'.

It was Christmas Eve and to get into the mood Terri had a compilation CD on her iPod playing Christmas songs and a small artificial Christmas tree flashing two long and one short every ten seconds in the bay window. At that moment, 'Jingle

Bells' was belting out its refrain and two apple and cinnamon candles permeated the air with Christmas cheer.

She didn't mind. This wasn't the first time she'd spent Christmas alone. 'It's only two days,' she kept saying as Doris Day's voice resonated around the room. 'What's the big deal anyway? Unless you have kids, all this Christmas cheer is a bit old hat.'

Pulling the belt of her new cashmere dressing-gown more tightly around her waist, she snuggled down, waiting to watch the annual repeats of Morecombe and Wise on the box as her fingers flicked through the photographs of her days on *Rum Punch*.

There was Sam, up close and personal with Lord Glenconner in Bang between the Pitons, then the film set at Wallilabou, George landing her first yellow finned tuna, Sam again, being suggestive with a banana in Bequia, and Evie standing wrapped inside Dale's arms on the stern of *Southern Cross*. Terri hesitated over a shot of Shadrach at the helm, his strong arms steering *Rum Punch* through the waves, the wind in the sails, his dreadlocks clubbed at his neck. Then again playing the guitar on Chatham Beach, before the group photograph at dawn with Shark Attack, taken by the French skipper. She sipped her Prosecco and relived the moment.

Then came the photos of Cyril naked in PSV followed by shots of secret compartments full of black packages. Then Evie strapping Shadrach's guitar case to the masthead followed by ones of the Grenadian Coastguard lashed onto *Rum Punch*'s hull and *Southern Cross* impounded in Prickly Bay.

'It was one hell of an experience,' she announced to the lounge, closing the album. 'I wouldn't have missed it for the world.' She raised her wine glass, a smile lifting the corners of her mouth and snuggled deeper into the old settee. 'Cheers, *Rum Punch*, and fair winds. It was great knowing you.'

She must have dozed because she woke to hear the front doorbell ringing and children singing carols. 'OK, OK, I'm coming.' She pushed herself off the settee, gathering up her purse as she headed down the hall, trying to fluff up her hair before opening the front door.

I must look like a geriatric in my dressing gown, she thought, as the light in the porch illuminated six young kids, lanterns in hand, singing away. With the second verse of 'Good King Wenceslas' ringing in her ears, Terri waited in the freezing cold until they had finished, then applauded with gusto and dropped a five-pound note into their hat. 'Merry Christmas,' she shouted as they rushed down the path, giggling with delight.

Did I go carol singing when I was their age? she wondered. She couldn't remember, shrugged and closed the door. On her way back to the settee the doorbell rang again.

'Oh, for Christ's sake, d'you think I'm made of money?' Terri flung the front door open and was about to give the local kids a piece of her mind when what she saw on her doorstep made her catch her breath. Standing under her Victorian portico was a Rastafarian strumming a guitar, his bright red nose peeking out below a Jamaican tea-cosy hat, carolling an amended version of a John Lennon classic. Terri's toes curled as she stood there and listened.

Rum Punch

So dis is Christmas,
Are you havin' fun?
Anudder year over,
And a new one just begun.

Or is Christmas lonely,
Just you on your own,
Still dreamin' of Rum Punch,
Still longin' to roam.

You could stay 'ere in England?
Or set yourself free,
De Caribe awaits you,
To say nuttin' of me.

But be safe in your old world,
Wid its tinsel and lights,
Just don't forget Rum Punch,
And dose warm starry nights.

'Ave a very merry Christmas, Terri,
Wid a glass full o' cheer,
Dis summer was special,
Why not repeat it next year?

They stood there getting pneumonia, Terri in her cashmere dressing gown, Shadrach in his knitted hat.

She finally broke the spell. 'Oh, for goodness' sake, come in.'

Shadrach crossed her threshold, his guitar strung behind his back. Blowing warm air onto his frozen hands, he stood in the hallway under her white-paper lampshade that needed dusting, and scrutinised Terri's new, slim-line appearance and bobbed hairstyle. She suddenly realised she was naked below her thin cashmere and recalled him staring at her transparent cheesecloth dress in the same way.

'Have you eaten?' she asked, feeling self-conscious.

'Yes, missy. D'you tink I'd cross London from me mam and dad's flat in de Elephant and Castle on an empty stomach?'

'However did you find me?'

'Evie. She gave me a neck massage for me spondylosis over on PSV. She told me where you live.'

Terri walked into the lounge, all thoughts of Morecombe and Wise gone. 'Shadrach, what the hell are you doing freezing to death on my doorstep when you're supposed to be in the Caribbean?'

'Well, now, dat's a good question.' His guitar slipped to the floor and he stood leaning against the lounge door, muffled in layers of clothing, his arms and legs crossed in that familiar way of his. 'Dere's a possibility dat I was tryin' out my latest lyrics on a connoisseur o' music, or I could 'ave been prayin' dat de lady of dis opulent establishment,' he took in the peeling chipboard wallpaper and distressed furniture, 'would be willin' to give a bloke a few coppers for his troubles at Christmas, or I could 'ave bin wooin' de woman I wants to spend de rest of me natural wid, cruisin' in de Caribbean.'

Terri was speechless, and stood in the centre of the room as the man of her dreams began to discard his outer layers all over her shag-pile rug.

'You now be lookin' at de new owner of *Sudden Cross*, Terri. Except she's now called *Sudden Comfort*, and in need of a woman's touch if she's gonna be acceptable to all dose fancy clients Georgie is gonna send a-cruisin' throughout de Caribbean.'

Terri wanted to interrupt but Shadrack lifted his finger.

'Now, Delilah reckons you might be just de one to fit de bill, and I tends to agree wid 'er.'

'I bloody knew that Delilah was my grannie reincarnated.'

Shadrach was now standing by the coffee table clad in a pair of cream chinos and a navy-blue polo shirt with a logo, in white, of *Southern Comfort,* embroidered across the pocket.

'So, Teresa Gillingham, what's it to be? *Sudden Comfort* or Deloitte Villas?'

Terri never got the chance to answer because Shadrach walked into her personal space and took over her world.

She later decided that Georgina had been wrong about the settee. It finally gave up the ghost that Christmas Eve as the legs crumbled under the weight of a pair of humans who couldn't get enough of each other, and who were still wrapped in each other's arms at eight o'clock on Christmas morning.

Terri never did get round to buying that replacement settee and as for British Electric, they began the New Year advertising for yet another BIE Marketing Manager while Shadrach and

Terri sailed into the sunset in their beautiful eighty-three-foot boat.

As for *Rum Punch*? CJ bought her from Shadrach for an undisclosed sum and donated her to the A-team. They based her in Prickly Bay, and the catamaran could often be seen around the Grenadines, her all-female crew behaving badly and pottering from one gorgeous anchorage to another sipping cocktails and reminiscing about their days at Beagle Air!

About the Author

Su Garcia was born in Nottingham in 1948 and by the age of nineteen had become an executive air-stewardess before starting her own successful company managing residential property for private owners working overseas.

Her passion for sailing became a lifestyle when, after twenty-three years, she sold her company, and went ocean-cruising with her husband, David, including crossing the Atlantic Ocean four times and covering over 50,000 nautical miles on their private yacht. During the long hours at sea, Su wrote articles for the sailing press and regular blogs for family and friends. Writing fiction was a natural progression beginning with her first novel, DEAD RECKONING, in 2015.

Su continues writing from both the current family yacht based in the Mediterranean, and from her home in Devon. After a lifetime of travel, her wealth of experiences form the basis for her intricate plots and characters.

Facebook.com/SuGarcia
twitter.com/sugarcia_author

www.baggatellepublishers.com

Acknowledgements

Having cruised the Lesser Antilles in the late 1990's and early 2000's on our yacht, *Saltwhistle III*, I experienced a number of the events which, with some poetic licence, have formed part of *Rum Punch*'s plot.

The Pirates of the Caribbean was filmed in Wallilabou, St Vincent, with sailors from the cruising community acting as extras. A rescue did take place of two young fishermen in Caribbean waters by an English-flagged yacht and a vessel was impounded by the Coastguard for drug running between South America and the USA. The Right Honourable James Fitz-Allen Mitchell is a very well-respected ex-Prime Minister of St Vincent and the Grenadines, who retired from that post in 2000. Members of his family continue to run the Frangipani Beach Hotel in Bequia to this day, a favourite watering hole for cruisers passing through Admiralty Bay. Bang between the Pitons in Jalousie Bay, St Lucia, was owned by Lord Glenconner and has since been sold to new owners, while the actors and film crew of 'A Touch of Class' did film this comedy-romance in areas around Malaga, Spain.

My thanks must go to both Yolanda López Segura and Idoia López from DCD Productions in Menorca, who created the novel's cover, and Lynn Curtis, whose professional editing skills shaped *Rum Punch*'s plot into a readable manuscript for publication.

My list of beta-readers would be endless. You know who you are, and I thank you all for your support and constructive critiques, including my husband, David, who was given the unenviable task off criticising his wife's creative musings while maintaining equilibrium within the marriage. Not an easy task.

My greatest thanks, however, go to the island people of St Lucia, St Vincent and the Grenadines and Grenada, for giving me some wonderful memories and the background for this novel. I will be back!

Author's Books

Dead Reckoning
by
Su Garcia

An action-packed novel, set in a stunning Aegean island and on the high seas. A great read for all those who enjoy a gripping, topical storyline with a nautical flavour, spiced with love, lust, revenge, conflict and danger.

Mac's Trilogy
by
Susie Baggaley

A story of dogged determination by a female Scottish medic trying to improve the plight of women and children of India during the Raj era and battling with the misogynistic attitude of her peers in the India Medical Service.

Published by Baggatelle Publishers Ltd
www.baggatellepublishers.com

Printed in Great Britain
by Amazon